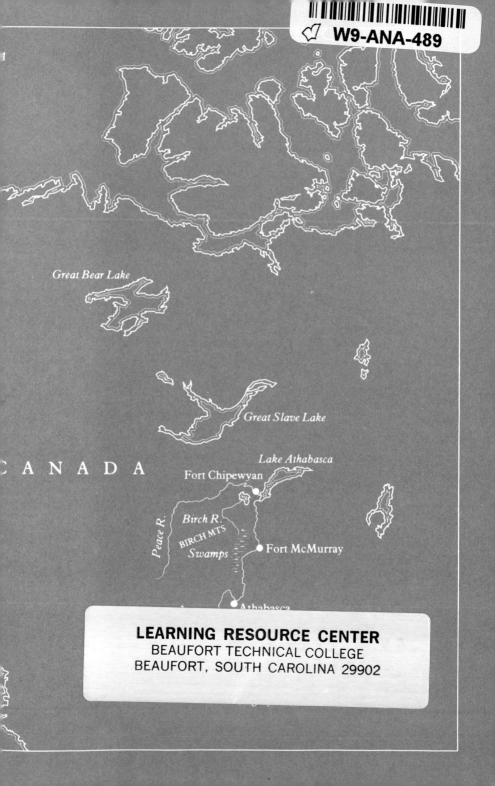

W9-ANA-489

Great Bear Lake

Great Slave Lake

Lake Athabasca

C A N A D A   Fort Chipewyan

Peace R.   Birch R.
BIRCH MTS
Swamps   Fort McMurray

Athabasca

ATHABASCA

ALISTAIR MacLEAN

Athabasca

DOUBLEDAY & COMPANY, INC.
GARDEN CITY, NEW YORK
1980

14126

ISBN: 0-385-17204-4
Library of Congress Catalog Card Number 80–1067

ATHABASCA

PROLOGUE

THIS BOOK IS NOT PRIMARILY ABOUT OIL, but is based on oil and the means whereby oil is recovered from the earth, so it may be of some interest and help to look briefly at these phenomena.

What oil is, and how it is formed in the first place, no one quite seems to know. The technical books and treatises on this subject are legion—I am aware that, personally, I haven't seen a fraction of them—and they are largely, so I am assured, in close agreement—except when they come to what one would have thought was a point of considerable interest: How, precisely, does oil become oil? There appear to be as many divergent theories about this as there *are about the origins of life. Confronted with complexities, the well-advised layman takes refuge in over-simplification —which is what I now do, as I can do no other.*

Only two elements were needed for the formation of oil—rock and the incredibly abundant plants and primitive living organisms that teemed in rivers, lakes and seas as far back as perhaps a billion years ago. Hence, the term fossil fuels.

The biblical references to the rock of ages give rise to misconceptions about the nature and permanency of rock. Rock—the material of which the earth's crust is made—is neither eternal nor indestructible. Nor is it even unchanging. On the contrary, it is in a state of constant change, movement and flux, and it is salutary to remind ourselves that there was a time when no rock existed. Even today there is a singular lack of agreement among geologists, geophysicists and astronomers as to how the earth came into being; but there is a measure of agreement that there was a primary incandescent and gaseous state, followed by a molten state, neither of which was conducive to the formation of anything, rock included. It is erroneous to suppose that rock has been, is and ever will be.

Yet we are not concerned here with the ultimate origins of rock, but rock as we have it today. It is, admittedly, difficult to observe this process of flux because a minor change may take ten million years; a major change, a hundred million.

Rock is constantly being destroyed and rebuilt. In the

destructive process weather is the main factor; in the rebuilding, the forces of gravity.

Five main weather elements act upon rock. Frost and ice fracture rock. It can be gradually eroded by airborne dust. The action of the seas, whether through the constant movement of waves and tides or the pounding of heavy storm waves, remorselessly wears away the coastlines. Rivers are immensely powerful destructive agencies—one has but to look at the Grand Canyon to appreciate their enormous power. And such rocks as escape all these influences are worn away over the eons by the effect of rain.

Whatever the cause of erosion, the end result is the same: The rock is reduced to its tiniest possible constituents—rock particles or, simply, dust. Rain and melting snow carry this dust down to the tiniest rivulets and the mightiest rivers, which, in turn, transport it to lakes, inland seas and the coastal regions of the oceans. Dust, however fine and powdery, is still heavier than water, and whenever the water becomes sufficiently still, it will gradually sink to the bottom, not only in lakes and seas but also in the sluggish lower reaches of rivers and where flood conditions exist, in the form of silt.

And so, over unimaginably long reaches of time, whole mountain ranges are carried down to the seas, and in the process, through the effects of gravity, new rock is born as layer after layer of dust accumulates on the bottom, building up to a depth of ten, a hundred, perhaps even a thousand feet, the lowermost layers being gradually compacted by the immense and steadily increasing pressures from above, until the particles fuse together and reform as new rock.

It is in the intermediate and final processes of this new rock formation that oil comes into being. Those lakes and seas of hundreds of millions of years ago were almost choked by water plants and the most primitive forms of aquatic life. On dying, they sank to the bottom of the lakes and seas along with the settling dust particles and were gradually buried deep under the endless layers of more dust and more aquatic and plant life that slowly accumulated above them. The passing of millions of years and the steadily increasing pressures from above gradually changed the decayed vegetation and dead aquatic life into oil.

Described thus simply and quickly, the process sounds reasonable enough. But this is where the gray and disputatious area arises. The conditions necessary for the formation of oil are known; the cause of the metamorphosis is not. It seems probable that some form of chemical catalyst is involved, but this catalyst has not been isolated. The first purely synthetic oil, as distinct from secondary synthetic oils such as those derived from coal, has yet to be produced. We just have to accept that oil is oil, that it is there, bound up in rock strata in fairly well-defined areas throughout the world but always on the sites of ancient seas and lakes, some of which are now continental land, some buried deep under the encroachment of new oceans.

Had the oil remained intermingled with those deeply buried rock strata, and were the earth a stable place, that oil would have been irrecoverable. But our planet is a highly unstable place. There is no such thing as a stable continent securely anchored to the core of the earth. The continents rest on the so-called tectonic plates which, in turn, float on the molten magma below, with neither anchor nor rudder, free to wander in whichever haphazard fashion they will. This they unquestionably do. They are much given to banging into each other, grinding alongside each other, overriding or dipping under each other in a wholly unpredictable fashion and, in general, resembling rocks in the demonstration of their fundamental instability. As this banging and clashing takes place over periods of tens or hundreds of millions of years, it is not readily apparent to us except in the form of earthquakes—which generally occur where two tectonic plates are in contention.

The collision of two such plates engenders incredible pressures, and two of the effects of such pressures are of particular concern here. In the first place the huge compressive forces involved tend to squeeze the oil from the rock strata in which it is imbedded and to disperse it in whichever direction the pressure permits—up, down or sideways. Secondly, a collision buckles or folds the rock strata themselves, the upper strata being forced upward to form mountain ranges—the northern movement of the Indian tectonic plate created the Himalayas—and the lower strata buckling to create what are virtually subterranean *mountains, folding the layered strata into massive domes and arches.*

It is at this point, insofar as oil recovery is concerned, that the nature of the rocks themselves become of importance. The rock can be porous or non-porous. The porous rock—such as gypsum—permits liquids, such as oil, to pass through them, while the non-porous—such as limestone— does not. In the case of porous rock, the oil, influenced by those compressive forces, will seep upward through the rock until the distributive pressure eases, when it will come to rest at or very close to the surface of the earth. In the case of non-porous rock, the oil will become trapped in a dome or arch, and in spite of the great pressures from below can escape neither sideways nor upward but must remain where it is.

In this latter case, what are regarded as conventional methods are used in the recovery of oil. Geologists locate a dome, and a hole is drilled. With reasonable luck they hit an oil dome and not a solid one, and their problems are over—the powerful subterranean pressures normally drive the oil to the surface.

The recovery of seepage oil which has passed upward through porous rock presents a quite different and far more formidable problem, the answer to which was not found until as late as 1967. Even then it was only a partial answer. The trouble, of course, is that this surface seepage oil does not collect in pools, but is inextricably intermixed with foreign matter, such as sand and clay, from which it has to be abstracted and refined.

It is, in fact, a solid and has to be mined as such; and although this solidified oil may go as deep as six thousand feet, only the first two hundred feet, in the limits of present-day knowledge and techniques, are accessible, and that only by surface mining. Conventional mining methods —the sinking of vertical shafts and the driving of horizontal galleries—would be hopelessly inadequate, as they would provide only the tiniest fraction of the raw material required to make the extraction process commercially viable. The latest oil extraction plant, which went into operation only in the summer of 1978, requires 10,000 tons of raw material every hour.

Two excellent examples of the two different methods of oil recovery are to be found in the far northwest of North America. The conventional method of deep drilling is well exemplified by the Prudhoe Bay oil field on the Arctic shore of northern Alaska: its latter-day counterpart, the surface mining of oil, is to be found—and, indeed, it is the only place in the world where it can be found—in the tar sands of Athabasca.

ATHABASCA

ONE

THIS," SAID GEORGE DERMOTT, "IS NO place for us." He eased his considerable bulk back from the dining table and regarded the remains of several enormous lamb chops with disfavor. "Jim Brady expects his field operatives to be lean, fit and athletic. Are we lean, fit and athletic?"

"There are desserts," Donald Mackenzie said. Like Dermott he was a large and comfortable man—a little larger and a little less comfortable than his partner—with a rugged, weatherbeaten face. Observers often took him and his partner for a pair of retired heavyweight boxers. "I can see cakes, cookies and a wide variety of pastries," he went on. "You read their food brochure? Says that the average man requires at least five thousand calories a day to cope with Arctic conditions. But we, George, are not average men. Six thousand would do better in a pinch. Nearer seven would be safer, I'd say. Chocolate mousse and double cream?"

"He had a notice about it on the staff bulletin board," Dermott said wryly. "Heavy black border, for some reason. Signed, too."

"Senior operatives don't look at staff boards." Mackenzie heaved his 220 pounds erect and headed purposefully for the food counter. There was no doubt that BP/ Sohio did extremely well by their staff. Here at Prudhoe Bay, on the bitter rim of the Arctic Ocean in midwinter, the spacious, light and airy dining room, with multicolored pastel walls backdropping the recurrent five-pointed-star motif, was maintained at a pleasantly fresh 72° F. by the air-conditioned central heating. The temperature difference between the dining room and the outside world was 105 degrees. The range of excellently cooked food was also astonishing.

"Don't exactly starve themselves up here," he said as he returned with a mousse for each of them and a pitcher of heavy cream. "I wonder what the old Alaskan sourdoughs would have made of it."

The first reaction of a prospector or trapper of yesteryear would have been that he was suffering from hallucinations. All in all, it was hard to say what feature he would have found the most astonishing. Eighty per cent of the items on the menu would have been unknown to him. But he would have been still more amazed by the forty-foot swimming pool and the glassed-in garden, with its pine trees, birches, plants and profusion of flowers, that abutted on the dining room.

"God knows what the old boys would have thought," said Dermott. "You might ask *him*, though." He indicated a man heading in their direction. "Jack London would have recognized this one right away."

Mackenzie said, "More the Robert Service type, I'd say."

The newcomer certainly wasn't of current vintage. He wore heavy felt boots, moleskin trousers and an incredibly faded mackinaw which went well enough with the equally faded patches on the sleeves. A pair of sealskin gloves were suspended from his neck, and he carried a coonskin cap in his right hand. His hair was long and white and parted in the middle. He had a slightly hooked nose and clear blue eyes with deeply entrenched crow's feet, which could have been caused by too much sun, too much snow or a too highly developed sense of humor. The rest of his face was obscured by a magnificent, grizzled beard and mustache, both of which were at that moment rimed by droplets of ice. The yellow hard hat swinging from his left hand struck a jarring note. He stopped at their table, and from the momentary flash of white teeth it could be assumed that he was smiling.

"Mr. Dermott? Mr. Mackenzie?" He offered his hand. "Finlayson. John Finlayson."

Dermott said, "Mr. Finlayson. Field operations manager's office?"

"I *am* the field operations manager." He pulled out a chair, sat, sighed and removed some ice particles from his beard. "Yes, yes, I know. Hard to believe." He smiled again, gestured at his clothing. "Most people think I've been riding the rods. You know, hobo on the boxcars. God knows why. Nearest railroad track's a long, long way from Prudhoe Bay. Like Tahiti and grass skirts. You know, gone native. Too many years on the North Slope." His oddly staccato manner of speech was indeed suggestive of a person whose contact with civilization was, at best, intermittent. "Sorry I couldn't make it. Meet you, I mean. Deadhorse."

Mackenzie said, "Deadhorse?"

"Airstrip. A little trouble at one of the gathering centers. Happens all the time. Sub-zero temperatures play hell with the molecular structure of steel. Being well taken care of, I hope?"

"No complaints." Dermott smiled. "Not that we require much care. There the food counter, here Mackenzie. The wateringhole and the camel." Dermott checked himself. He was beginning to talk like Finlayson. "Well, one little complaint, perhaps. Too many items on the lunch menu, too large a helping of any item. My colleague's waistline—"

"Your colleague's waistline can take care of itself," Mackenzie said comfortably. "But I do have a complaint, Mr. Finlayson."

"I can imagine." Another momentary flash of teeth, and Finlayson was on his feet. "Let's hear it in my office. Just a few steps." He walked across the dining hall, stopped outside a door and indicated another door to the left. "Master Operations Control Center. The heart of Prudhoe Bay—or the western half of it, at least. All the computerized process control facilities for the supervision of the field's operations."

Dermott said, "An enterprising lad with a satchelful of grenades could have himself quite a time in there."

"Five seconds and he could close down the entire oil field. Come all the way from Houston just to cheer me up? This way."

He led them through the outer door, then through an inner one to a small office. Desks, chairs and filing cabinets, all in metal, all in battleship gray. He gestured them to sit and smiled at Mackenzie. "As the French say, a meal without wine is like a day without sunshine."

"It's this Texas dust," Mackenzie said. "Sticks in the gullet like no other dust. Laughs at water."

Finlayson made a sweeping motion with his hand. "Some big rigs out there. Damned expensive and damned difficult to handle. It's pitch dark, say, forty below and you're tired—you're always tired up here. Don't forget we work twelve hours a day, seven days a week. A couple of scotches on top of all that, and you've written off a million dollars' worth of equipment. Or you damage the pipeline. Or you kill yourself. Or, worst of all, you kill some of your mates. Comparatively, they had it easy in the old prohibition days—bulk smuggling from Canada, bathtub gin, illicit stills by the thousand. Rather different on the North Slope here—get caught smuggling in a teaspoonful of liquor, and that's it. No argument, no court of appeal. Out. But there's no problem—no one is going to risk eight hundred dollars a week for ten cents' worth of bourbon."

Mackenzie said, "When's the next flight out to Anchorage?"

Finlayson smiled. "All is not lost, Mr. Mackenzie." He unlocked a filing cabinet, produced a bottle of scotch and two glasses and poured with a generous hand. "Welcome to the North Slope, gentlemen."

"I was having visions," said Mackenzie, "of travelers stranded in an Alpine blizzard and a St. Bernard lolloping toward them with the usual restorative. You're not a drinking man?"

"Certainly. One week in five when I rejoin my family in Anchorage. This is strictly for visiting VIPs. One would assume you qualify under that heading?" Thoughtfully, he mopped melting ice from his beard. "Though frankly, I never heard of your organization until a couple of days ago."

"Think of us as desert roses," Mackenzie said. "Born to blush and bloom unseen. I think I've got that wrong, but the desert bit is appropriate enough. That's where we seem to spend most of our time." He nodded toward the window. "A desert doesn't have to be made of sand. I suppose this qualifies as an Arctic desert."

"I think of it that way myself. But what do you do in those deserts? Your function, I mean."

"Our function?" Dermott considered. "Oddly enough, I'd say our function is to reduce our worthy employer, Jim Brady, to a state of bankruptcy."

"*Jim* Brady? I thought his initial was A."

"His mother was English. She christened him Algernon. Wouldn't *you* object? He's always known as Jim. Anyway, there are only three people in the world any good at extinguishing oil-field fires, particularly gusher fires, and all three are Texas-based. Jim Brady's one of the three.

"It used to be commonly accepted that there are just three causes of such oil fires: spontaneous combustion, which should never happen but does; the human factor, i.e., sheer carelessness; and mechanical failure. After twenty-five years in the business Brady recognized that there was a fourth and more sinister element involved that would come, broadly speaking, under the heading of industrial sabotage.

"Who would engage in sabotage? What would the motivation be?

"Well first we can rule out the most obvious—rivalry among the big oil companies. It doesn't exist. This notion of cut-throat competition exists only in the sensational press and among the more feeble-minded of the public. To be a fly on the wall at a closed meeting of the oil lobby in Washington is to understand once and for all the meaning of the expression 'two minds with but a single thought, two hearts that beat as one.' Multiplied by twenty, of course. Let Exxon put up the price of gas by a penny today, and Gulf, Shell, BP, Elf, Agip and all the others will do the same tomorrow. Or even take Prudhoe Bay here. The classic example, surely, of co-operation—umpteen companies working hand-in-glove for the mutual benefit of all concerned—benefit of all the oil companies, that is. The state of Alaska and the general public might adopt a rather different and more jaundiced viewpoint.

"So we rule out business rivalries. This leaves another kind of energy. Power. International power politics. Say Country X could seriously weaken enemy Country Y by slowing down its oil revenues. That's one obvious scenario. Then there's *internal* power politics. Suppose disaffected elements in an oil-rich dictatorship see a means of demonstrating their dissatisfaction against a regime that clasps the ill-gotten gains to its mercenary bosom or, at best, distributes some measure of the largesse to its nearest and dearest, while ensuring that the peasantry remains in the properly medieval state of poverty. Starvation does nicely as motivation. This kind of setup leaves room for personal revenge, the settling of old scores, the working off of old grudges.

"And don't forget the pyromaniac who sees in oil a ludicrously easy target and the source of lovely flames. In short, there's room for practically everything, and the more bizarre and unimaginable, the more likely to happen. A case in point."

He nodded at Mackenzie. "Donald and I have just returned from the Gulf. The local security men and the
police were baffled by an outbreak of small fires—small, so-
called, but with damage totaling two million dollars.
Clearly the work of an arsonist. We tracked him down,
apprehended him, and punished him. We gave him a bow
and arrow."

Finlayson looked at them as if their scotch had taken
hold too quickly.

"Eleven-year-old son of the British consul. He had a
powerful Webley air pistol. Webley makes the traditional
ammunition for this—hollow, concave lead pellets. They
do *not* make pellets of hardened steel, which give off a
splendid spark when they strike ferrous metal. This lad
had a plentiful supply obtained from a local Arab boy who
had a similar pistol and used those illegal pellets for hunting desert vermin. Incidentally, the Arab boy's old man, a
prince of the blood royal, owned the oil field in question.
The English boy's arrows have rubber tips."

"I'm sure there's a moral there somewhere."

"Sure, there's a lesson: The unpredictable is always
with you. Our industrial sabotage division—that's Jim
Brady's term for it—was formed six years ago. There are
fourteen of us in it. At first it was a purely investigative
agency. We went to a place after the deed had been done
and the fire put out—as often as not it was Jim who put it
out—and tried to find out who had done it, why, and what
his *modus operandi* had been. Frankly, we had very lim-

ited success. Usually the horse had gone, and all we were doing was locking the empty stable door.

"Now the emphasis has changed—we try to lock the damned door in such a fashion that no one can open it. In other words, prevention: The maximum tightening of both mechanical and human security. The response to this service has been remarkable—we're now the most profitable side of Jim's operations. By far. Capping off runaway wells, putting fires out, can't hold a candle, if you'll pardon the expression, to our security work. Such is the demand for our services that we could triple our division and still not cope with all the calls being made upon us."

"Well, why don't you? Triple the business, I mean."

"Trained personnel," Mackenzie said. "Just not there. More accurately, there are next to no experienced operatives, and there's an almost total dearth of people qualified to be trained for the job. The combination of qualifications is difficult to come by. You have to have an investigative mind, and that, in turn, is based on an inborn instinct for detection—the Sherlock Holmes genes, shall we say. You've either got it or not. It can't be inculcated. You have to have an eye and a nose for security, an *obsession*, almost—and this can only come from field experience. You have to have a pretty detailed knowledge of the oil industry worldwide. And, above all, you have to be an oilman."

"And you gentlemen are oilmen." It was a statement, not a question.

"All our working lives," Dermott said. "We've both been field operation managers."

"If your services are in such demand, how come we should be so lucky as to jump to the head of the queue?"

Dermott said, "As far as we know this is the first time any oil company has received notification of *intent to* sabotage. First real chance we've had to try out our preventive medicine. We're just slightly puzzled on one point, Mr. Finlayson. You say you never heard of us until a couple of days ago. How come we're here, then? I mean, we knew of this three days ago when we arrived back from the Mideast. We spent a day resting up, another day studying the layout and security measures of the Alaskan pipeline and—"

"You did that, eh? Isn't it classified information?"

Dermott was patient. "We could have sent for it immediately on receiving the request for assistance. We didn't have to. The information, Mr. Finlayson, is not classified. It's in the public domain. Big companies tend to be incredibly careless about such matters. Whether to reassure the public or burnish their own image by taking thorough-going precautions, they not only release large chunks of information about their activities but positively bombard the public with them. The information, of course, comes in disparate and apparently unrelated lumps. It requires only a moderately intelligent fella to piece them all together.

"Not that those big companies, such as Alyeska, who built your pipeline, have much to reproach themselves about. They don't even begin to operate in the same league of indiscretion as the all-time champs, the U. S. Government. Take the classic example of the declassification of the secret of the atom bomb. When the Russians got the bomb, the Government thought there was no point in being secretive anymore and proceeded to tell all. You want to know how to make an atom bomb? Just send a pittance to the AEC in Washington and you'll have the necessary information by return mail. That this information could be used by Americans against Americans apparently never occurred to the towering intellects of Capitol Hill and the Pentagon, who seem to have been under the impression that the American criminal classes voluntarily retired *en masse* on the day of declassification."

Finlayson raised a defensive hand. "Hold. Enough. I accept that you haven't infiltrated Prudhoe Bay with a battalion of spies. Answer's simple. When I received this unpleasant letter—it was sent to *me*, not to our H.Q. in Anchorage—I talked to the general manager, Alaska. We both agreed that it was almost certainly a hoax. Still, I regret to say that many Alaskans aren't all that kindly disposed toward us. We also agreed that if it was *not* a hoax, it could be something very serious indeed. People like us, although we're well enough up the ladder in our own fields, don't make final decisions on the safety and future of a ten-billion-dollar investment. So we notified the grand panjandrums. Your directive came from London. Informing me of their decision must have come as an afterthought."

"Head offices being what they are," Dermott said. "Got this threatening note here?"

Finlayson retrieved a single sheet of notepaper from a drawer and passed it across.

"'My dear Mr. Finlayson,'" Dermott read. "Well, that's civil enough. 'I have to inform you that you will be incurring a slight spillage of oil in the near future. Not much, I assure you, just sufficient to convince you that we can interrupt oil flow whenever and wherever we please. Please notify ARCO.'"

Dermott shoved the letter across to Mackenzie. "Understandably unsigned. No demands. If this is genuine, it's intended as a softening-up demonstration in preparation for the big threat and big demand that will follow. A morale-sapper, if you will, designed to scare the pants off you."

Finlayson's gaze was on the middle distance. "I'm not so sure he hasn't done that already."

"You notified ARCO?"

"Yup. Oil field's split more or less half-and-half. We run the western sector. ARCO—Atlantic Richfield, Exxon, some smaller groups—they run the eastern sector."

"What's their reaction?"

"Like mine. Hope for the best, prepare for the worst."

"Your security chief. What's his reaction?"

"Downright pessimistic. It's his baby, after all. If I were in his shoes, I'd feel the same way. He's convinced of the genuineness of this threat."

"Me too," Dermott said. "This came in an envelope?

Ah, thank you." He read the address. " 'Mr. John Finlayson, B.Sc., A.M.I.M.E.' Not only punctilious, but they've
done their homework on you. 'BP/Sohio, Prudhoe Bay,
Alaska.' Postmarked Edmonton, Alberta. That mean anything to you?"

"Nary a thing. I have neither friends nor acquaintances there, and certainly no business contacts."

"Your security chief's reaction?"

"Same as mine. Zero."

"What's his name?"

"Bronowski. Sam Bronowski."

"Let's have him in, shall we?"

"You'll have to wait, I'm afraid. He's down in Fairbanks. Back tonight if the weather holds up. Depends on
visibility."

"Blizzard season?"

"We don't have one. Precipitation on the North Slope
is very low, maybe six inches in a winter. High winds are
the bugaboo. They blow up the surface snow so that the
air can be completely opaque for thirty or forty feet above
the ground. Just before Christmas a few years ago a Hercules, normally the safest of aircraft, tried to land in those
conditions. Didn't make it. Two of the crew of four killed.
Pilots have become a bit leery since—if a Hercules can
crash, any aircraft can. These high winds and the surface
snowstorms they generate—that snow can be driving along
at seventy miles an hour—are the bane of our existence up
here. That's why this operations center is built on pilings
seven feet above ground—lets the snow blow right under-

neath. Otherwise we'd end the winter season buried under a massive drift. The pilings, of course, also virtually eliminate heat transfer to the permafrost, but that's secondary."

"What's Bronowski doing in Fairbanks?"

"Stiffening the thin red line. Hiring extra security guards for Fairbanks."

"How does he set about that?"

"Approach varies, I suppose. Really Bronowski's department, Mr. Dermott. He has *carte blanche* in those matters. I suggest you ask him on his return."

"Oh, come on. You're his boss. Bosses keep tabs on their subordinates. Roughly, how does he recruit?"

"Well, he's probably built up a list of people whom he's personally contacted and who might be available in a state of emergency. I'm honestly not sure about this. I may be his boss, but when I delegate responsibility, I do just that. I do know that he approaches the chief of police and asks for suitable recommendations. He may or may not have put in an ad in the *All-Alaska Weekly*—that's published in Fairbanks." Finlayson thought briefly. "I wouldn't say he's deliberately close-mouthed about this. I suppose when you've been a security man all your life you naturally don't let your left hand know what the right hand's doing."

"What kind of men does he recruit?"

"Almost all ex-cops—you know, ex-State Troopers."

"But not trained security men?"

"As such, no, although I'd have thought security would have come as second nature to a State Trooper."

Finlayson smiled. "I imagine Sam's principal criterion is whether the man can shoot straight."

"Security's a mental thing, not physical. You said 'almost all.'"

"He's brought in two first-class security agents from outside. One's stationed at Fairbanks, the other at Valdez."

"Who says they're first class?"

"Sam. He handpicked them." Finlayson rubbed his drying beard in what could have been a gesture of irritation. "You know, Mr. Dermott, friendly, even genial you may be, but I have the odd impression that I'm being third-degreed."

"Rubbish. If that were happening, you'd know all about it because I'd be asking you questions about yourself. I've no intention of doing so, now or in the future."

"You wouldn't be having a dossier on me, would you?"

"Tuesday, September 5, 1939, was the day and date you entered your secondary school in Dundee, Scotland."

"Jesus!"

"What's so sensitive about the Fairbanks area? Why strengthen your defenses there particularly?"

Finlayson shifted in his seat. "No hard-and-fast reason, really."

"Never mind whether it's hard and fast. The reason?"

Finlayson drew in his breath as if he were about to sigh, then seemed to change his mind. "Bit silly, really. You know how whisperings can generate a hoodoo. People on the line are a bit scared of that sector. You'll know that the pipeline has three mountain ranges to traverse on its eight-hundred-mile run south to the terminal at Valdez. So, pump stations, twelve in all. Pump Station Number Eight is close to Fairbanks. It blew up in the summer of seventy-seven. Completely destroyed."

"Fatalities?"

"Yes."

"Explanations given for this blow-up?"

"Of course."

"Satisfactory?"

"The pipeline construction company—Alyeska—were satisfied."

"But not everyone?"

"The public was skeptical. State and federal agencies withheld comment."

"What reason did Alyeska give?"

"Mechanical and electrical malfunction."

"Do *you* believe that?"

"I wasn't there."

"The explanation was generally accepted?"

"The explanation was widely disbelieved."

"Sabotage, perhaps?"

"Perhaps. I don't know. I was here at the time. I've never even seen Pump Station Number Eight. Been rebuilt, of course."

Dermott sighed. "This is where I should be showing some slight traces of exasperation. Don't believe in committing yourself, do you, Mr. Finlayson? Still, you'd probably make a good security agent. I don't suppose you'd like to venture an opinion as to whether there was a cover-up or not?"

"My opinion hardly matters. What matters, I suppose, is that the Alaskan press was damned certain there was, and said so loud and clear. The fact that the papers appeared unconcerned about the possibility of libel action could be regarded as significant. They would have welcomed a public inquiry. One assumes that Alyeska would not have."

"Why were the newspapers stirred up—or is that an unnecessary question?"

"What incensed the press was that they were prevented for many hours from reaching the scene of the accident. What doubly incensed them was that they were prevented not by peace officers of the state but by Alyeska's private guards who, incredibly, took it upon themselves to close state roads. Even their local PR man agreed that this amounted to illegal restraint."

"Anybody sue?"

"No court action resulted."

"Why?"

When Finlayson shrugged, Dermott went on, "Could it have been because Alyeska is the biggest employer in the state, because the life blood of so many companies depends on their contracts with Alyeska? In other words, big money talking big?"

"Possibly."

"Any minute now I'll be signing you up for Jim Brady. What *did* the press say?"

"Because they'd been prevented for a whole day from getting to the scene of the accident, they believed Alyeska employees had been working feverishly during that time to clean up and minimize the effects of the accident, to remove the evidence of a major spillage and to conceal the fact that their fail-safe system had failed dangerously. Alyeska had also—the press said—covered up the worst effects of the fire damage."

"Might they also have removed or covered up incriminating evidence pointing to sabotage?"

"No guessing games for me."

"All right. Do you or Bronowski know of any disaffected elements in Fairbanks?"

"Depends what you mean by disaffected. If you mean environmentalists opposed to the construction of the pipeline, yes. Hundreds—and very strongly opposed."

"But I assume they're open about it—always give their full names and addresses when writing to the papers."

"Yes."

"Besides, environmentalists tend to be sensitive and non-violent people who work within the confines of the law."

"About any other disaffected types, I wouldn't know. There are fifteen thousand people in Fairbanks, and it would be optimistic to expect they're all as pure as the driven snow."

"What did Bronowski think of the incident?"

"He wasn't there."

"That wasn't what I asked . . ."

"He was in New York at the time. He hadn't even joined the company then."

"A relative newcomer, then?"

"Yes. In your book, I suppose that automatically makes him a suspect. If you wish to go ahead and waste your time investigating his antecedents, by all means do so, but I could save you time and effort by telling you that we had him checked, double-checked and triple-checked by three separate top-flight agencies. The New York Police Department gave him a clean bill of health. His record and that of his company are—were—impeccable."

"I don't doubt it. What were his qualifications, and what was his company?"

"One and the same thing, really. He headed up one of the biggest and arguably the best security agencies in New York. Before that he was a cop."

"What did his company specialize in?"

"Nothing but the best. Guards, mainly. Additional guards for a handful of the biggest banks when their own security forces were understaffed by holidays or illness. Guarding the homes of the richest people in Manhattan and Long Island to prevent the ungodly making off with the guests' jewelry when large-scale social functions were being held. His third specialty was providing security for exhibitions of precious gems and paintings. If you could ever persuade the Dutch to lend you Rembrandt's 'Night Watch' for a couple of months, Bronowski would be the man you'd send for."

"What would induce a man to leave all that and come to this end of the world?"

"He doesn't say. He doesn't have to. Homesickness. More specifically, his wife's homesickness. She lives in Anchorage. He flies down there every weekend."

"I thought you were supposed to do a full four weeks up here before you got time off."

"Doesn't apply to Bronowski—only to those whose permanent job is here. This is his nominal base, but the whole line is his responsibility. For instance, if there's trouble in Valdez, he's a damn sight nearer it in his wife's flat in Anchorage than he would be if he were up here. And he's very mobile, is our Sam. Owns and flies his own Comanche. We pay his fuel, that's all."

"He's not without the odd penny to his name?"

"I should say not. He doesn't really need this job, but he can't bear to be inactive. Money? He retains the controlling interest in his New York firm."

"No conflict of interests?"

"How the hell could there be a conflict of interests? He's never even been out of the state since he arrived here over a year ago."

"A trustworthy lad, it would seem. Damn few of them around these days." Dermott looked at Mackenzie. "Donald?"

"Yes?" Mackenzie picked up the unsigned letter from Edmonton. "FBI seen this?"

"Of course not. What's it got to do with FBI?"

"It might have an awful lot to do with them, and soon. I know Alaskans think that this is a nation apart, that this is your own special and private fiefdom up here, and that you refer to us unfortunates as the lower forty-eight, but you're still part of the United States. When the oil from the pipeline arrives at Valdez, it's shipped to one of the West Coast states. Any interruption in oil transfer between Prudhoe Bay and, say, California, would be regarded as an unlawful interference with interstate commerce and would automatically bring in the FBI."

"Well, it hasn't happened yet. Besides, what can the FBI do? They know nothing of oil or pipeline security. Look after the pipeline? They couldn't even look after themselves. We'd just spend most of our time trying to thaw out the few of them who didn't freeze to death during their first ten minutes here. They could only survive under cover, so what could they do there? Take over our computer terminals and master communications and alarm detection stations at Prudhoe Bay, Fairbanks and Valdez? We have highly trained specialists to monitor over three thousand sources of alarm information. Asking the FBI to do that would be like asking a blind man to read Sanskrit. Inside or out, they'd only be in the way and a useless burden to all concerned."

"Alaska State Troopers could survive. I guess they'd survive where even some of your own men couldn't. Have you been in touch with them? Have you notified the state authorities in Juneau?"

"No."

"Why not?"

"They don't love us. Oh, sure, if there was physical trouble—violence—they'd move in immediately. Until then, they'd rather not know. I can't say I blame them. And before you ask me why I'll tell you. For good or bad, we've inherited the Alyeska mantle. Alyeska built the pipeline and they run it, but we use it. I'm afraid there's a wide gray area of non-discrimination here. In most people's eyes they *were* pipeline, we *are* pipeline."

Finlayson reflected on his next words. "It's hard not to feel a bit sorry for Alyeska. They were pretty cruelly pilloried. Sure, they bore the responsibility for a remarkable amount of waste, and incurred vast cost overruns, but they did complete an impossible job in impossible conditions and, what's more, brought it in on schedule. Best construction company in North America at the time. Brilliant engineering and brilliant engineers—but the brilliance stopped short of their PR people, who might as well have been operating in downtown Manhattan for all they knew about Alaskans. Their job should have been to sell the pipeline to the people. All they succeeded in doing was in turning a large section of the population solidly against the line and the construction company."

He shook his head. "You had to be truly gifted to get it as wrong as they did. They sought to protect the good name of Alyeska, but all they did, by blatant cover-ups—it was alleged—and by deliberate lying, was to bring whatever good name there was into total disrepute."

Finlayson reached into a drawer, took out two sheets

of paper and gave them to Dermott and Mackenzie. "Photostats of a classic example of the way they handled those under contract to them. One would assume they learned their trade in one of the more repressive police states. Read it. You'll find it instructive. You'll also understand how by simple thought transference we're not in line for much public sympathy."

The two men read the photostats.

Alyeska Pipeline Service   Supplement No. 20
   Company   Revision No. 1
Pipeline and Roads   April 1, 1974
Job Specification   Page 2004

C. IN NO EVENT SHALL CONTRACTOR OR ITS PERSONNEL REPORT A LEAK OR AN OIL SPILL TO ANY GOVERN- MENTAL AGENCY. Such reporting shall be the sole responsibility of ALYESKA. CONTRACTOR shall emphasize this to all its supervisory personnel and employees.

D. Further, IN NO EVENT SHALL CON- TRACTOR OR ITS PERSONNEL DIS-

CUSS, REPORT, OR COMMUNICATE
IN ANY WAY WITH NEWS MEDIA
whether the news media be radio, television,
newspapers or periodicals. Any such communication by CONTRACTOR shall be
deemed to be a material breach of CON-
TRACT by CONTRACTOR. All contracts
with news media regarding leaks or oil spills
shall be made by ALYESKA. If news media
people contact CONTRACTOR or CON-
TRACTOR's personnel, they shall refer news
media to ALYESKA without further discussing, reporting or communicating. CON-
TRACTOR shall emphasize the afore-
mentioned ALYESKA news media require-
ments to all its supervisory personnel and employees.

Dermott rested the photostat on his knee. "An *American* wrote this?"

"An American of foreign extraction," Mackenzie said,
"who obviously trained under Goebbels."

"A charming directive," Dermott said. "Hush-up,
cover-up or lose your contract. Toe the line or you're
fired. A shining example of American democracy at its

finest. Well, well." He glanced briefly at the paper, then at Finlayson. "How did you get hold of this? Classified information, surely?"

"Oddly enough, no. What you would call the public domain. Editorial page, *All-Alaska Weekly*, July 22, 1977. I don't question it *was* classified. How the paper got hold of it, I don't know."

"Nice to see a little paper going against the might of a giant company and getting away with it. Restores one's faith in something or other."

Finlayson picked up another photostat. "The same editorial also made a despairing reference to the 'horrendous negative impact of the pipeline on us.' That's as true now as it was then. We've inherited this horrendous negative impact, and we're still suffering from it. So there it is. I'm not saying we're entirely friendless, or that the authorities wouldn't move in quickly if there were any overt violations of the law, but, because votes are important, those in charge of our destinies rule from behind. They sense the wind of public opinion, then enact acceptable legislation and adopt correspondingly safe attitudes. Whatever happens, they're not going to antagonize those who keep them in power. They are not, with the public's eye on both them and us, going to come and hold our hands because of any anonymous threat by some anonymous crackpot."

Mackenzie said, "So it amounts to this. Until actual sabotage occurs, you can expect no outside help. So far as preventative measures are concerned, you're dependent solely upon Bronowski and his security teams. In effect, you're on your own."

"It's an unhappy thought, but there it is."

Dermott stood up and walked back and forth. "Accepting this threat as real, who's behind it and what does he want? Not a crackpot, that's sure. If it were, say, some environmentalist running amok, he'd go ahead and do his damnedest without any prior warning. No, could be with a view to extortion or blackmail, which do not have to be the same thing. Extortion would be for money; blackmail could have many different purposes in mind. Stopping the flow of oil is unlikely to be that primary purpose. More likely, it'll be a stoppage for another and more important purpose. Money, politics—local or international—power, misguided idealism, genuine idealism or just crackpot irresponsibility. Well, I'm afraid speculation will have to wait on developments. Meantime, Mr. Finlayson, I'd like to see Bronowski as soon as possible."

"I told you, he has business to finish. He'll be flying up in a few hours."

"Ask him to fly up now, please."

"Sorry. Bronowski's his own man. Overall, he's answerable to me, but not in field operations. He'd walk out if I tried to usurp his authority. Unless he had the power to act independently, he'd be effectively hamstrung. You don't hire a dog and bark yourself."

"I don't think you quite understand. Mr. Mackenzie and I have not only been promised total co-operation, we've been empowered to direct security measures if, in our judgment, such extreme measures are dictated by circumstances."

Finlayson's Yukon beard still masked his expression, but there was no mistaking the disbelief in his voice. "You mean, take over from Bronowski?"

"If, again in our judgment, he's good enough, we just sit by the sidelines and advise. If not, we will exercise the authority invested in us."

"Invested by whom? This is preposterous. I will not, I cannot permit it. You walk in here and imagine—no, no way. I have received no such directive."

"Then I suggest you seek such a directive, or confirmation of it, immediately."

"From whom?"

"The grand panjandrums, as you call them."

"London?" Dermott said nothing. "That's for Mr. Black."

Dermott remained silent.

"General manager, Alaska."

Dermott nodded at the three telephones on Finlayson's desk. "He's as far away as one of those."

"He's out of state. He's visiting our offices in Seattle, San Francisco and Los Angeles. At what times and in what order I don't know. I do know he'll be back in Anchorage at noon tomorrow."

"Are you telling me that is the soonest you can—or will—contact him?"

"Yes."

"You could phone those offices."

"I've told you, I don't know where he'd be. He could be at some other place altogether. Like as not, he's in the air."

"You could try, couldn't you?" Finlayson remained silent and Dermott spoke again. "You could call London direct."

"You don't know much about the hierarchy in oil companies, do you?"

"No. But I know this." Now Dermott's customary geniality was gone. "You're a considerable disappointment, Finlayson. You are, or very well may be, in serious trouble. In the circumstances, one does not expect an executive in top management to resort to stiff outrage and wounded pride. You've got your priorities wrong, my friend—the good of the company comes first, not your feelings or protecting your ass."

Finlayson's eyes showed no expression. Mackenzie was staring at the ceiling as if he had found something of absorbing interest there. Dermott, he had learned over the years, was a past master at pinning an adversary into a corner. The victim either surrendered or placed himself in an impossible situation of which Dermott would take ruthless advantage. If he couldn't get co-operation, he would settle for nothing less than domination.

Dermott went on, "I have made three requests, all of which I regard as perfectly reasonable, and you have refused all three. You persist in your refusals?"

"Yes, I do."

Dermott said, "Well, Donald, what are my options?"

"There are none." Mackenzie sounded sad. "Only the inevitable."

"Yes." Dermott looked at Finlayson coldly. "You have a radio microwave band to Valdez that links up with the continental exchanges." He pushed a card toward Finlayson. "Or would you refuse me permission to talk to my head office in Houston?"

Finlayson said nothing. He took the card, lifted the phone and talked to the switchboard. After three minutes' silence, which only Finlayson seemed to find uncomfortable, the phone rang. Finlayson listened briefly then handed over the phone.

Dermott said, "Brady Enterprises? Mr. Brady, please . . . Dermott." There was a pause, then, "Good afternoon, Jim."

"Well, well, George." Brady's strong carrying voice was clearly audible in the office. "Prudhoe Bay, is it? Coincidence, coincidence. I was just on the point of phoning you."

"Well. My report, Jim. News, rather. There's nothing to report."

"And I have news for you. Mine first, it's more important. Open line?"

"One moment." Dermott looked at Finlayson. "What security classification does your switchboard operator have?"

"None. Jesus, she's only a telephone girl."

"As you so rightly observe, Jesus! Heaven help the

trans-Alaska pipeline." He pulled out a notebook and pencil and addressed the phone. "Sorry, Jim. Open. Go
ahead."

In a clear, precise voice Brady began to recite a seem-
ingly meaningless jumble of letters and figures which Dermott noted down in neatly printed script. After about two
minutes Brady paused and said, "Repeat?"

"No thanks."

"You have something to say?"

"Just this. Field manager here unco-operative, unrea-
sonable and obstructive. I don't think we can profitably
operate here. Permission to pull out."

There was only a brief pause before Brady said
clearly, "Permission granted." There came the click of a
replaced receiver and Dermott rose to his feet.

Finlayson was already on his. "Mr. Dermott—"

Dermott looked down at him icily and spoke in a
voice as cold as winter, "Give my love to London, Mr.
Finlayson, if you're ever there."

TWO

THIRTEEN HUNDRED MILES SOUTHEAST of Prudhoe Bay, at ten P.M., Brady's men met Jay Shore in the bar of the Peter Pond Hotel in Fort McMurray. Among those qualified to pass judgment on such matters, it was readily agreed that as an engineering construction manager Shore had no peer in Canada. His face was dark, saturnine, almost piratical—which was rather an unfair trick for nature to play on him, since that same nature had made him easygoing, companionable, humorous and cheerful.

Not that he felt in the least humorous and cheerful at that moment. Nor did the man who sat beside him, Bill

Reynolds, Sanmobil's operations manager, a rubicund and normally smiling man to whom nature had given precisely the kind of diabolical mind that Shore appeared to have but didn't.

Bill Reynolds looked across the table to Dermott and Mackenzie, whom he and Shore had met thirty seconds previously, and said, "You make fast time, gentlemen. Remarkable service, if one may say so."

"We try," Dermott said comfortably. "We do our best."

"Scotch?" asked Mackenzie.

"Thanks." Reynolds nodded. "Twin jet—is that it?"

"Right."

"A shade expensive, a man would think."

"Gets you around." Dermott smiled.

"Head office—that's Edmonton—told us you might take up to four days. We didn't expect you in four *hours*." Reynolds eyed Dermott speculatively over his newly poured glass. "I'm afraid we don't know much about you."

"Fair enough. We probably know even less about you."

"Not oilmen, then?"

"Of course. But drilling oilmen. We're not familiar with mining the stuff."

"And your full-time job is security?"

"That's right."

"So there's no need to ask what you were doing up on the North Slope?"

"Right again."

"How long were you up there?"

"Two hours."

"Two hours! You mean you can lick a security—"

"We licked nothing. We left."

"May one ask why?"

"Operations manager was . . . unhelpful, let's say."

"Me and my big mouth."

"Meaning?"

"I'm the operations manager here. But I get the message."

Dermott said pleasantly, "No message. You asked a question, I answered."

"And you decided to walk out—"

"We have a backlog of cases all over the world, and no time to waste trying to help those who won't help themselves. Let's not get off on the wrong foot, gentlemen —your company expects Mackenzie and me to do the questioning while you do the answering. When was this threat received?"

Shore said, "Ten o'clock this morning."

"You have it with you?"

"Not exactly. It came by phone."

"Where from?"

"Anchorage. International call."

"Who took the message?"

"I did. Bill here was with me, listening in. Caller gave us his message twice. Word for word he said, 'I have to inform you that Sanmobil will be incurring a slight interruption in oil production in the near future. Not much, I assure you, just sufficient to convince you that we can interrupt oil flow whenever and wherever we please.' That was all."

"No demands?"

"No—surprisingly."

"Don't worry. The demands will come when the big threat does. Would you recognize this voice again?"

"Would I recognize the voices of a million other Canadians who talk exactly as he does? You take this threat seriously?"

"I do. We take most things seriously. How good is security at the plant?"

"Well—fair enough for normal circumstances, I suppose."

"These promise to be highly abnormal circumstances. How many guards?"

"Twenty-four, under Terry Brinckman. He knows what he's doing."

"I don't doubt it. Guard dogs?"

"None. The usual police dogs—alsatians, dobermans, boxers—can't survive in these extreme conditions. Huskies can, of course, but they make lousy watchdogs—they're more interested in fighting each other than looking for intruders."

"Electric fences?"

Shore rolled his eyes upward and looked sorrowful. "You want to equip the environmentalists with a gallows right on the site? Why, if even the meanest old wolf were to singe its mangy hide . . ."

"Okay, okay. I suppose it's pointless to ask about electronic beams, sensor devices and the like?"

"Pointless is right."

Mackenzie said, "How big is this plant site?"

Reynolds looked unhappy. "About eight thousand acres."

"Eight thousand acres." Mackenzie's voice was all doom. "What kind of perimeter would that make for?"

"Fourteen miles."

"Yes. We have a problem here," Mackenzie said. "I take it your security duties are twofold: the guarding of vital installations in the plant itself and patrolling the perimeter to keep intruders out?"

Reynolds nodded. "The guards are in three shifts, eight men per shift."

"Eight men, without any protective aids at all, to guard the plant itself and at the same time patrol fourteen miles of perimeter in the blackness of a winter night."

Shore was defensive. "Ours is a twenty-four-hour operation. The plant is brilliantly lit day and night."

"But the perimeter isn't. A blind man could drive a coach and four—hell, why go on? A couple of army regiments might help, although I doubt even that. As I say, a problem."

"Not only that," Dermott said, "all the brilliant illumination in the world isn't of the slightest help. Not when you've got hundreds of workers on each of the three shifts a day."

"Meaning?"

"Subversives."

"Subversives! Less than two per cent of the work force are non-Canadians."

"There's been a royal decree abolishing Canadian criminals? When you hire, you investigate backgrounds?"

"Well, not intensive questioning, third degree, lie detector tests or any of that rubbish. Try that and you'd never hire anyone. We check on previous experience, qualifications, recommendations and, most important, criminal records."

"That's the least important. Really clever criminals never *have* criminal records." Dermott looked like a man who had been about to sigh, explode, curse or quit, but had changed his mind. "Well—it's late. Tomorrow, Mr. Mackenzie and I would like to talk to your Terry Brinckman and look over the plant."

"If we have a car here at ten o'clock—"

"How about seven o'clock? Yes, seven will be fine."

Dermott and Mackenzie watched the two men go, looked at each other, emptied their glasses, signaled the barman, then looked out through the windows of the Peter Pond Hotel, named after the first white man ever to see the tar sands.

Pond went down the Athabasca River by canoe almost exactly two hundred years before. He did not take too much interest in the sands, it appears, but ten years later the much more famous explorer Alexander Mackenzie was intrigued by the sticky substance oozing from outcrops high above the river, and wrote: "The bitumen is in a fluid state, and when mixed with gum, or the resinous substance collected from the spruce fir, serves to gum the Indians' canoes. In its heated state it emits a smell like that of sea-coal."

Oddly, the significance of the words "sea-coal" wasn't appreciated for more than a hundred years; nobody realized that the two eighteenth-century explorers had stumbled across one of the world's largest reservoirs of fossil fuels. But had they not so stumbled, there would have been no Peter Pond Hotel where it is today nor, indeed, the township beyond its windows.

Even in the mid-nineteen-sixties Fort McMurray was little more than a rough, primitive frontier outpost, with a population of only thirteen hundred, and streets covered with dust, mud or slush according to season. By now, though still a frontier town, it had become a frontier town with a difference. Treasuring its past, but with an eye to the future, it was the epitome of a boomtown and, in terms of burgeoning population, the fastest expanding township in Canada. Where there were thirteen hundred citizens fourteen years earlier, there were now thirteen thousand. Schools, hotels, banks, hospitals, churches, supermarkets and, above all, hundreds of new houses stood and more were being built. And, wonder of wonders, the streets were paved. This seeming miracle stemmed from one factor and one factor only: Fort McMurray sits squarely in the heart of the Athabasca tar sands, the biggest such known deposits in the world.

It had been snowing heavily earlier in the evening and

had still not completely stopped. Everything—houses, streets, car tops, trees—was under a smooth cover of white. Hundreds of lights shone hospitably through the gently falling flakes. The scene would have gladdened the eye and heart of a Christmas postcard artist. Some such thought had occurred to Mackenzie.

"Santa Claus should be here tonight."

"Indeed." Dermott sounded morose. "Especially if he brought along some of that peace on earth and goodwill to all men. Whatever happened to peace on earth? We're running low on goodwill toward men. Shortage of everything. What did you make of that telephone message to Sanmobil?"

"Same thing you did. Practically identical to the letter Finlayson received up in Prudhoe Bay. Obviously the work of the same man or group of men."

"And what do you make of the fact that Alaskan oil people got a threatening message from Alberta, while the Albertan oil interests received the same threat from Alaska?"

"Nothing—except that both threats had the same origin. That call from Anchorage. For a certainty, from a public telephone booth. Untraceable."

"Probably. Not certainly. I don't know if you can dial direct from Anchorage to here. I don't think so, but we can find out. If not, the telephone operator will have a record. There's a chance that we might locate the phone."

Mackenzie briefly surveyed Fort McMurray through the base of his glass and said, "That'll be a big help."

"It might be a small help. Two ways. That call came in at ten this morning. That's six A.M. Anchorage time. Who except a nut—or some night-shift worker—is going to be out in the black and freezing streets of Anchorage at that hour? That sort of odd behavior, I suggest, isn't likely to go unnoticed."

"If there's anyone there to notice."

"State Troopers in a patrol car. Taxi driver. Snow-plow driver. Mailman on the way to work. You'd be surprised at the number of people who go about their lawful occasions in the dark watches of the night."

"I would not be surprised." Mackenzie spoke with some feeling. "We've done it often enough in this damned job of ours. Two ways, you said. What's the second way?"

"*If* we locate this pay phone, we have the police remove the coin box and give it to their fingerprint boys. The chances are good that the person who made the call to Fort McMurray used more high-denomination coins than anyone else who went into the pay phone that day—or night. Get two or three large coins with the same prints, and that's our man."

"Objection. Coins are handled by many people. You'll get prints, all right. A plethora, shall we say, of fingerprints."

"Objection overruled. It's established that on a metal surface—the overlay—the last person to touch such a surface leaves the dominant print. By the same token, we'd print the area around the dial. People don't dial in fur mittens. Then we'd check with criminal records. The prints may be on file. If they are, we'll get the man and ask him all sorts of interesting questions."

"You do have a devious mind, George. Low cunning, but albeit a mind. First catch your man, though."

"If we get a description or prints with history, it shouldn't be too difficult. If he's gone to ground, it would be different. But there's no reason why he should think he has to take cover. Might be awkward for him anyway. May well be a pillar of the Anchorage business and social communities."

"I'll bet the other Anchorage pillars would love to hear you say that. They'd have the same opinion of you as our friend John Finlayson has now. What are we going to do about Finlayson, anyway? *Rapprochement* doesn't seem advisable—it's essential. With the tie-up so obvious—"

"Let him stew in his own juice for a while. I don't mean that the way it sounds, but just let him worry awhile in Prudhoe Bay until we're ready. He's a good man, intelligent, honest. He reacted precisely the way you or I would have if a couple of interlopers had tried to take over. The longer we stay away, the more certainly we're guaranteed his co-operation when we get back. Jim Brady may have been the bearer of bad news, but that call of his couldn't have come at a more opportune time. Gave us the perfect excuse to take off. Speaking of Jim—"

"I've been thinking that I don't much like any of this. Presentiments. My Scottish forebears, one presumes. You know that Prudhoe Bay and this place here contain well over half the oil reserves of North America. It's an awful lot of oil. A man wouldn't want anything to happen to these two."

"You haven't worried about such things before. An investigator is supposed to be cold, clinical, detached."

"That's about other people's oil. This is *our* oil. Massive responsibilities. Awesome decisions at the highest levels."

"We were talking of Jim Brady."

"I still am."

"You think we should have him up here?"

"I do."

"So do I. Must be why I raised the subject. Let's go call him."

THREE

JIM BRADY, THAT PASSIONATE BELIEVER IN leanness, keenness, fitness and athleticism for his field operatives, stood five feet eight in his elevator shoes and turned the scales at around 240 pounds. Never a believer in traveling light, he brought with him on the flight from Houston not only his attractive, blond wife, Jean, but also his positively stunning daughter Stella, another natural blond, who acted as his secretary on these field trips. He left Jean behind at the hotel in Fort McMurray, but kept Stella with him in the minibus that Sanmobil had sent to ferry him out to the plant.

The first impression he made on the hard men of

Athabasca was less than favorable. He wore a superbly cut dark-gray business suit—it had to be well cut even to approximate a frame as spherical as his—a white shirt and a conservative tie. On top of these indoor clothes, however, he wore two woolen overcoats and a vast beaver coat, the combined effect being to render his vertical and horizontal dimensions approximately equal. He sported a soft felt hat the same color as his suit, but this too was almost invisible, anchored by a gray woolen scarf that passed twice over the crown and under his chins.

"Well I'll be damned!" he exclaimed. His voice was muffled by the ends of the scarf, tied across his face just below the eyes, which were the only part of him that could be seen. Even so, it was clear to his companions that he was impressed.

"This sure is something. You boys must have a lot of fun digging away here and building these nice little ol' sand castles."

"That's one way of putting it, Mr. Brady." Jay Shore spoke with restraint. "Not much, perhaps, by Texas standards, but it's still the biggest mining operation in the history of mankind."

"No offense, no offense. You don't expect a Texan to admit there's something bigger and better outside his own state?" One could almost feel him bracing himself for a handsome admission. "That beats anything I've ever come across."

"That" was a dragline, but a dragline such as Brady had never seen before. A dragline is essentially an engine housing with a control cabin that operates a cranelike boom. The boom is hinged and swiveled at the base of the engine housing, and so can be both raised and lowered and swung from side to side. Control is achieved by cables from the engine housing which pass over a massive steel super-structure and reach out to the tip of the boom. Another cable, passing over the tip of the boom, supports a bucket which can be lowered to scoop up material, raised again and then swung to one side to dump its load.

"Biggest thing that ever moved on earth," said Shore.

"*Move?*" Stella said.

"Yes, it can move. Walks, shuffles would be a better word, on those two huge shoes at the base, step by step. You wouldn't want to enter it for the Kentucky Derby—it takes seven hours to travel a mile. Not that it's ever required to travel more than a few yards at a time. Point is, it gets there."

"And that long nose . . ." she said.

"The boom. The comparison most generally used is that it's as long as a football field. Wrong—it's longer. From here the bucket doesn't look all that big, but that's only because everything is dwarfed out of perspective. It scoops up eighty cubic yards at a time or enough to fill a two-car garage. A large two-car garage. The dragline weighs sixty-five hundred tons—about the same as a light-medium cruiser. Cost? About thirty million dollars. Takes fifteen to eighteen months to build—on the site, of course. There are four of them, and between them they can shift up to a quarter of a million tons a day."

"You win. This is a boomtown." Brady said. "Let's get inside. I'm cold." The other four—Dermott, Mackenzie, Shore and Brinckman, the security chief—looked at him in mild astonishment. It seemed impossible that a man so extravagantly upholstered and insulated, both naturally and otherwise, could possibly feel even cool, but if Brady said he was cold, he was cold.

They clambered into the minibus, which if a bit short on other creature comforts, did at least have heaters in excellent condition. Also in excellent condition was the girl who sat down in the back seat, lowered her parka hood, and beamed at them. Brinckman was much the youngest of the men, and had not paid much attention to Stella. Now he touched the rim of his fur cap and lit up like a lamp. His enthusiasm was hardly surprising, for the white fur parka made her as cuddly looking as a polar bear cub.

"Wanna' dictate anything, Dad?" she asked.

"Not yet," Brady grunted. Once safely sheltered from the vicious cold, he undid the ends of the scarf that concealed his face. Somewhere in the distant past there must have been signs of the character that had driven him from the back streets of poverty to his present millions, but years of gracious living had eradicated all trace of them. Bone structure had vanished under a fatty accumulation which had left him without a crease, line or even the hint of crow's feet. It was a fat, spoiled face like a cherub's. With one exception: There was nothing cherubic about the eyes. They were blue, cool, appraising and shrewd.

He looked through the window at the dragline. "So that's the end of the line."

"The beginning of it," Shore said. "The tar sands may lie as deep as fifty feet down. The stuff above, the over-burden, is useless to us—gravel, clay, muskeg, shale, oil-poor sand—and has to be removed first of all." He pointed to an approaching vehicle. "Here's some of that rubbish being carried away now—it's been excavated by another dragline on a new site.

"To impress you further, Mr. Brady, those trucks are also the biggest in the world. A hundred and twenty-five tons empty, payload of a hundred and fifty, and all this on just four tires. But, you will admit, they are some tires."

The truck was passing now, and they were indeed some tires; to Brady, they looked at least ten feet high and proportionately bulky. The truck itself was monstrous—twenty feet high at the cab and about the same width, with the driver mounted so high as to be barely visible from the ground.

"You could buy a very acceptable car for the price of one of those tires," Shore said. "As for the truck itself, if you went shopping for one at today's prices, you wouldn't get much change from three quarters of a million." He spoke to his driver, who started up and moved slowly off.

"When the overburden is gone, the same dragline scoops up the tar sand—as the one we've just looked at is doing now—and dumps it in this huge pile we call a windrow." A weird machine of phenomenal length was nosing into the pile. Shore pointed and said, "A bucket-wheel reclaimer—there's one paired with every dragline. Four hundred and twenty-eight feet long. You can see the revolving bucket wheel biting into the windrow. With fourteen buckets on a forty-foot-diameter wheel, it can remove a fair tonnage every minute. The tar sands are then transported along the spine of the reclaimer—the bridge, we call it—to the separators. From there—"

Brady interrupted, "Separators?"

"Sometimes the sands come in big, solid lumps as hard as rock, which could damage the conveyor belts. The separators are just vibrating screens that sort out the lumps."

"And without the separators the conveyor belts could be damaged?"

"Certainly."

"Put out of commission?"

"Probably. We don't know. It's never been allowed to happen yet."

"And then?"

"The tar sands go into the traveling hoppers you see there. They drop the stuff onto the conveyor belt, and off it goes to the processing plant. After that—"

"One minute." It was Dermott. "You have a fair amount of this conveyor belting?"

"A fair bit."

"How much exactly?"

Shore looked uncomfortable. "Sixteen miles." Dermott stared at him and Shore hurried on. "At the end of the conveyor system radial stackers direct it to what are called surge piles—just really storage dumps."

"Radial stackers?" said Brady. "What are they?"

"Elevated extensions of the conveyor belts. They can rotate through a certain arc to direct the tar sands to a suitable surge pile. They can also feed bins that take the sands underground to start the processes of chemical and physical separation of the bitumen. The first of those processes—"

"Jesus!" said Mackenzie incredulously.

"That about sums it up," Dermott said. "I have no wish to be rude, Mr. Shore, but I don't want to hear about the extraction processes. I've already heard and seen all I want to."

"Good God Almighty!" exclaimed Mackenzie by way of variation.

Brady said, "What's the matter, gentlemen?"

Dermott picked his words carefully. "When Don and I were talking to Mr. Shore and Mr. Reynolds, the operations manager, last night, we thought we had reason to be concerned. I now realize we were wasting our time on trifles. But, by God, now I am worried.

"Last night we had to face the fact of the ridiculous ease with which the perimeter can be penetrated and the almost equal ease with which subversives could be introduced onto the plant floor. In retrospect, those are but bagatelles. How many points did you pick up, Don?"

"Six."

"My count also. First off, the draglines. They look as impregnable as the Rock of Gibraltar. They are, in fact, pathetically vulnerable. A hundred tons of high explosive would hardly dent the Rock of Gibraltar, but I could take out a dragline with two five-pound charges of wrap-around explosive placed where the boom is hinged to the machine house."

Brinckman, an intelligent and clearly competent person in his early thirties, spoke for the first time in fifteen minutes, then immediately wished he hadn't. He said, "Fine, if you could approach the dragline—but you can't. The area is lit by brilliant floodlights."

"Jesus!" Mackenzie's limited repertoire was in use again.

"What do you mean, Mr. Mackenzie?"

"What I mean is I would locate the breaker or switch or whatever that supplies the power to the floodlights and immobilize it by smashing it or by the brilliantly innovative device of turning it off. Or, I'd cut the power lines. Simpler still, with a five-second burst from a submachine gun I'd shoot them out. Assuming, of course, that they're not made of bulletproof glass."

Dermott saved Brinckman the embarrassment of a long silence. "Five pounds of commercial Amatol would take out the bucket wheel for an indefinite period. A similar amount would take care of the reclaimer's bridge. Two pounds to buckle the separator plate. That's four ways. Getting at the radial stackers would be another excellent device—that would mean Sanmobil couldn't even get the tar sands stockpiled in the surge piles down below for processing. And then, best of all, is this little matter of sixteen unpatrolled miles of conveyor belting."

There was quiet in the bus until Dermott rumbled on. "Why bother sabotaging the separation plant when it's so much simpler and more effective to interrupt the flow of raw material? You can't very well carry out a processing operation if you've got nothing to process. It'd be childishly simple. Four draglines. Four bucket wheels. Four reclaimers' bridges. Four separators. Four radial stackers. Sixteen miles of conveyor, fourteen miles of unpatrolled perimeter, and eight men to cover. Situation's ludicrous. I'm afraid, Mr. Brady, there's no way in the world we can stop our Anchorage friend from carrying out his threat."

Brady turned what appeared to be one cold, blue eye on the unfortunate Brinckman. "And what do you have to say?"

"What can I say except to agree? Even if I had ten times the number of men at my disposal, we still wouldn't be geared to meet a threat like this." He shrugged. "I'm sorry, I didn't even dream of anything like this."

"Nor did anyone else. Nothing to reproach yourself about. You security people thought you were in the oil business, not at war. What are your normal duties, anyway?"

"We're here to prevent three things—physical trouble

among members of the work force, petty pilfering, and drinking on the plant site. But so far we've had few instances of any of them."

Visibly, Brinckman's words struck a chord in Brady. "Ah, yes. Trouble in moments of stress and all that." He turned in his seat. "Stella!"

"Yes, Dad." She opened a wicker basket, produced a flask and glass, poured a drink and handed it to her father.

"Daiquiri," he said. "We also have scotch, gin, rum—"

"Sorry, Mr. Brady," Shore said. "No. The company has very strict regulations."

Brady gave him some terse suggestions as to what he could do with company regulations and turned to Brinckman again.

"So, in effect, you've been pretty superfluous up till now and, if anything, are going to be even more so in the future?"

"I'd agree with half of that. The fact that we've had little to do up to now doesn't mean we've been superfluous. Presence is important. You don't heave a brick through a jeweler's window if there's an interested cop standing by five feet away. As to the future, yes, I agree. I feel pretty helpless."

"If you were carrying out an attack somewhere, what would you go for?"

Brinckman was not of two minds. "The conveyor belting every time."

Brady looked at Dermott and Mackenzie. Both men nodded.

"Mr. Shore?"

"Agreed." Shore was absentmindedly sipping some scotch that had found its way into his hand. "Apart from the fact that there's so damn much of it, it's fragile. Six feet wide, but the steel cord belting is only an inch and a half thick. With a sledgehammer and chisel I could wreck it myself." Shore looked and sounded tense. "Not many people are aware of the vast quantities of material that are processed here. To keep the plant operating at capacity and to make the project commercially viable, we need close on a quarter of a million tons of tar sands a day. As I said, the biggest mining operation ever. Cut off the supplies, and the plant closes down in a few hours. That's a hundred and thirty thousand barrels of oil a day lost. Even Sanmobil couldn't stand this kind of loss indefinitely."

"How much did it cost to set up this plant?" Brady asked.

"Two billion, near enough."

"Two billion dollars. And a potential operating loss of a hundred and thirty thousand barrels of oil a day." Brady shook his head. "No one's arguing about the brilliance of the men who dreamed up this idea. Same goes for the engineers who made it work. But there's another thing no one would question—at least *I* would never question—and that is that those towering intellects had a huge blind spot. Why didn't the bosses foresee this? I know it's easy to be wise after the event, but, goddamn, you don't need much foresight to think of that. Oil is not just another business. Couldn't they have seen the giant potential for hate or crackpots—or blackmail? Couldn't they have foreseen that they'd built the biggest industrial hostage to fortune of all time?"

Shore gazed gloomily at his glass, gloomily drank its contents, and maintained a gloomy silence.

Dermott said, "Well, not quite."

"What do you mean 'not quite'?"

"Sure, it's an industrial hostage to fortune. But not the biggest of all time. That dubious distinction belongs without any question to the trans-Alaska pipeline. Their capital outlay wasn't two billion—it was eight billion. They don't transport a hundred and thirty thousand barrels a day—they transport one million two hundred thousand. And they don't just have sixteen miles of conveyor belting to guard—they have eight hundred miles of pipeline."

Brady handed his glass back for a refill, digested this unpleasant thought, fortified himself and said, "Don't they have *any* means of protecting the damned thing?"

"To the extent that they can limit damage, certainly. They have magnificent communication and electronic control systems, with every imaginable fail-safe and back-up device, even to the extent of a satellite emergency control station." Dermott produced a paper from his pocket. "They have twelve pump stations, locally or remotely controlled. They have sixty-two remote gate valves, all radio-controlled from the pump station immediately to the north. Those gate valves can stop the flow of oil in either direction.

"There are eighty check valves to prevent the oil from flowing backward, and, well, all sorts of other weird valves that would only make sense to an engineer. Altogether they have a remote-control capability at well over a thousand points. In other words, they can isolate any section of the line at any time they want. Because it takes six minutes to shut down a big pump, some oil is bound to escape—up to fifty thousand barrels, it's estimated. That may seem a lot, but it's a drop in the bucket compared to what's in the pipeline. But there's no way the oil can keep on pumping out indefinitely."

"All very interesting." Brady sounded cool. "You can bet they try harder to protect the environment. You can also bet that crooks and extortionists don't give a damn about the environment one way or another. All they want is to interrupt the flow of oil. Can the line be protected?"

"Well, about this huge blind spot you mentioned—"

"What you're trying not to tell me is that the pipeline can be breached any place, any time."

"That's right."

Brady looked at Dermott. "You've thought about this problem?"

"Of course."

"And you, Donald?"

"Me, too."

"Well then, what have you come up with?"

"Nothing. That's why we sent for you. We thought *you* might come up with something."

Brady looked at him maliciously and resumed his pondering. By and by he said, "What happens if there's a break and the oil is stopped in the pipe? Does it gum up?"

"Eventually. But it takes time. The oil is hot when it comes out of the ground and it's still warm when it reaches Valdez. The pipeline is very heavily insulated, and the oil passing through the pipe generates friction heat. They reckon they might get it flowing again after a twenty-one-day standstill, maximum. After that—" He spread his hands.

"No more oil flow?"

"No."

"Not ever again?"

"I shouldn't think so. I don't really know. Nobody's talked to me about it. I don't think anyone really wants to talk about it."

No one did until Brady said, "Do you know what I wish?"

"I know," Dermott said. "You wish you were back in Houston."

The radio-phone rang. The driver listened briefly then turned to Shore.

"Operations manager's office. Will we return immediately. Mr. Reynolds says it's urgent." The bus driver picked up speed.

Reynolds was waiting for them. He indicated a phone lying on his table and spoke to Brady. "Houston. For you."

Brady said, "Hello." Then he made a gesture of irritation and turned to Dermott.

"Horseshit. Damn code. Take it, huh?" This was hardly reasonable of Brady, since it was he who had invented the code and insisted on using it for almost everything except "Hello" and "Good-bye." Dermott reached for a pad and pencil, took the phone and started writing. It took him about a minute to record the message and two more to decode it.

He said into the phone, "Is that all you have?" A pause. "When did you get this message, and when did this happen?" Another pause. "Fifteen minutes and two hours. Thank you." He turned to Brady, his face bleak. "The pipeline's been breached. Pump Station Number Four. Near Atigun Pass in the Brooks Range. No hard details yet. Damage not severe, it seems, but enough to close down the line."

"No chance of an accident?"

"Explosives. They took out two gate valves."

There was a brief silence while Brady surveyed Dermott curiously.

"No need to look so goddamned grim, George. We were expecting something like this. It's not the end of the world."

"It is for two of the men on Pump Station Four. They've been murdered."

FOUR

IT WAS HALF-PAST TWO IN THE AFTER-
noon, Alaskan time, almost dark, but with good visibility,
a ten-knot wind and a temperature of $-4°$F. $-36°$C.
below when the twin-jet touched down again on one of
the Prudhoe Bay airstrips. Brady, Dermott and Mackenzie
had moved quickly after receipt of the message from
Houston. They had driven back to Fort McMurray,
packed essentials, which in Brady's case consisted primarily of three flasks, said good-bye to Jean and Stella and
driven straight to the airport. Brady was asleep when they
entered Yukon air space, and Mackenzie dozed off shortly
afterward. Only Dermott remained awake, trying to puz-

zle out why the enemy, in carrying out what they said
would be—and, in fact proved to be—no more than a token
demonstration, should have found it necessary to kill in the
process.

As the jet came to a halt, a brightly lit minibus pulled
up alongside and slid open a front door. Brady, third out
of the aircraft, was first into the bus. The others followed
him in and the door was quickly closed. As the bus moved
off the man who had ushered them aboard came and sat
down beside them. Aged anywhere between forty and
fifty, he was a broad, chunky man with a broad, chunky
face. He looked tough, but he also looked as if he could be
humorous—although he had nothing to smile about at that
moment.

"Mr. Brady, Mr. Dermott, Mr. Mackenzie," he said,
in the unmistakably flat accent of one who had been born
within commuting distance of Boston, "welcome. Mr. Finlayson sent me to meet you—as you can imagine, he's
right now practically a prisoner in the Master Operations
Control Center. My name's Sam Bronowski."

Dermott said, "Security chief."

"For my sins." He smiled. "You'll be Mr. Dermott,
the man who's going to take over from me?"

Dermott looked at him. "Who the hell said that?"

"Mr. Finlayson. Or words to that effect."

"I'm afraid Mr. Finlayson must be slightly over-
wrought."

Bronowski smiled again. "Well, now, that wouldn't

surprise me either. He's been talking to London, and I think he suffered some damage to his left ear."

Brady said, "We're not out to take over from anyone. That's not how we work. But unless we get co-operation— I mean total co-operation—we might as well have stayed home. For instance, Mr. Dermott here wanted to talk to you right away. The chairman of your company himself had guaranteed me complete co-operation. Yet Finlayson refused point-blank to co-operate with Dermott and Mackenzie."

"I'd have come at once if I'd known," said Bronowski quickly. "Unlike Mr. Finlayson, I've been a security man all my life, and I know who you are and the reputation you have. In a set-up like this I can do with all the expert help I can get. Go easy with him, will you? This isn't his line of country. He treats the pipeline as his favorite daughter. This is a new experience for him and he didn't know what to do. He wasn't stalling—just playing it safe until he'd consulted on the highest level."

"You don't need lessons in sticking up for your boss, do you?"

"I'm being fair to him. I hope you will be, too. You can imagine how he feels. Says that if he hadn't been so ornery, those two men up at Pump Station Four might be alive now."

"That's plain daft," Mackenzie said. "I appreciate his feelings, but this would have happened if there had been fifty Dermotts and fifty Mackenzies here."

"When," Brady asked, "are we going out there?"

"Mr. Finlayson asked if you and your colleagues would come first to see him and Mr. Black. The helicopter is ready to go any moment after that."

"Black?"

"General manager, Alaska."

"You been out at the station?"

"I was the man who found them. Rather, I was the first man on the scene after the attack. Along with my section chief, Tim Houston."

"You fly your own plane?"

"Yes. Not this time, though. That section of the Brooks Range is like the mountains on the moon. Helicopter. We've been making a continuous check on the pump stations and the remote gate valves since this damned threat came through, and we'd stayed at Station Five last night. We were just approaching Four, a mile away, I'd reckon, when we saw this damned great explosion."

"*Saw* it?"

"You know, oil smoke and flames. You mean, did we *hear* anything? You never do in a helicopter. You don't have to—not when you see the roof take off into the air. So we put down and got out, me with a rifle, Tim with two pistols. Wasting our time. The bastards had gone. Being oilmen yourselves, you'll know it requires quite a group of men and a complex of buildings to provide the care and maintenance for a couple of thirteen-thousand-five-hundred-horsepower aircraft-type turbines, not to mention

all the monitoring and communications they have to handle.

"It was the pump room itself that was on fire, not too
badly but badly enough for Tim and me not to go inside
without fire extinguishers. We'd just started looking when
we heard shouting come from a store room. It was locked,
naturally, but the key had been left in the lock. Poulson—
he's the boss—came running out with his men. They had
the extinguishers located and the fire out in three minutes.
But it was too late for the two engineers inside—they'd
come down the previous day from Prudhoe Bay to do a
routine maintenance job on one of the turbines."

"They were dead?"

"Very." Bronowski's face registered no emotion.
"They were brothers. Fine boys. Friends of mine . . . and
Tim's."

"No possibility of accidental death? From the effects
of the explosion?"

"Explosions don't shoot you. They were pretty badly
charred, but charring doesn't hide a bullet wound between
the eyes."

"You searched the area?"

"Certainly. Conditions weren't ideal—it was dark,
with a little snow falling. I thought I saw helicopter ski
marks on a wind-blown stretch of rock. The others
weren't so sure. On the remote off-chance, I contacted
Anchorage and asked them to alert every public and private airport and strip in the state. Also to have radio and

TV stations ask the public to report hearing or sighting a helicopter in an unusual place. I haven't but one hope in ten thousand that the request will bring any results."

He grimaced. "Most people never realize how huge this state is. It's bigger than half of Western Europe, but it's got a population of just over three hundred thousand, which is to say it's virtually uninhabited. Again, helicopters are an accepted fact of life in Alaska, and people pay no more attention to them than you would to a car in Texas. Third, we've still only got about three good hours of light, and the idea of carrying out an air search is laughable—anyway, we'd require fifty times the number of planes we have, and even then it would be sheer luck to find them.

"But, for the record, we did find out something unpleasant. In case anything should happen to the pump station, there's an emergency pipeline that can be switched in to bypass it. Our friends took care of that also. They blew up the control valve."

"So there's going to be a massive oil spillage?"

"No chance. The line is loaded with thousands of sensors all the way from Prudhoe Bay to Valdez, and any section of it can be closed down and isolated immediately. Even the repairs would normally present no problem. But neither metal nor men work too well in these abnormally low temperatures."

"Apparently that doesn't apply to saboteurs," Dermott said. "How many were there?"

"Poulson said two. Two others said three. The remainder weren't sure."

"Not a very observant lot, are they?"

"I wonder if that's fair, Mr. Dermott. Poulson's a good man and he doesn't miss much."

"Did he see their faces?"

"No. That much is for certain."

"Masked?"

"No. Their fur collars were pulled high up and their hats low down so that only their eyes were visible. You can't tell the color of a man's eyes in the darkness. Besides, our people had just been dragged from bed."

"But not the two engineers. They were working on the engines. How come at that very early hour?"

Bronowski spoke with restraint. "Because they had been up all night. Because they were going home to their families in Fairbanks for their week's leave. And because I had arranged to pick them up there shortly after that time."

"Did Poulson or any of his friends recognize the voices?"

"If they had, I'd have the owners behind bars by this time. Their collars were up to their eyes. Of course their voices would have been muffled. You ask a lot of questions, Mr. Dermott."

"Mr. Dermott is a trained interrogator," Brady said cheerfully. "Trained him myself, as a matter of fact. What happened after that?"

"Poulson and his men were marched across to the food store and locked in there. We keep it locked because of bears. Unless bears are near starving, they aren't very partial to human beings, but they're partial indeed to all human goodies."

"Thank you, Mr. Bronowski. One last question. Did Poulson or his men hear the fatal shots?"

"No. Both the men Poulson saw were carrying silenced guns. That's the great advantage of those modern educational pictures, Mr. Dermott."

There was a pause in the questioning. Brady said, "Because I am an acute observer of character, George, I can tell something's eating you. What's on your mind?"

"It's only a thought. I'm wondering if the murderers are employees of the trans-Alaska pipeline."

The silence was brief but marked. Then Bronowski said, "This beats everything. I speak as Dr. Watson, you understand. I know that Sherlock Holmes could solve a crime without leaving his armchair, but I never knew of any cop or security man who could come up with the answer without at least visiting the scene of the crime."

Dermott said mildly, "I'm not claiming to have solved anything. I'm just putting forward a possibility."

Brady said, "What makes you even think that?"

"In the first place, you pipeline people aren't just the biggest employer of labor around here . . . you're the *only* one. Where the hell else could the killers have come from? What else could they have been? Lonely trappers or prospectors on the North Slope or the Brooks Range in

the depth of winter? They'd freeze to death the first day
out. They wouldn't be prospectors, because the tundra is
frozen solid, and beneath that there's two thousand feet of
solid permafrost. As for trappers, they'd be not only cold
and lonely, but very hungry, indeed, because they
wouldn't find any form of food north of Brooks Range
until the late spring comes."

Brady grunted. "What you're saying in effect is that
the pipeline is the sole means of life-support in those
parts."

"It's a fact. Had this happened at Pump Station Seven
or Eight, circumstances would have been quite different—
those stations are only a hop, skip and jump from Fairbanks by car. But you don't take a car over the Brooks
Range in the heart of winter. And you don't backpack
over the Range at this time of year, unless you're bent on
quick suicide. So the question remains, how did they get
there and away again?"

"Helicopter," Bronowski said. "Remember I said I
thought I saw ski marks? Tim—Tim Houston—saw the
marks too, although he was less sure. The others were
frankly skeptical, but admitted the possibility. But I've
been flying helicopters for as long as I can remember."
Bronowski shook his head in exasperation. "God's sake,
how else could they have got in and out?"

"I thought," Mackenzie said, "that those pump stations had limited-range radarscopes."

"They do." Bronowski shrugged. "But snow plays
funny tricks on radar. Also, they may not have been look-

ing, or maybe they had the set switched off, not expecting company in such bad weather."

Dermott said, "They were expecting you, surely."

"Not for another hour or so. We'd had deteriorating weather at Number Five, so we left ahead of schedule. Another thing—even if they had picked up an incoming helicopter, they'd automatically have assumed it was one of ours and would have had no reason to be suspicious."

"Be that as it may," said Dermott, "I'm convinced. It was an inside job. The killers are pipeline employees. The note announcing their intention of causing a slight spillage of oil seemed civil and civilized enough, with no hint of violence, but violence there has been. The saboteurs blundered, and so they had to kill."

"Blundered?" Mackenzie was a lap behind.

"Yes. Bronowski said the key had been left in the storeroom door. Don't forget, all the engineers locked inside *were* engineers. With the minimum of equipment they could have either turned the key in the lock or slipped a piece of paper, cardboard, linoleum, anything, under the bottom of the door, pushed the key out to fall on it and hauled the key inside. Me, I'd have thrown that key a mile away. But the killers didn't. Their intention was to bring the two pump-house engineers to the storeroom and usher them in to join their friends, and lock them in, too. But they didn't do that either. Why? Because one of the saboteurs said or did something that betrayed their identity to the two engineers. They were recognized by the engineers, who evidently knew them well enough to penetrate their disguises. The saboteurs had no option, so they killed them."

Brady said, "How's that for a hypothesis, Sam?"

Bronowski was pondering his reply when the minibus pulled up outside the main entrance to the administrative building. Brady, predictably, was the first out and scuttled —as far as a nearly spherical human being could be said to scuttle—to the welcoming shelter that lay behind the main door. The others followed more sedately.

John Finlayson rose as they entered his room. He extended his hand to Brady and said, "Delighted to meet you, sir." He nodded curtly toward Dermott, Mackenzie and Bronowski, then turned to a man seated to his right behind a table. "Mr. Hamish Black, general manager, Alaska."

Mr. Black didn't look like the general manager of anything, far less the manager of a tough and ruthless oil operation. The rolled umbrella and bowler hat were missing, but even without them his lean, bony face, immaculately trimmed pencil moustache, thinning black hair parted with millimetric precision over the center of his scalp and the eyes behind pince-nez made him the epitome of a top City of London accountant, which he was.

That such a man, who could hardly tell a nut from a bolt, should head up a huge industrial complex was not a new phenomenon. The tea boy who had painstakingly fought his way up through the ranks to boardroom level had become a man of no mean importance. It was Hamish Black, so adept at punching the keyboard of his pocket calculator, who called the industrial tune. It was rumored that his income ran into six figures—pounds Sterling, not dollars. His employers, evidently, thought he was worth every penny of it.

He waited patiently while Finlayson made the introductions.

"I would not go as far as Mr. Finlayson and say I'm delighted to meet you." Black's smile was as thin as his face. His flat, precise, controlled voice belonged to the City—London's Wall Street—just as surely as did his appearance. "Under other circumstances, yes. Under these, I can only say that I'm glad you, Mr. Brady, and your colleagues are here. I assume Mr. Bronowski has supplied you with details. How did you propose we proceed?"

"I don't know. Do we have a glass?"

The expression on Finlayson's face could have been interpreted as reluctant disapproval: Black, it seemed, didn't believe in using expressions. Brady produced, poured the inevitable daiquiri, waved the flask at the others, who waved it on and said, "The FBI have been notified?"

Black nodded. "Reluctantly."

"Reluctantly?"

"There's a legal obligation to notify of any interruption of interstate commerce. Quite frankly, I don't see what they can achieve."

"They're out at the pump station now?"

"They haven't arrived here yet. They're waiting for

some specialist Army Ordnance officers to accompany them—experts on bombs, explosives and the like."

"Waste of time. Among the people who built and run this line there are as good—if not better—explosives experts than in any Army Ordnance Corps. The killers wouldn't have left a trace of explosives at Pump Station Number Four."

If a silence can be said to be cold, the ensuing silence was downright chilly. Finlayson said stonily, "Does that statement mean what I think it means?"

"I should imagine it does," said Brady. "Explain, George."

Dermott explained. When he had finished, Finlayson said, "Preposterous. Why should any of our pipeline employees want to do a thing like that? It doesn't make sense."

"It's never a pleasant thing to nurture a viper in your bosom," Brady said agreeably. "Mr. Black?"

"Makes sense to me, if only because no other immediate explanation occurs. What do *you* think, Mr. Brady?"

"Exactly what I was asking Mr. Bronowski as we touched down."

"Yes. Well." Bronowski didn't seem any too comfortable. "I don't like it. An inside job is all too damn plausible. Point is, carry this line of thinking a little further and the finger points at Tim Houston and myself as the two prime suspects." Bronowski paused. "Tim and I had a helicopter. We were in the right place at approximately the right time. We know of a dozen ways to sabotage the pipeline. It's no secret that we're both pretty experienced in the use of explosives, so taking out Station Four would have presented no problem for us." He paused. "But who's going to suspect the security chief and his number two?"

"Me, for one," said Brady. He sipped his drink and sighed. "I'd have you clapped behind bars right now were it not for your impeccable record, lack of apparent motive and the fact that it's incredible that you should have acted in such a clumsy fashion."

"Not clumsy, Mr. Brady. The killers were stupid to the point of insanity . . . or badly frightened. The job certainly wasn't the work of professional hit men. Why shoot the two engineers? Why leave any evidence that murder had been done? Just knock them unconscious—a dozen ways that can be done without leaving a mark—then blow them to pieces along with the pump station. Act of God, and no hint of foul play."

"Amateurism is a grievesome thing, is it not?" Brady turned to Finlayson. "Could we have a line to Anchorage, please? Thank you. Give him the number, then take the call, George." Dermott did so and within four minutes had hung up, his part of the conversation having been limited mainly to monosyllables.

"Wouldn't you know," Dermott said.

"No luck?" said Mackenzie.

"Too much. The Anchorage police have located not one but four hot phone booths. Suspicious characters either inside them or lurking in the vicinity, and this at that most ungodly hour. All four of them, dammit, with a disproportionate number of high-denomination coins inside them. All four have been dismantled and taken along to the cop shop. But they haven't been fingerprinted yet, and it may be hours before the cops can check the prints against their files."

Black said with sardonic restraint, "The relevance of this call escapes me. It has something to do with Pump Station Four?"

"Maybe," said Brady. "Maybe not. All we know for certain is that Sanmobil—the people who have the tar-sands concession north of Fort McMurray, in Alberta—have also received a threat against their oil production lines. Couched in almost identical terms with the threat you received, the only difference being that while yours arrived by mail, theirs came from a public phone booth in Anchorage. We're trying to trace which booth and, with any fingerprint luck, who the caller may have been."

Black thought briefly, then said, "Curious. A threat against Alaskan oil from Alberta, and one against Albertan oil from Alaska. Must tie up with Pump Station Four . . . the arm of coincidence isn't all that long. And while you're sitting here, Mr. Brady, some ill-intentioned person or persons may be planting an explosive device at some strategic point in Sanmobil's tar sands."

"The thought had not escaped me. However, surmise and speculation will serve no point until we turn up one or two hard facts. We hope that one may even result from a close inspection of Pump Station Four. Coming out there, Mr. Black?"

"Good heavens, no. I'm very much a desk-bound citizen. But I shall await your return with interest."

"Return? I'm going no place. Those frozen wastes— not for me. My excellent representatives know what to look for. Besides, someone has to stay and run the command post. How far to the pump station, Mr. Bronowski?"

"Helicopter miles? Hundred and forty, give or take."

"Splendid. That will leave us ample time for a belated lunch. Your commissary is still open, Mr. Finlayson, I trust, and your wine cellar tolerable?"

"Sorry about that, Mr. Brady." Finlayson made no effort to conceal the satisfaction in his voice. "Company regulations forbid alcohol."

"No need to distress yourself," Brady said urbanely. "Aboard my jet is the finest cellar north of the Arctic Circle."

FIVE

THREE GENERATOR-FED ARC LAMPS threw the half-demolished pump house and its shattered contents into harsh relief, glaring white and stygian blackness, with no intermediate shading between. Snow drifted silently down through the all-but-vanished roof, and a high wind blew a fine white cloud through a gaping hole in the northern wall. Already the combined effects of the two snows had softened and blurred the outlines of the machinery, but not sufficiently to conceal the fact that engines, motors, pumps and switchgear had been either destroyed or severely damaged. Mercifully, the snow had already covered the two mounds that lay side by side before the mangled remains of a switchboard. Dermott looked slowly around with a face again as bleak as the scene that lay before him.

"Damage evenly spread," he said, "so it couldn't have come from one central blast. Half-a-dozen charges, more likely." He turned to Poulson, the head man, a black-bearded man with bitter eyes. "How many explosions did you hear?"

"Just the one, I think. We really can't be sure. If there were more after the first one, our eardrums were sure in no condition to register them. But we're agreed that one was all we heard."

"Triggered electrically, by radio or, if they used fulminate of mercury, by sympathetic detonation. Experts, obviously." He looked at the two shapeless, snow-covered mounds. "But not so expert in other ways. Why have those two men been left here?"

"Orders."

"Whose orders?"

"Head office. Not to be moved until the postmortems have been carried out."

"Rubbish! You can't do a postmortem on a frozen body." Dermott stooped, began to clear away the snow from the nearest of the mounds, then looked up in surprise as a heavy hand clamped on his left shoulder.

"You deaf or something, mister?" Poulson didn't sound truculent, just annoyed. "I'm in charge here."

"You were. Donald?"

"Sure." Mackenzie eased Poulson's hand away and

said, "Let's go talk to the head office man, Black, and hear what he has to say about obstructing murder investigations."

"That won't be necessary, Mr. Mackenzie," Bronowski said. He nodded to Poulson. "John's upset. Wouldn't you be?"

Poulson hesitated briefly, turned and left the pump room. Dermott had most of the snow cleared away when he felt a light touch on his shoulder. It was Poulson again, proffering him, of all things, a long-handled clothes brush. Dermott took it, smiled his thanks and delicately brushed away the remaining snow.

The dreadfully charred skull of the dead man was barely recognizable as that of a human being, but the cause of the round hole above the eyeless left socket was unmistakable. With Mackenzie's help—the corpse was frozen solid—he lifted the body and peered at the back of the skull. The skin was unbroken.

"Bullet's lodged in the head," Dermott said. "Rifling marks on it should be of interest to the police ballistics department."

"I suppose," Bronowski agreed reluctantly. "But Alaska covers just over half a million square miles. I'm afraid optimism is not my long suit."

"We're agreed there." They lowered the body to the ground and Dermott tried to unzip the shredded green parka, but it, too, was frozen. There was a slight crackling of ice as he eased the jacket away from the shirt beneath and peered into the gap between the two layers of clothing. He could see some documents, including a buff-colored envelope, tucked away in the inside right pocket. By sliding his hand in flat he tried to extract them with his fore and middle fingers, but because he could achieve so little grip, and because they seemed frozen—not only together but also to the side of the pocket—they proved impossible to move. Dermott straightened to an upright kneeling position, looked at the dead man thoughtfully, then up at Bronowski.

"Could we have the two bodies moved to someplace where they can be thawed out a bit? I can't examine them in this state, nor, by the same token, can the doctors carry out their postmortems."

"John?" Bronowski looked at Poulson, who nodded, albeit with some reluctance.

"Another thing," Dermott said. "What's the quickest way of clearing away the snow here from the floor and machinery?"

"Canvas covers and a couple of hot-air blowers. No time at all. Want me to fix it now? And the two men?"

"Please. Then there's a question or two I'd like to ask. In your living quarters, perhaps?"

"Straight across. Be with you in a few minutes."

Outside, on their way, Mackenzie said, "Your hound-dog instincts have been aroused. What gives?"

"Dead man back there. Index finger on his right hand is broken."

"That all? Wouldn't be surprised if half the bones in his body are broken."

"Could be. But this bone appears to have been broken in a rather peculiar fashion. Be able to tell better, later."

Bronowski and Poulson joined them around the table of the comfortable kitchen living quarters. Poulson said, "Okay, fixed. Snow in the pump room should be gone in fifteen minutes. About the two engineers—well, I wouldn't know."

"Considerably longer," Dermott said. "Thanks. Now, then. Bronowski, Mackenzie and myself think it likely that the murderers were employees of the trans-Alaska pipeline. What would you think of that?"

Poulson glanced enquiringly at Bronowski, found no inspiration there, looked away and pondered. "It figures," he said at last. "The only living souls for ten thousand square miles around here—a hundred thousand as far as I know—are employed by the pipeline. More than that, while any mad bomber could have blown up the pump station, it took an oilman to know where to locate and destroy the bypass control valve."

"We also theorize that the engineers—what were their names, by the way?"

"James and James. Brothers."

"We think that the bombers gave themselves away in one fashion or another, that the Jameses recognized them and had to be silenced for keeps. But you and your men didn't recognize them. That's for sure?"

"For sure." Poulson smiled without much humor. "If what you suppose is correct, it's just as well for us that we didn't. But then it's not surprising that we didn't. Don't forget that up here in Number Four we're no better than hermits living on a desert island. The only time we see anybody is when we go on leave every few weeks. Traveling maintenance engineers like the Jameses—or, come to that, Mr. Bronowski here—see ten times as many people as we do, and so are likely to recognize ten times as many people. Which makes your idea that it was an inside job all the more likely."

"You and your men are certain there wasn't the remotest peculiarity about them, either in speech or dress, that struck a chord?"

"You're flogging a dead horse, Dermott."

"I suppose. There's a possibility that those saboteurs came by helicopter."

"Damned if I can see how else they could have come. Mr. Bronowski here thought he saw skid marks. I wasn't sure one way or another. It was a bad night for being sure of anything . . . dark, with a strong wind and drifting snow. Circumstances like that, you can imagine almost anything."

"You didn't *hear* this helicopter approaching—or imagine you heard it?"

"We heard nothing. Don't forget we were all asleep and—"

"I thought you mounted a radar watch?"

"In a fashion. Any errant bleep triggers off an alarm. But we don't sit with our eyes glued to the screen night and day. Then, because of the extremely heavy insulation, it's difficult for any sound to penetrate from outside. The generator running next door doesn't help much either. Finally, of course, the wind was blowing—as it still is—almost directly from the north and would have carried away the sound of any craft approaching from the opposite direction. I know that a helicopter is one of the most rackety bits of machinery in existence but—even though we were wide awake then—we didn't hear Mr. Bronowski's chopper coming in from the south. Sorry, that's all I can tell you."

"How long will it take to repair the pump room?"

"A few days, a week. I'm not sure. We'll need new engines, switchgear, pipelines, a mobile crane and a bulldozer. All those we already have at Prudhoe except the engines, and I expect a Herc will fly those in this evening. Then a chopper or two can fly the stuff out here. The repair crews will be on the job in the morning."

"So a week before the oil starts flowing again?"

"No, no. Tomorrow, with luck. The bypass control valve is not a major repair job . . . parts replacement mainly."

Dermott said, "You might look at all this as just a minor disruption?"

"Technically, yes. The ghosts of the James brothers might see it differently. Want to look at the pump room now? Most of the stuff should have melted by this time."

The snow in the pump room had gone, and the atmosphere was warm and humid. Without the protective white covering, the scene was more repellent than before, the extent of the devastation more clearly and dishearteningly evident, and the stench of oil and charring more pungent and penetrating. Each with a powerful flashlight to lighten the shadows cast by the arc lamps, Dermott, Mackenzie and Bronowski embarked on a search of every square inch of the floors and walls.

After ten minutes Poulson said curiously, "What *are* you looking for?"

"I'll let you know when I find it," Dermott said. "Meantime, I haven't a clue."

"In that case, can I join in the search?"

"Sure. Don't touch or turn anything over. The FBI wouldn't like it."

Ten minutes later, Dermott straightened and switched off his light. "That's it, then, gentlemen. If you've found no more than I have, among the four of us we've found nothing. Looks as if fire or blasts have wiped the platter clean. Let's have a look at the James brothers. They should be in a fairly examinable state by now."

They were. Dermott moved first to the man he'd looked at in the pump room. This time the zip on the green parka unfastened easily. The blast effect that had shredded the parka had not penetrated it, for the plaid shirt beneath bore no signs of damage. Dermott removed some papers, cards and envelopes from the inside right pocket of the jacket, leafed through and replaced them. He then lifted both charred wrists, examined them and the hands in an apparently cursory fashion and lowered them again. He repeated the process with the other victim, then rose to his feet. Poulson bent a quizzical eye on him.

"That's the way a detective examines a murdered man?"

"I don't suppose it is. But then, I'm not a detective." He turned to Bronowski. "You all through?"

"If you are." Sam Bronowski led the way to the helicopter, Dermott and Mackenzie following through the thinly driving snow that reduced visibility to a few yards. It was intensely cold.

"Clues," Mackenzie said into Dermott's ear, not from any wish for privacy but simply to make himself heard. "Man can't move around without tripping over them."

"None in the pump room, that's sure. Place had been pretty comprehensively quartered before we ever got there. Almost certainly before the snow had started to cover anything."

"What do you mean?"

"The old fine-tooth comb is what I mean."

"Poulson and his men?"

"And/or. Who else?"

"Perhaps there was nothing to find?"

Dermott said—or rather shouted, "That dead man's forefinger had been deliberately broken. Bent in at forty-five degrees toward the thumb. Never seen anything like it before."

"Freak accident."

"'Odd' is better. Something else odd, too. When I

searched him first there was a buff envelope in his inner pocket. I was unable to get it out."

"But you were when you unzipped it later?"

"No. It was gone."

"'And/or' at work, you think?"

"So it seems."

"All very curious," Mackenzie said.

Jim Brady was of the same opinion. After reporting the results of their investigation, Dermott and Mackenzie had retired with him to the room he'd been allocated for the night.

Brady said, "Why didn't you mention those things to Black and Finlayson? Those are hard facts—an oddly broken finger, a missing envelope?"

"Hard facts? There's only my word for it. I've no idea what was in the envelope anyway, and although I'd say the forefinger had been deliberately broken, I'm no osteologist."

"But no harm in mentioning those things, surely?"

"Bronowski and Houston were there too."

"You really don't trust anyone, do you, George?" Brady's tone was admiring, not reproachful.

"As you never fail to remind people, sir, you taught me yourself."

"True, true," Brady said complacently. "Very well,

then, have them up. I'll do my Olympian act while you
ply them with questions and strong drink."

Dermott spoke on the phone and within a minute
Bronowski and Houston had knocked, entered and taken
seats.

"Kind, gentlemen, kind." Brady was at his most
avuncular. "Long day, I know, and you must be damnably
tired. But we're babes in the wood up here. We're not
only *short* of necessary information, we're totally devoid
of it, and we believe you two gentlemen are those best
equipped to supply us with that information. But I forget
myself, gentlemen. I suggest a pre-inquisitional restorative."

Mackenzie said, "What Mr. Brady means is a drink."

"That's what I said. You gentlemen like scotch?"

"Off-duty, yes. But you know the company regulations, sir, and how strictly Mr. Finlayson interprets those."

"Strict? I am ironclad in the interpretation of my own
regulations." The wave of Brady's arm was, indeed, Olympian. "You are off-duty. Off regular duty, anyhow.
George, refreshments. Mr. Dermott will ask the questions,
alternating, I do not doubt, with Mr. Mackenzie. You
gentlemen, if you will be so kind, will fill in the gaps in
our knowledge."

He took his daiquiri from Dermott, savored it, laid
down his glass, relaxed in his chair and steepled his hands
under his chin. "I shall but listen and evaluate." Nobody
was left with any doubt as to which was the most demand-
ing task of the three. "Health, gentlemen."

Bronowski lifted his own glass, which he had accepted with no great show of reluctance. "And confusion to our enemies."

Dermott said, "That's precisely the point. The enemy aren't confused. We are. The taking out of Pump Station Four is only the opening skirmish in what promises to be a bloody battle. They—the enemy—know where they're going to hit again. We have not the vaguest idea. But you must have—by the very nature of your job you must be more aware of the points most vulnerable to attack than anyone else between Prudhoe Bay and Valdez. Take off your security hats and put on those of the enemy. Where would *you* strike next?"

"Jesus!" Bronowski fortified himself with some of Brady's malt. "That's more than a sixty-four-dollar question. It's an eight-hundred-mile question—and every damned mile is virtually a sitting target."

"The boss is right," Tim Houston said. "If we sit here and drink your whiskey while pretending to help, we're only abusing your hospitality. There's nothing we or anyone else can do to help. A combat-ready division of the U. S. Army would be about as useful as a gaggle of Girl Scouts. The task is impossible and the line indefensible."

Mackenzie said, "Well, George, at least we're operating on a bigger scale than with the tar-sands boys in Athabasca. There they said a battalion wouldn't be big enough to guard their installation. Now it's a division." Mackenzie turned to Bronowski. "Let's switch hats with the enemy. Where *wouldn't* you strike next?"

Bronowski said, "Well, I wouldn't strike at any of the pump stations again on the assumption that, until this matter is cleared up, they will be heavily guarded. I'd have been sorely tempted to go for Pump Station Ten at the Isabel Pass in the Alaska Range, or Number Twelve at the Thompson Pass in the Chugach Mountains. All pump stations are vital of course, but some are more vital than others, and those are Number Ten and Number Twelve—along with Number Four here." He considered briefly. "Or maybe I *would* go for them . . . I mean, maybe you'd be so damned certain that I wouldn't hit again in the same place that you wouldn't much bother—"

Dermott held up his hand. "Start in on the double-guessing, and we're up all night. On with the hazards—the low priority ones, I mean."

"I wouldn't go for the two Master Operations Control Centers at Prudhoe Bay. They could be taken out easily enough and, sure, they'd stall all production from the wells immediately, but not for long. It's no secret that contingency plans for bypassing the centers are already in hand. Repairs wouldn't take all that long. In any event, security will be now tightened to the extent that the game wouldn't be worth the candle. So we can be pretty certain that there will be no attempt made to sabotage the oil supply before it enters the pipeline. Same goes for when it leaves the pipe at Valdez. Maximum damage there could be inflicted at the Oil Movements Control Center, where the pipeline controller can monitor and control the flow of oil all the way from Prudhoe to Valdez, and the terminal controller—he's in the same room, actually—controls practically everything that moves in the terminal itself. Both of those, in turn, are dependent on what's called the Backbone Supervisory System Computer. Knock out any of those three and you're in dead trouble. But they're pretty secure as they are. From now, they'll be virtually impregnable. Again, not worth it."

Dermott said, "How about the storage tanks?"

"Well, now. If one or two of them were attacked or ruptured—it would be impossible to get them all at once— the containment dikes would take care of the spillage. Fire would be another thing, but even then the snow would have a blanketing effect—we may only have an annual dusting of snow up here, but down there they have over three hundred inches. Anyway, the tank farms are the most open and easily guarded complex on the entire pipeline. There's no way you can really get at them without bombing the area. Not very likely, one would think."

"What about the tanker terminals?"

"Again, easily guarded. I hardly think they're likely to run to underwater demolition squads. Even if they did, they couldn't do much damage, and that would be easily repaired."

"The tankers themselves?"

"Sink a dozen and there's always a thirteenth. No way you can interrupt the oil flow by hitting the tankers."

"The Valdez Narrows?"

"Block them?" Dermott nodded and Bronowski shook his head. "The Narrows aren't as narrow as they look on a small-scale chart. Three thousand feet—that's the minimum channel width—between the Middle Rock and the east shore. You'd have to sink an awful lot of vessels to block that channel."

"So we cross off the unlikely targets. Where does that leave us?"

"It leaves us with eight hundred miles." Bronowski shifted.

"The air temperature is the overriding factor," Houston said. "No saboteur worth his salt would consider wrecking anything except the pipeline itself. This time of the year any attack has to be in the open air."

"Why?"

"This is only early February, remember, and to all intents we're still in the depth of winter. As often as not the temperature is well on the wrong side of thirty below, and in these parts thirty below is the crucial figure. Rupture the pipeline at, say, thirty-five below, and it stays ruptured. Repair is virtually impossible. Men can work, although well below their norm, but unfortunately the metal they may try to repair or the machine tools they use to make the repairs won't co-operate with them. At extreme temperatures, profound molecular changes occur in metal and it becomes unworkable. Given the right—or wrong— conditions, a tap on an iron rod will shatter it like glass."

Brady said, "You mean, all I need is a hammer and a few taps on the pipeline—"

Houston was patient. "Not quite. What with the heat of the oil inside and the insulation lagging outside, the steel of the pipeline is always warm and malleable. It's the repair tools that would fracture."

Dermott said, "But surely it would be possible to erect canvas or tarpaulin covers over the fracture and bring the temperature up to workable levels by using hot-air blowers? You know, the way Poulson did at Station Four?"

"Of course. Which is why I wouldn't attack the pipeline directly. I'd attack the structures that support the pipeline, those that are already frozen solid at air temperature and would require days, perhaps weeks, to bring up to a working temperature."

"Structures?"

"Indeed. The terrain between Prudhoe and Valdez is desperately uneven and traversed with innumerable watercourses which have to be forded or spanned in one way or another. There are over six hundred streams and rivers along the run. The six-hundred-fifty-foot free-span suspension bridge over the Tazlina River would make a dilly of a target. Even better would be the twelve-hundred-foot span—a similar type of construction—over the Tanana River. But one doesn't even have to operate on such a grandiose scale, and I, personally, would prefer not to." He looked at Bronowski. "Wouldn't you agree?"

"Completely. Operate on a much more moderate and undramatic scale, but one equally effective. I'd go for the VSMs every time."

Dermott said, "VSMs?"

"Vertical support members. Roughly half the length

of the pipeline is above ground and lies on a horizontal cradle or saddle supported by vertical metal posts. That makes for a fair number of targets—seventy-eight thousand of them, to be precise. They would be a snap to take out—wrap-around beehive plastic explosives which would need all of a minute to fix in position. Take out twenty of those, and the line would collapse under its own weight and the weight of the oil inside it. Take weeks to repair."

"They could still use those hot-air canvas shelters."

"A hell of a lot of help that would be," Bronowski said, "if they couldn't bring up the cranes and crawler equipment to effect the repairs. Anyway, there are places where, at this time of year, it just couldn't be done. There is, for instance, one particularly vulnerable stretch that gave the designers headaches, the builders sleepless nights and security nightmares. This steep and dangerous stretch is between Pump Station Five and the summit of Atigun Pass, which is between four and five thousand feet high."

Houston said, "Four thousand seven hundred and seventy-five feet."

"Four thousand seven hundred and seventy-five feet. In a run of a hundred miles from the pass the pipe comes down to twelve hundred feet, which is quite a drop."

"With a corresponding amount of built-up pressure?"

"That's not the problem. In the event of a break in the line, a special computer linkage between Four and Five will automatically shut down the pumps in Four and close every remote valve between the stations. The fail-safe procedures are highly sophisticated, and they work. At the very worst the spillage could be restricted to fifty thousand barrels. But the point is, in winter the line couldn't be repaired."

Brady coughed apologetically and descended from his Olympian heights.

"So a break in this particular section, about now, could immobilize the line for weeks on end?"

"No question."

"Then forget it."

"Mr. Brady?"

"The burdens I have to bear alone," Brady sighed. "Let me have men about me who can think. I begin to understand why I am what I am. I find it extraordinary that the construction company never carried out any tests to discover what happens to the viscosity of oil in low temperatures. Why didn't they seal off a couple of hundred feet of experimental pipe with oil inside it and see how long it would take before it gummed up to the extent that it would cease to flow?"

"Never occurred to them, I suppose," Bronowski said. "An eventuality that would never arise."

"It has arisen. An estimate of three weeks has been bandied about. Based on scientific calculations, one assumes?"

Bronowski said, "I wouldn't know. Not my field. Maybe Mr. Black or Mr. Finlayson would know."

"Mr. Black knows nothing about oil, and I doubt whether Mr. Finlayson or any other professional oilman on the line has anything but the vaguest idea. Could be ten days. Could be thirty. You take my point, George?"

"Yes. Blackmail, threats, extortion, some positive and very material advantages to be gained. Interruption is one thing, cessation another. They require a lever, a bargaining counter. Close down the line completely, and the oil companies would laugh at their threats, for then they would have nothing to lose. The bargaining arm would have gone. The kidnapper can't very well hold a kidnappee for ransom if it's known that the kidnappee is dead."

"I question if I could have put it better myself," Brady said. He had about him an air of magnanimous self-satisfaction. "We are, clearly, not dealing with clowns. Our friends would have taken such imponderables into account and would err on the side of caution. You are with me, Mr. Bronowski?"

"I am now. But when I was talking about hazards, I wasn't taking that side of it into account."

"I know you weren't. Nobody was. Well, I think that will do, gentlemen. We appear to have established two things. It is unlikely that any attack will be carried out on any major installation—that is Prudhoe, Valdez or the intervening twelve major pump stations. It is further unlikely that any attack will be carried out in regions so inaccessible that repairs may be impossible for weeks on end.

"So we're left with the likelihood that any further sabotage will take the form of attacks on accessible stretches of VSMs or the taking out of minor bridges—the possibility of destroying the Tazlina or Tanana bridges is remote, as those could well take weeks to repair. We may not have come up with too much, but at least we have clarified matters and established some sort of system of priorities."

Not without difficulty Brady heaved himself to his feet to indicate that the interview was over. "Thank you, gentlemen, both for your time and information. I'll see you in the morning—at, of course, a reasonably Christian hour."

The door closed behind Bronowski and Houston. Brady asked, "Well, what did you make of that?"

Dermott said, "As you said, just a limitation of possibilities, which, unfortunately, still remain practically limitless. Three things I'd like to do. First, I'd like the FBI or whoever to carry out a rigorous investigation into the pasts of Poulson and his pals at Pump Station Four."

"You have reason to suspect them?"

"Not really. But I've an odd feeling. Something is wrong at Number Four. Don shares my feeling, but there's nothing we can put a finger on except that buff envelope that was missing from the dead engineer's pocket. Even with that I'm beginning to question whether my eyes or imagination were playing tricks on me. The lighting was damned harsh, and I could have got my colors wrong. No matter—as you'd be the first to agree, every pipeline employee is a suspect until his innocence is established."

"You bet. You said Poulson and Bronowski seemed on pretty cordial terms?"

"Bronowski is the sort of character who seems on pretty cordial terms with everyone. If you're suggesting what I think you are, I might mention that according to Finlayson there have been three security checks carried out on Bronowski."

"And passed with flying colors, no doubt. What does Finlayson know about security checks and how to evaluate them? Has he any guarantee that none of those three professedly unbiased investigators was not, in fact, a bosom friend of Bronowski? Now, *I* have a very good and very discreet friend in New York. As you say yourself, every pipeline operator is as guilty as hell until proved otherwise."

"I didn't quite say that."

"Hair-splitting. The second thing?"

"I'd like a medical opinion, preferably that of a doctor with some osteopathetic knowledge, on how the dead engineer's finger came to be broken."

"How can that help?"

"How should I know?" Dermott sounded almost irritable. "God knows, Jim, you've emphasized often enough never to overlook anything that seems odd."

"True, true," Brady said pacifically. "There was a third matter?"

"Let's find out how the fingerprint boys in Anchorage are getting on with that telephone-booth affair. Three tiny things, I know, but it's all we have to go on."

"Four. There's also Bronowski. And now?"

The telephone rang. Brady picked it up, listened

briefly, scowled and handed the phone over to Dermott. "For you." Dermott lifted an eyebrow. "It's that damnable code again."

Dermott gave him a familiar look, put the phone to his ear, reached for a pad and started to take notes. After barely a minute he hung up and said, "And now? That was your last question, wasn't it?"

"What? Yes. So?"

"And now it's back to the old jet and heigh-ho for Canada." Dermott gave Brady an encouraging smile. "Should be all right, sir. Still plenty of daiquiris in your airborne bar."

"What the devil is that meant to mean?"

"Just this, sir." Dermott's smile had gone. "You will recall our three brilliant minds sitting around in Sanmobil's office and coming to the unanimous conclusion that there were six points vulnerable to attack—the draglines, the bucket wheels, the reclaimers' bridges, the separator plates, the radial stackers and, above all, the conveyor belting? Some joker up there obviously didn't see it our way at all. He's taken out the main processing plant."

SIX

FOUR HOURS LATER THE BRADY ENTER-
prises team stood shivering in Sanmobil's sabotaged
processing plant at Athabasca. Brady himself was enveloped in his usual cocoon of coats and scarves, his temper
not improved by the fact that the flight from Alaska had
deprived him of dinner.

"How did it *happen?*" he repeated. "Here we have an
easily patrolled area, brilliantly lit, as you pointed out
yourself, and staffed with one hundred per cent—I beg
your pardon, ninety-eight per cent—loyal and patriotic Canadians." He peered through a large hole that had been

blown in a cylindrical container. "How can such things be?"

"I don't think that's quite fair, Mr. Brady." Bill Reynolds, the fair-haired and ruddy-faced operations manager, spoke up for his colleague Terry Brinckman, the security chief at whom Brady's remarks had been directed. "Terry had only eight men on duty last night—and that was his second shift of the day. In other words, he himself had been continuously on duty for fifteen hours when this incident occurred. You can see how hard he was trying."

Brady did not nod in assent.

Reynolds went on, "You remember we had all agreed on the priorities—the areas most liable to attack. Those were the places that Terry and his men were doing their best to protect—which didn't leave any men for patrolling the plant itself. You will recall, Mr. Brady, that you were in complete agreement. You also said Terry had nothing to reproach himself with. If we're going to apportion blame, let's not forget ourselves."

"Nobody's blaming anybody, Mr. Reynolds. How extensive is the damage?"

"Enough. Terry and I figure that these guys let off three charges here—that's the gas-oil hydrotreater—and the same number next door at the Naptha hydrotreater. In fact, we've been extremely lucky—we could have had gas explosions and fuel fires. We had none. As it is, damage is comparatively slight. We should be on stream again in forty-eight hours."

"Meantime, everything is shut down?"

"Not the draglines. But the rest is. The radial stackers are full."

"One of the plant operatives, you think?"

Brinckman said, "I'm afraid we're sure. It's a big plant but it takes surprisingly few people to operate it, and everybody on a shift knows everybody else. A stranger would have been spotted at once. Besides, we *know* it was an inside job—six thirty-ounce explosive charges were taken from the blasting shed last night."

"Blasting shed?"

Reynolds said, "We use explosives to break up large chunks of tar sand that have become too tightly bound together. But we've only got small charges."

"Big enough, it would seem. The blasting shed is normally kept locked?"

"Double-locked."

"Somebody forced the door?"

"Nobody forced anything. That's why Brinckman told you we're sure it was an inside job. Somebody used keys."

"Who normally holds the keys?" Dermott asked.

Reynolds said, "There are three sets. I hold one, Brinckman has two."

"Why two?"

"One I keep permanently," Brinckman explained. "The other goes to the security supervisor for the night shift, who passes it on to the person in charge of the morning and afternoon shifts."

"Who are those other security shift supervisors?"

Brinckman said, "My number two, Jorgensen—this is his shift, really—and Napier. I don't think that any of the three of us is much given to stealing explosives, Mr. Dermott."

"Not unless you're certifiable. Now, it seems unlikely anyone would risk abstracting keys and having copies made. Not only would they be too likely to be missed, but there's also more than a fair chance that we could trace the key cutter and so the thief."

"There could be illegal key cutters."

"I still doubt the keys would have been taken. Much more likely someone took an impression. That would need seconds only. And that's where the illegal side would come in—no straight key cutter would touch an impression. How easy would it be for anyone to get hold of the keys, even briefly?"

Brinckman said, "About Jorgensen's and Napier's I wouldn't know. I clip mine to my belt."

Mackenzie said, "Everybody's got to sleep."

"So?"

"You take your belt off then, don't you?"

"Sure." Brinckman shrugged. "And if you're going to ask me next if I'm a heavy sleeper, well, yes, I am. And if you're going to ask me if it would have been possible for anyone to sneak into my room while I was asleep, borrow my key for a couple of minutes and return it unseen, well, yes that would have been perfectly possible too."

"This," Brady said, "is not going to take us very far.

Sticky-fingered characters with an affinity for keys are legion. Would there have been *any* security man in this area tonight?"

"Jorgensen would know," Brinckman said. "Shall I get him?"

"Won't he be out patrolling sixteen miles of conveyor belting or something?"

"He's in the canteen."

"But surely he's in charge—on duty?"

"In charge of what, Mr. Brady? There are four men keeping an eye on the four draglines. The rest of the plant is closed down. We think it unlikely that this bomber will strike again tonight."

"Not much is unlikely."

"Bring him along to my office," Reynolds said. Brinckman left. "I think you'll find it warmer and more comfortable there, Mr. Brady."

They followed Reynolds to the office block, through an external room where a bright-eyed and pretty young woman at the desk gave them a charming smile, and on into Reynolds' office where Brady began divesting himself of several outer layers of clothing even before Reynolds had the door closed. Reynolds took his chair behind the desk while Brady sank wearily into the only armchair in the room.

Reynolds said, "Sorry to drag you all over the northwest like this. No sleep, no food, jet lags, all very upsetting. In the circumstances, I feel entitled to bend company regulations. Come to think of it, I'm the only person in Sanmobil who can. A refreshment would be in order?"

"Ha!" Brady pondered. "Early in the morning. Not only no dinner but no breakfast either." A hopeful look crept into his eye. "Daiquiri?"

"But I thought you always—"

"We had an unfortunate experience over the Yukon," Dermott said. "We ran out."

Brady scowled. Reynolds smiled. "No daiquiris here. But a really excellent twelve-year-old malt." A few seconds later Brady lowered his half-tumbler and nodded appreciatively.

"A close second. Now you two"—this to Dermott and Mackenzie—"I've done all the work so far."

"Yes, sir." Not even the shadow of a smile touched Mackenzie's face. "Three questions, if I may. Who suggested checking up on the amount of explosives in the blasting shed?"

"Nobody. Terry Brinckman did it right off the bat. We have a meticulous checking system and an easy one. The tally sheet's kept up to date twice a day. We just count the numbers of each particular type of explosive, subtract that number from the latest entry on the tally sheet, and that's the number that's been issued that day. Or stolen, as the case may be."

"Well, that's certainly a mark in favor of your security chief."

"You have reservations about him?"

"Good heavens no. Why on earth should I? Number two—where do you hang up your keys at night?"

"I don't." He nodded toward a massive safe in a corner. "Kept there day and night."

"Ah! In that case I'll have to rephrase what was going to be my third question. You are the only person with a key to that safe?"

"There's one more key. Corinne has it."

"Ah. That lovely lassie in the outer office?"

"That, as you say, lovely lassie in the outer office, is my secretary."

"And why does *she* have a key?"

"Various reasons. All big companies, as you must know, have their codes. We're no exception. Code books are kept there. Corinne's my coding expert. Also, I can't be here all the time. Undermanagers, accountants, our legal people and the security chief all have access to the safe. I can assure you the safe contains items of vastly more importance than the keys to the blasting shed. Nothing has ever been missing yet."

"People just walk in, help themselves and walk out?"

Reynolds lifted his eyebrows and looked hard at Mackenzie. "Not quite. We are security conscious to a degree. They have to sign in, show Corinne what they've taken and sign out again."

"A couple of keys in a trouser pocket?"

"Of course she doesn't search them. There has to be a certain amount of trust at executive levels."

"Yes. Could we have her in, do you think?"

Reynolds spoke into the box on his desk. Corinne entered looking good standing up, in her khaki cord Levi's and nicely distorted plaid shirt, a person with a smile for everyone. Reynolds said, "You know who those gentlemen are, Corinne?"

"Yes, sir. I think everybody does."

"I think Mr. Mackenzie here would like to ask you some questions."

"Sir?"

"How long have you been with Mr. Reynolds?"

"Just over two years."

"Before that?"

"I came straight from secretarial school."

"You have a pretty sensitive and responsible position here?"

She smiled again, but this time a little uncertainly, as if unsure where the questions were leading. "Mr. Reynolds lists me as his confidential secretary."

"May I ask how old you are?"

"Twenty-two."

"You must be the youngest confidential secretary of any big corporation I've ever come across."

This time she caught her lip and glanced at Reynolds, who was leaning back in his chair, hands clasped lazily behind his neck, with the air of a man who was almost enjoying himself. He smiled and said, "Mr. Mackenzie is an industrial sabotage investigator. He has a job to do, and asking questions is part of that job. I know he's just made a

statement, not asked a question, but it's one of those state-
ments that expects comment."

She turned back to Mackenzie, with a swing of her
long chestnut hair. "I suppose I've been pretty lucky at
that."

She spoke with marked coolness, and Mackenzie felt
it. "None of my questions are directed against you,
Corinne, okay? Now, you must know the executive-level
people pretty well?"

"I can hardly help it. They all come through me to
get to Mr. Reynolds."

"Including those who have business with that safe
there?"

"Of course. I know them all well."

"All good friends, I take it?"

"Well"—she smiled, but the smile had an edge to
it—"lots of them are much too senior to be my friends."

"But on good terms, shall we say?"

"Oh, yes." She smiled again. "I don't think I've made
any enemies."

"Perish the thought!" This came from George Der-
mott, who took over the questioning on a brisker note.
"Any of the people using the safe ever give you trouble?
Like trying to take away what they shouldn't?"

"Not often, and then it's only absentmindedness or because they haven't studied the classified list. And surely,
Mr. Dermott, if anyone wanted to get something past me
they'd hide it in their clothing."

Dermott nodded. "That's true, Miss Delorme." The

girl was inspecting his rough-and-ready good looks with a spark of humor in her eyes, as if amused by his blunt approach. He caught the expression and, in his turn, watched her for a reflective moment. "What do you think now?" he asked her. "Do you think anyone might have smuggled something past you out of the safe?"

She looked him in the eye. "They might," she said, "but I doubt it."

"Could I have a list of the people who used the safe in the past four or five days?"

"Certainly." She left and returned with a sheet which Dermott studied briefly.

"Good Lord! The safe appears to be the Mecca for half of Sanmobil. Twenty entries at least in the last four days." He looked up at the girl. "This is a carbon. May I keep it?"

"Of course."

"Thank you."

Corinne Delorme smiled at the room in general, but the blue eyes came back to Dermott before she went out.

"Charming indeed," said Brady.

"Plenty of spunk," Mackenzie said ruefully. "She built a whole generation gap between you and me, George." He frowned. "What gave you the idea her name was Delorme?"

"There was a plaque on her desk. 'Corinne Delorme,' it said." Dermott shook his head. "Hawkeye Mackenzie," he said.

The other men laughed. Some of the tension that had

grown in the room during the questioning of the girl fell away again.

"Well. Anything more I can do for you?" Reynolds asked.

Dermott said, "Yes, please. Could we have a list of the names of your security staff?"

Reynolds bent over the intercom and spoke to Corinne. He had just finished when Brinckman arrived accompanied by a tall, red-haired man whom he introduced as Carl Jorgensen.

Dermott said, "You were in charge of the night security shift, I understand. Were you around the sabotaged area at all tonight?"

"Several times."

"So often? I thought you would have been concentrating on what we regarded—mistakenly—as the more vulnerable areas."

"I went around them a couple of times, but by jeep only. But I had this funny feeling that we might have been guarding the wrong places. Don't ask me why."

"Your funny feeling didn't turn out to be so funny after all. Anything off-beat? Anything to arouse suspicion?"

"Nothing. I know everybody on the night shift and I know where they work. Nobody there that shouldn't have been there, nobody in any place that he hadn't any right to be."

"You've got a key to the blasting shed. Where do you keep it?"

"Terry Brinckman mentioned this. I have it only during my tour of duty and then I hand it over. I always carry it in the same button-down pocket on my shirt."

"Could anybody get at it?"

"Nobody except a professional pickpocket, and even then I'd know."

The two security men left and Corinne came in with a sheet of paper. Reynolds said, "That was quick."

"Not really. They were typed out ages ago."

Brady said to the girl, "You must come and meet my daughter, Stella. I'm sure you'd get on. Both the same age. Stella is very like you, actually."

"Thank you, Mr. Brady. I think I'd like that."

"I'll have her call you."

When she had gone, Dermott said, "What do you mean, like your daughter? I've never seen anyone less like Stella."

"Dancing eyes, my boy, dancing eyes. One must learn to probe beneath the surface." Brady heaved himself to his feet. "The years creep on. Breakfast and bed. I'm through detecting for the day. It's tougher than capping fires."

Dermott drove the rented car back to the hotel, Mackenzie sitting beside him. Brady took his ease across the entire width of the back seat. He said, "I'm afraid I wasn't quite leveling with Reynolds there. Breakfast, yes. But it'll be some hours before I—we—retire. I have come up with a plan." He paused.

Dermott said courteously, "We're listening."

"I think I'll do some listening first. Why do you think I employ you?"

"That's a fair question," Mackenzie said. "Why?"

"To investigate, to detect, to think, to plot, to scheme, to plan."

"All at once?" Mackenzie said.

Brady ignored him. "I don't want to come up with a proposal and then, if it goes wrong, have to spend the rest of my days listening to your carping reproaches. I'd like you two to come up with an idea and then if it's a lemon we can all share the blame. Incidentally, Donald, I take it you have your bug-box with you?"

"The electronic eavesdropping locator-detector?"

"That's what I said."

"Yes."

"Splendid. Now, George, let's have your reading of the situation."

"My reading of the situation is that for all the good we're doing we haven't a hope in hell of stopping the bad guys from doing exactly what they want and when they want. There is no way to forestall attacks on Sanmobil or the Alaska pipeline. They're calling the shots and we're the sitting ducks, if you'll pardon the mixing of the metaphors. They call the tune and we dance to it. They're active, we're passive. They're offensive, we're defensive. If we have any tactics, I'd say it's time we changed them."

"Go on," his leader urged him from behind.

"If that's meant to sound encouraging," Dermott said, "I don't know why. But how's this for a positive thought? Instead of letting them keep us off-balance, why don't we keep them off-balance? Instead of their harassing us, let us harass them."

"Go on, go on," the back seat exhorted.

"Let's attack them and put them on the defensive. Let *them* start worrying, instead of us." He paused. "I see things as through a glass darkly, but I say plant a light at the end of the tunnel. What we'll do is, we'll provoke them. Provoke a reaction. Provoke the hell out of them. We'll hang it on this one factor: Our own pasts, our backgrounds, can be probed until the cows come home, and nothing will be turned up. But you can say *that* about how many people in a hundred?"

Dermott twisted his head briefly to locate a peculiar noise from the back of the car. Brady was actually rubbing his hands together. "Well, Donald, what's your reading of it?"

"Simple enough when you see it," Mackenzie said. "All you have to do is to antagonize anywhere between sixty and eighty people to hell and back again. Investigate them as openly as possible. Deploy maximum indiscretion."

Brady beamed. "What sixty to eighty people do we investigate?"

"In Alaska *all* the security agents. Here, the security agents again, plus everybody who's had access to Reynolds' safe in the past few days. Going to include Reynolds himself?"

"Good heavens, no."

Mackenzie said inconsequentially, "She *is* a lovely girl."

Brady looked aloof. Mackenzie asked him, "Do you really expect to find your panjandrum among that lot?"

"Panjandrum?"

"The prime mover. Mr. Big. Messrs. Big."

"Not for a moment. But if there's a rotten apple in the barrel, he may well find him for us."

Mackenzie said, "Right. So we get all their names and past histories. Later on—sooner rather than later—we'll have the lot fingerprinted. Sure, they're going to stand on their civic rights and yell blue murder, and that will please you no end—refusal to co-operate will point the finger of suspicion at the refusee, if that's the word I want. Then you feed the information to your investigators in Houston, Washington and New York. Cost no object, urgency desperate. Not that you'll care a damn whether the investigators come up with anything or not. All that matters is that the suspects get to hear such inquiries are under way. That's all the provocation they'll need."

"What kind of reactions do we expect to provoke?" Dermott asked.

"Unpleasant ones, I should hope. For the villains, I mean."

"The first thing I'd do," Dermott told Brady, "is send your family back to Houston. Jean and Stella could really become a liability. The scheme might rebound on you. Can't you see the word coming through—lay off, Brady, or something unpleasant's going to happen to your family? These people are playing for high stakes. They've killed once, they won't hesitate to kill again. They can't be hung twice."

"Same thought occurred to me." Mackenzie turned to face the back seat. "Either get the girls right back home, or have the RCMP protect them."

"Hell—I *need* them!" Brady sat forward with indignation. "Number one, I have to be looked after. Number two, Stella's handling the Ekofisk business for me."

"Ekofisk?" Dermott almost turned backward. "What's that?"

"Big fire in the North Sea, Norwegian half. Started after you'd come north. We have a team going in there today."

"Well, okay," Dermott gave way a little. "So you have to keep in touch. But why not work through the locals? That brunette of Reynolds'—Corinne. She could field calls for you."

"What happens when we go back to Alaska?"

"Use somebody up there. Finlayson's got a secretary—must have."

"No substitute for the personal touch," said Brady magisterially. He sank back in the seat as though the argument were over.

His two heavyweights turned forward again with an exchange of looks. Having been through all this a hundred times before, they knew that further pressure would be useless for the moment. Wherever he went, Brady maintained the fiction that his wife and daughter were part of his essential life-support system, and he kept them with him regardless of the expense. Or danger.

SEVEN

NOT THAT DERMOTT AND MACKENZIE in the least minded having Jean and Stella around. Like mother, like daughter: whereas Jean was a strikingly handsome woman in her middle-forties, with that lovely, naturally blond hair and intelligent gray eyes, Stella looked the spittin' image of her mother, only younger, and even livelier, with, as her father was so fond of claiming, dancing eyes.

The men found Jean awaiting their return in the lounge bar of the Peter Pond Hotel. Tall and elegant, she advanced to meet them with her usual expression of tolerant, kindly amusement. This look, Dermott knew from experience, reflected her genuine feelings: An equable temperament was no small advantage for someone who had to spend her life humoring Jim Brady.

"Hi, honey!" He reached up slightly to kiss her on the forehead. "Where's Stella?"

"In your room. She's got some messages for you—been pretty busy on the phone."

"Excuse me, then, gentlemen. Maybe one of you would be so kind as to buy my wife a drink."

He waddled off along the corridor, while Dermott and Mackenzie settled comfortably into the warmth of the bar. In marked contrast to her husband, Jean scarcely drank alcohol at all, and she sipped carefully at a pineapple juice while the two men addressed themselves to the scotch. Nor did she try to talk shop in Brady's absence. Instead, she chatted pleasantly about Fort McMurray and its modest midwinter pleasures until her husband returned.

When he came back, Stella was with him, swinging along with her easy, loose-hipped walk. Dermott—not normally given to flights of fancy—was suddenly struck by the absurd disparity between the two figures. Jesus, he thought to himself: a hippo and a gazelle. What a pair!

Scarcely had Brady subsided into an armchair, with an outsize glass of daiquiri in his pudgy hand, than he made a slight sign to Dermott and Mackenzie, who muttered something and slipped off.

Brady seemed in buoyant form, and began to regale his family with an edited account of his movements around the far north. After a while Jean said doubtfully, "It doesn't seem to me you've *accomplished* very much."

Brady was unruffled. "Ninety per cent of our business is cerebral, my dear. When we move into action, what happens is merely the almost mechanical and inevitable culmination of all the invisible hard work that's gone on before." He tapped his head. "The wise general doesn't fling his troops into battle without reconnoitering beforehand. We've been reconnoitering."

Jean smiled. "Let us know when you've identified the enemy." Suddenly she became serious. "It's a nasty business, isn't it?"

"Murder always is, my dear."

"I don't like it, Jim. I don't like you being in it. Surely this is for the law. You've never come across murder before in your business."

"So I run away?"

She looked at his ample frame and laughed, "That's one thing you're not built for."

"Run?" Stella said, mock-scornfully. "Dad couldn't jog from here to the john!"

"Please!" Brady beamed. "I trust no such haste will be necessary."

"Where did Donald go?" Jean asked.

"Upstairs, doing a little job for me."

Mackenzie was at that moment moving slowly around Brady's apartment with a calibrated metal box in one hand, a portable antenna in the other and a pair of earphones on his head. He moved purposefully, a man who knew what he was about. He soon found what he was looking for.

When he came back to the bar he headed straight for Brady's family encampment.

"Two," he reported.

"Two what, Uncle Donald?" Stella asked sweetly.

Mackenzie appealed to his boss. "When are you going to start training this incorrigibly nosy daughter of yours?"

"I've stopped. Failed. Mother's job, anyway." He jerked his head upward. "Got them all, did you?"

"Guess so."

Dermott also reappeared to report.

"Ah, George," Brady greeted him. "How did it go?"

"Reynolds seems very co-operative. Unfortunately, all records are stored at the head office in Edmonton. He says by the time they've been dug out and flown up here, it may be late this evening or even tomorrow morning."

"What records?" Stella asked.

"Affairs of state," Brady told her. "Well, can't be helped. Anything else?"

"Naturally enough he's got no fingerprinting equipment."

"Fix it after lunch."

"He says he'll fix it himself—the police chief's a pal of his, apparently. Thinks the chief might be a bit stuffy about the delay in reporting the crime." He grinned across at Stella. "And don't ask 'what crime?'"

"No, sir, Mr. Dermott, sir!" She wrinkled her upper

lip in a fetching manner. "I *never* ask questions if I'm just permitted to fetch and carry, mend and clean."

Brady went on, "Reynolds can always claim that at first he thought it was an industrial accident."

"I understand the chief of police has twenty-twenty vision and intelligence to match."

"Well—Reynolds'll have to handle it as best he can. What about Prudhoe Bay?"

"An hour's hold. They'll page me."

"Fair enough." Brady shifted his attention to Stella. "We met an enchanting girl this morning—didn't we, George? Knock spots off you, any day. Wouldn't she, gentlemen?"

"Unquestionably," said Mackenzie.

Stella looked at Dermott. "Foul, aren't they?"

"Dead heat," said Dermott, "but she's very nice."

"The manager's secretary," Brady said. "Corinne Delorme. I thought maybe you'd like to meet her. She said she'd like to meet you. She must know all the nightclubs, discos and other iniquitous dens in Fort McMurray."

Stella said, "News for you, Dad. You've got to be talking about another town. I don't know what this place is like in summer, but whatever it is, it's a dead city in midwinter. You might have warned us that this is an *Arctic* town."

"Lovely choice of phrase. Wonderful sense of geography. That's education for you," Brady said to no one in particular. "Maybe you should have stayed in Houston."

Stella looked at her mother. "Did you hear what I just heard, Mom?" she asked with a scornful shake of the head at her father, which brought the pale blond hair swinging around her face.

Jean smiled. "I heard. Sooner or later, my dear, you have to face up to the fact that your father is no more and no less than a fearful old hypocrite."

"But he dragged us up here, kicking and screaming against our wills, and now . . ." Remarkably, words failed her.

As much as it was possible for so rubicund a face to register an expression, Brady's was registering unhappiness. "Well, now you've found out you don't like it, maybe you'd rather get back down to Houston." A note of wistfulness crept into his voice. "It'll be nearly seventy degrees back there now."

Silence descended. Brady looked at Dermott and Dermott looked at him. Jean Brady looked at both of them. "Something goes on that I don't understand," she said. Brady dropped his eyes, so she switched her attention to Dermott. "George?"

"Yes, ma'am?"

"George!" He looked at her. "And don't call me 'ma'am.'"

"No, Jean." He sighed and spoke with some feeling. "The boss of Brady Enterprises is not only a fearful old hypocrite, he's a fearful old coward as well. What he wants, in the good old-fashioned western phrase, is that you should get out of town."

"Why? What on earth have we done?"

Dermott looked hopefully at Mackenzie, who said, "You've done nothing. He has—or is about to." Mackenzie shook his head at Dermott. "This is difficult," he said.

Dermott explained, "We've decided on a course of action to flush the ungodly into the open, make them show their hand. Don and I have this unpleasant feeling that their reaction may be directed against Brady Enterprises in general and its boss in particular. The reaction may be violent—these people don't play by any rules but their own. We don't think they'd go for Jim himself. It's well known that he can't be intimidated. But what's equally well known is what he thinks of his own family. If they got you or Stella, or both of you, they might figure they could force him to pull out."

Jean reached out to take Stella's hand. "But this must be nonsense," she said. "Drama. Things like that don't happen anymore. Don, I appeal to you . . ." She looked anxiously at her daughter, gave her hand a little shake and released it.

Mackenzie was dogged. "Don't appeal to me, Jean. When they snip off your finger with the wedding ring on it, will you still be saying things like that don't happen anymore?" She looked hurt. "Sorry if I sound brutal, but things like that have never stopped happening. It may not come to anything so bad. I'm looking on the blackest possible side. But that's the only sensible way to look. We've got to find a safe place for you and Stella. How can Jim operate at his best if you're on his mind?"

"He's right," muttered Brady. "Go pack your bags, please."

During Mackenzie's speech Stella had sat with her hands clasped together on her lap, like a schoolgirl, listening gravely. Now she said, "I can't do that, Dad."

"Why not?"

"Who's going to make your daiquiris for you?"

Her mother cut in sharply. "There's a little more to this than the damned daiquiris. If we left, who's going to be number one target?"

"Dad," said Stella flatly. She glowered at Dermott. "You know that, George."

"I do," he answered mildly. "But Donald and I are pretty good at looking after people."

"That would be just fine, wouldn't it?" She threw herself back in her chair, hazel eyes blazing. "All three of you shot or blown up or something."

"Getting upset isn't going to help," said Jean soothingly. "Logic will, though." She transferred her attention to Brady. "If we went, you'd still be worried stiff about us, and we'd be worried stiff about you. So where would that get us?"

Brady said nothing, and she went on, "But there's only one point that really matters. Not only will I not run away from my husband, I'll be damned if Jean Brady will run, period."

Stella said, "And *I'll* be damned if Stella Brady runs either. Who's gonna maintain communications, for one thing? You know how long I spent on the phone today—to

England and all that? *Four hours.*" She stood up deci-
sively. "Another drink, Dad?" She cocked an ear at him
ostentatiously. "I'm sorry, I didn't hear that."

" 'Monstrous regiment of women,' was what I said."

"Ah!" she smiled, collected the empty glasses and
headed for the bar. Brady glared at Dermott and Mackenzie. "Hell of a lot of good you two are. Why didn't you
back me up?" He sighed heavily and changed his tack.
"Why don't we all get something to eat? Lunch, and after
that I'll catch up on some sleep. What are you girls pro-
posing to do this afternoon?"

Stella came back with full glasses. "We're going for a
sleigh ride. Won't that be nice!"

"Good God! You mean *outside?*" Brady gloomily
surveyed the few flakes drifting past the window. "Very
nice for some, I'm sure, but not for the sane." He struggled to his feet. "The dining room in two minutes, then.
George, if you will." He took Dermott aside.

With a giant Caribou T-bone steak, a quarter of
blueberry pie and some excellent California burgundy inside him, Brady watched his befurred wife and daughter
go out through the main entrance and sighed with satisfaction at the feeling of physical well-being that enveloped
him.

"Well, gentlemen, I really believe I might manage a brief snooze after all. Yourselves too?"

Dermott said, "Off and on. Donald and I thought we'd chivvy up Prudhoe Bay and Sanmobil and get those names and records through as soon as possible."

"Well, thank you, gentlemen. Very considerate. Do not wake me up unless Armageddon is nigh. Aha! Here, not unexpectedly, return the ladies." He waited until his wife had reached the table. "Something up, then?"

"Something *is* up." Jean did not sound pleased. "There are two men on the driving bench of that sleigh. Why two?"

"My dear, I'm not the arbiter of local customs. Are you afraid they're homosexual?"

She lowered her voice. "They're both carrying guns. You can't see them, but you can, if you know what I mean."

Brady said, "Members of the Royal Canadian Mounted Police are entitled to bear arms at all times. Says so in their constitution."

Jean stared at him, snorted with resignation, turned and left. Jim Brady beamed in satisfaction. Mackenzie said airily, "They tell me there are some very handsome young constables in the RCMP."

Apart from chatting with Ferguson, Brady's pilot, Dermott spent the afternoon alone in the lounge, consum-

ing one cup of coffee after the other. About mid-afternoon
Jean and Stella returned, rosy-cheeked and in high spirits.
Stella, it appeared, had learned from their escorts of a
place where the younger people congregated of an evening, and had called Corinne Delorme at work to invite
her out. Whether they intended to invite their erstwhile
escorts along, Stella did not say nor did Dermott inquire.
Brady would have the place comprehensively checked out
before he would let them near it. Shortly afterward Dermott received a call from Alaska. It was Bronowski in
Prudhoe Bay. John Finlayson, he said, was out at Pump
Station Four but was expected back soon. He, Bronowski,
would immediately set about obtaining what Dermott
wanted and would arrange for the services of a fingerprint
expert from Anchorage.

At five o'clock Reynolds came through to say that the
fingerprinting was well in hand. The records Dermott
required were even then being delivered to Edmonton airport and would be delivered straight from McMurray airport to the hotel. At six-thirty Mackenzie appeared, looking refreshed but at the same time reproachful.

"You should have called me. I'd meant to come down
a couple of hours ago."

"I'll sleep tonight," Dermott said. "That's four hours
you owe me."

"Three and a half. I put a call through to Houston,
explained what we had in mind, told them to alert Washington and New York, and emphasized the urgency."

"I trust your unofficial listener got it all down."

"He could hardly fail to," Mackenzie said. "There was a bug installed inside the base plate of the telephone."

"Well, that should be the final stirring-up of the hornets' nest. Let's hope the wrong people don't get stung. How's Jim?"

"Peered around his door on the way down. Looked like he'd died in his sleep."

At seven o'clock a call came through from Sanmobil. Dermott indicated to Mackenzie that he should listen in on the extension earphone slotted onto the back of the receiver.

"Mr. Reynolds? Not more bad news, I hope."

"For me it is. I've been told to shut down the plant for a week."

"When?"

"Now. Well, a few minutes ago. And I'm to be contacted in forty-eight hours to see if I've complied."

"Was the message from Anchorage?"

"Where else?"

"Phone?"

"No. Telex."

"They sent an open message?"

"No. Code. Our own company code."

Dermott looked at Mackenzie. "Pretty sure of themselves, aren't they?"

Reynolds said, "What was that?"

"Talking to Donald Mackenzie. He's listening in. So they know that we know it's an inside job. They must be pretty sure of themselves. Who's got access to the code books?"

"Anybody who's got access to my safe."

"How many people does that make?"

"Twenty. Give or take."

"What do you intend to do?"

"Consult Edmonton. With their approval I intend to be on stream again inside forty-eight hours."

"I wish you luck." Dermott replaced the receiver and looked at Mackenzie. "Now what?"

"Do you think Armageddon is nigh enough to justify waking up the boss?"

"Not yet. Nothing he, we or anybody can do. Infuriating. Let's try Anchorage. Want to bet they've had a similar threat to close down the pipeline?" He lifted the phone, asked for the number, listened briefly then hung up. "Hold, they say. One hour, two hours. They're not sure."

The telephone rang. Dermott picked it up. "Anchorage? No it can't be. I've just been told—ah, I see." He looked at Mackenzie. "Police." Mackenzie picked up the extension receiver. They both listened in silence. Dermott said, "Thank you. Thank you very much," and both hung up.

Mackenzie said, "Well, they seem pretty confident."

"They're certain. Perfect copies of the prints from the Anchorage phone booths. But they can't match them up with any on their lists."

"It all helps," Mackenzie said gloomily.

"It's not all that bad. The photostat is promised for tomorrow. Might just match up with some of the prints we hope to collect. The Alaskan ones, I mean. It would be too easy to check up on anyone here who made a brief stopover in Anchorage."

Stella came into the lounge, all set for dancing in black sequinned silk and colored tights, and carrying her coat. Dermott said, "And where do you think you're going?"

Stella said, "I'm going out with Corinne. First a snack and then the bright lights and the light fantastic."

"You'll confine your dancing activities strictly to this hotel. You're not going any place."

When she had got through a diatribe, calling him a stuffed shirt and a spoilsport, she added, "Mr. Reynolds said it's all right."

"When did he say this?"

"We phoned about an hour ago."

"It's not up to Mr. Reynolds to give you permission."

"But he knows Corinne is coming with me. She lives near here. You don't think he'd let his secretary walk into danger, do you?"

"*She* wouldn't be walking into danger. Nobody would be interested in her. But in you, yes."

Stella said, "You sound as if you're convinced something is going to happen to me."

"That's the way to make sure that nothing will happen to you—by taking precautions. See what your father says anyway."

"But how would *he* know what's safe and what isn't? How would he check up?"

"He'd go to the top—the chief of police, I'm certain."

Stella smiled brilliantly and said, "But we've talked already to him. Over the phone. He was with Mr. Reynolds. He says it's perfectly okay." She smiled again, impishly. "Besides, we won't lack protection."

"Your friends of this afternoon?"

"John Carmody and Bill Jones."

"Well, I suppose that does make a difference. Ah, here comes Corinne." He beckoned her across, made the introductions and watched as they moved off. "Well, I suppose we worry too much." He glanced at the doorway. "When I look at that lot coming in, I hardly think we need worry at all."

"That lot" were a pretty formidable looking pair—big men in their late twenties or early thirties who looked eminently capable of taking care not only of themselves but of anyone who might be along with them. Dermott and Mackenzie rose and crossed to meet them.

Dermott said, "I could be wrong, but you wouldn't be two policemen disguised as civilians?"

"There we go," said the fair-haired man. "Can't be very good at undercover work if it's as obvious as that. I'm John Carmody. This is Bill Jones. You must be Mr. Dermott and Mr. Mackenzie. Miss Brady described you to us."

Mackenzie asked, "You gentlemen on overtime tonight?"

Carmody grinned. "Tonight? Two gallant volunteers. Labor of love. Doesn't look like being any great hardship."

"Watch them. Beautiful she may be, but Stella's a conniving young minx. One other thing. You know we have a feeling some bad actors might try to hurt her. Or take her out of circulation. Just a suspicion, but you never know."

"I think we might be able to take care of that."

"I'm sure you can. Most kind of you gentlemen. Very much appreciated, I can tell you. I know Mr. Brady would like to thank you himself, but as he's in the land of dreams, I'll do it on his behalf. The girls are through there. I hope you have a pleasant evening."

Dermott and Mackenzie returned to their table, where they talked in desultory fashion. Then the phone rang again. This time it was Alaska: Prudhoe Bay.

"Tim Houston here. Bad news, I'm afraid. Sam Bronowski is in the hospital. I found him lying unconscious on the floor of Finlayson's office. Appears to have been struck over the head with a heavy object. He was hit over the temple where the skull is thinnest. Doctor says there may be a fracture—he's just finishing some X rays. He's certainly concussed."

"When did this happen?"

"Half hour ago. No more. But that's not all. John Finlayson is missing. He vanished soon after coming back from Pump Station Four. Searched everywhere. No trace of him. Not in any of the buildings. If he's outside on a night like this, well"—there was a grim pause—"he won't be around for long. We've got a high wind and heavy drifting, and the temperature's between thirty and forty below. Every man in the place is out looking for him. Maybe he was attacked by the same person who attacked Bronowski. Maybe he wandered out dazed. Maybe he was forcibly removed—although I don't see how that could be possible with so many people around. Are you coming up?"

"Are the FBI and the State Police there?"

"Yes. But there's been another development."

"A message from Edmonton?"

"Yes."

"Telling you to close down the line?"

"How did you know?"

"They made similar demands. We've got one here. I'll talk to Mr. Brady. If you don't hear, you'll know we're on our way." He replaced the receiver and said to Mackenzie, "Armageddon? Enough to wake Jim?"

"More than enough."

EIGHT

FERGUSON, THE PILOT, WAS UNHAPPY AND with good reason. Throughout the flight he was in more or less continuous touch with the operations center in Prudhoe Bay, and knew that the weather ahead was dangerous. The wind was gusting at 40 miles per hour. Flying snow had cut ground visibility to a few feet, and the thickness of the drifting surface snow storm was estimated at sixty feet or even more—less than ideal circumstances for landing a fast jet in darkness.

Ferguson had every modern navigational and landing aid, but although he could make a hands-off touchdown if he had to, he preferred to see *terra firma* before he put his wheels down on it. One factor in Ferguson's favor was that he was a profound pessimist. His three passengers well knew that he was not given to endangering his own life, let alone those of other people on board, and would have turned back had the risks been too great.

Brady, who had been wakened from a deep sleep and was in a sour mood, spoke scarcely a word on the way north. Mackenzie and Dermott, aware that the flight might be their last opportunity for some time, spent most of the trip asleep.

The landing, with much advancing and retarding of the throttles, was a heavy, bouncing one, but nonetheless safely accomplished. Visibility was down to twenty feet, and Ferguson crept cautiously forward until he picked up the lights of a vehicle. When the cabin door was opened, freezing snow whirled in, and Brady lost no time in making his customary elephantine dash for the shelter of the waiting minibus. At the wheel was Tim Houston, lieutenant to the invalided Bronowski.

"Evening, Mr. Brady." Houston wore no welcoming smile. "Filthy night. I won't ask if you had a good flight because I'm sure you didn't. Afraid you haven't had too much sleep since you came to the northwest."

"I'm exhausted." Brady didn't mention that he'd had six hours' sleep before leaving Fort McMurray. "What's the word about John Finlayson?"

"None. We've examined every building, every pump house, every last shack within a mile of the Operations

Center. We thought there was a remote chance that he'd gone across to the ARCO Center, but they searched and found nothing."

"What's your feeling?"

"He's dead. He must be." Houston shook his head. "If he isn't—or wasn't—under cover, he couldn't have lasted a quarter of the time he's been missing. What makes that even more certain is that he didn't take his outdoor furs with him. Without furs? Ten minutes, if that."

"The FBI or police come up with anything?"

"Zero. Conditions are bad, Mr. Brady."

"I can see that." Brady spoke with feeling and shivered. "I suppose you'll have to wait for daylight before you can carry out a proper search?"

"Tomorrow will be too late. Even now it's too late. Anyway, even if he is around, the chances are we won't find him. We might not find him until warmer weather comes and the snow goes."

"Drifting, you mean?" This was Mackenzie.

"Yes. He could be in a gully or by the roadside—our roads are built five feet high on gravel—and he could be lying at the bottom of a ditch with not even a mound to show where he is." Houston gave a shrug.

"What a way to die," Mackenzie said.

"I'm accepting the fact that he is gone," Houston said, "and though it sounds callous, maybe, it's not such a bad way to go. Perhaps the easiest way to go. No suffering. You just go to sleep and never wake up again."

Dermott said, "You make it sound almost pleasant. How's Bronowski?"

"No fracture. Heavy contusions. Dr. Blake reckons the concussion is only slight. He was stirring and seeming to make an effort to surface when I left the camp."

"No further progress in that direction?"

"Nothing. Very much doubt whether there will be either. Sam was the only person who could have told us anything or identified his assailant. It's a thousand to one that he was attacked from behind and never caught a glimpse of his attacker. If he had, the attacker would probably have silenced him for keeps. After you've killed two people, what's a third?"

"The same people, you reckon?"

Houston stared. "It's too much of a coincidence to be different people, Mr. Brady."

"I suppose. This Telex from Edmonton?"

Houston scratched his head. "Told us to close down the line for a week. Says they're going to check in forty-eight hours."

"And in your own company code, you said?" Dermott asked him.

"They didn't give a damn about letting us see it was an inside job. Damned arrogance. And the Telex was addressed to Mr. Black. Only someone working on the pipeline would know that he was up here. He spends nearly all his time in Anchorage."

Dermott said, "How's Black taking this?"

"Difficult to say. Bit of a cold fish—not much given to showing his feelings. I know how I'd feel in his shoes. He's the general manager, Alaska, and the buck stops with him."

Houston was doing Black a degree less than justice. When they arrived at his office in the Operations Center, he had a distinctly unhappy and *distrait* air about him. He said, "Good of you to come, Mr. Brady. Must have been a highly unpleasant trip—and in the middle of a winter's night." He turned to a tall tanned man with iron-gray hair. This is Mr. Morrison. FBI."

Morrison shook hands with all three. "Know of you, of course, Mr. Brady. I'll bet you don't get too much of this sort of thing out in the Gulf States."

"Never. Don't get any of this damnable snow and cold either. Mr. Houston here tells me that you're all up against a blank wall. Finlayson's just vanished."

Morrison said, "We were hoping that a fresh mind might be of use."

"I'm afraid your hopes are misplaced. I leave detection to the professionals. I'm merely, as are my colleagues here, a sabotage investigator, although in this case it's clear that sabotage and crimes of violence have a common ground. You've had Mr. Finlayson's office fingerprinted, of course."

"From top to bottom. Hundreds of prints, and not one seems to be of any use. No prints there that shouldn't have been there."

"You mean that the owners of those prints all had regular and legitimate access to the office?"

Morrison nodded. "Just that."

Brady scowled. "And since we're convinced that this character is someone working on the pipeline, any one of those fingerprints might be his."

Mackenzie asked the FBI man, "Any sign of the weapon used on Bronowski?"

"Nothing. Dr. Blake believes the blow was administered by the butt of a gun."

Dermott asked, "Where's the doctor?"

"In the sick bay, with Bronowski, who's just recovered consciousness. He's still dazed and incoherent, but it seems he'll be okay."

"Can we see the two of them?"

"I don't know," Black said. "The doctor, certainly. I don't know whether he'll allow you to talk to Bronowski."

"He can't be all that bad if he's conscious," said Dermott. "It's a matter of urgency. He's the only person who *might* be able to give us a clue about what happened to Finlayson."

When they arrived in the sick bay, Bronowski was speaking coherently enough to Dr. Blake. He was very pale, the right hand side of his head had been shaved, and a huge bandage, stretching from the top of his skull to the lobe of the ear, covered the right temple. Dermott looked at the doctor, a tall, swarthy man with an almost cadaverous face and a hooked nose.

"How's the patient?"

"Coming on. The wound's not too bad. He's just been soundly stunned, which is apt to addle anyone's brains a bit. Headache for a couple of days."

"A couple of brief questions for Bronowski."

"Well, brief." Dr. Blake nodded at Dermott's companions.

Dermott asked, "Did you see the guy who knocked you down?"

"See him?" Bronowski exclaimed. "Didn't even hear him. First thing I knew of anything was when I woke up in this bed here."

"Did you know Finlayson was missing?"

"No. How long's he been gone?"

"Some hours. Must have gone missing before you were clobbered. Did you see him at all? Speak to him?"

"I did. I was working on those reports you asked me to get for you. He asked about the conversation I had with you, then left." Bronowski thought about it. "That was the last I saw of him." He looked at Black. "Those papers I was working on. Are they still on the table?"

"I saw them."

"Can you have them put back in the safe, please? They're confidential."

"I'll do that," Black said.

Dermott asked, "May I see you a minute, doctor?"

"You're seeing me now." The doctor looked quizzically at Dermott down his long nose.

Dermott smiled heavily. "Do you want me to discuss my chilblains and gout in public?"

In the consulting room Dr. Blake said, "You look in pretty good shape to me."

"Advancing years is all. Have you been up to Pump Station Four?"

"Ah, so it's that business! What stopped you discussing it out there?"

"Because I'm naturally cagey, distrustful and suspicious."

"I went up with Finlayson." Blake made a grimace at the memory. "Place was a ghastly mess. So were the two murdered men."

"They were all that," Dermott agreed. "Did you carry out an autopsy on them?"

There was a pause. "Have you the right to be asking me these questions?"

Dermott nodded. "I think so, Doctor. We're all interested in justice. I'm trying to find out who killed those two men. May be three, by now, if Finlayson stays missing."

"Very well," Blake said. "I carried out an autopsy. It was fairly perfunctory, I admit. When men have been shot through the forehead, it's pointless to try to establish the possibility that they died of heart failure instead. Although, mind you, from the mangled state of their bodies, it's clear that the blast effect of the explosion would in itself have been enough to kill them."

"The bullets were still lodged in the head?"

"They were and are. A low-velocity pistol. I know

they'll have to be recovered, but that's a job for the police surgeon, not for me."

"Did you search them?"

Blake lifted a saturnine eyebrow. "My dear fellow, I'm a doctor, not a detective. Why should I search them? I did see that one had some papers in an inside coat pocket, but I didn't examine them. That was all."

"No gun? No holster?"

"I can testify to that. I had to remove coat and shirt. Nothing of that nature."

"One last question," Dermott said. "Did you notice the index finger on the same man's right hand?"

"Fractured just below the knuckle bone? Odd sort of break in a way, but it could have resulted from a variety of causes. Don't forget the blast flung both of them heavily against some machinery."

"Thank you for your patience." Dermott made for the door, then turned. "The dead men are still at Pump Station Four?"

"No. We brought them back here. I understand their families want them buried in Anchorage, and that they'll be flown down there tomorrow."

Dermott looked around Finlayson's office and said to Black, "Anything been altered since Bronowski was discovered here?"

"You'd have to ask Mr. Morrison. At the time, I was across seeing my opposite number in ARCO and didn't get here for twenty minutes."

The FBI man said, "Some things have been touched, naturally. My men had to when they were carrying out their fingerprinting."

Mackenzie nodded to the buff folders on Finlayson's desk. "Are those the reports on the security men? The ones that Bronowski said he was studying when he was clobbered?"

Black looked at Houston, and the security man said, "Yes."

"There were fingerprints, too." Mackenzie raised an eyebrow.

"Those will be in the safe," Houston said.

"We'd like to see those and the records," Dermott said. "In fact, we'd like to see everything in that safe."

Black intervened. "But that's where all our company confidential information is kept."

"That's precisely why we'd like to examine it."

Black compressed his lips. "That's a very large order, Mr. Dermott."

"If our hands are to be tied, we might as well go back to Houston. Or have you something to hide?"

"I consider that remark offensive."

"I don't." Brady had spoken from the depths of the only armchair in the room. "If you have something to hide, we'd like to know what it is. If you haven't, open up your safe. You may be the senior man in Alaska, but the people in London are the ones that matter, and they've promised me we would be afforded every co-operation. You are showing distinct signs of lack of co-operation. I must say that gives me food for thought."

Black's lips were very pale now. "That could be construed as a veiled threat, Mr. Brady."

"Construe it any damned way you like. We've been through this up here once before. And John Finlayson has gone on a walk-about or somewhere even less attractive. Co-operate or we leave—and leave you with the task of explaining to London the reason for your secretiveness."

"I am not being secretive. In the best interests of the company—"

"The best interest of your company is to keep that oil flowing and head off these killers. If you don't let us examine that safe, we can only conclude that for some reason you choose to obstruct the best interest of your company." Brady poured himself a daiquiri as if to indicate that his part of the discussion was over.

Black surrendered. "Very well." The lips had now thinned almost to nothing. "Under protest and under, I may say, duress, I agree to what I regard as an outrageous request. The keys are in Mr. Finlayson's desk. I will bid you good night."

"One moment." Dermott didn't sound any more friendly than Black. "Do you have records of *all* your employees on the pipeline?"

It was clear that Black was considering some further opposition, and then decided against it. "We do. But very concise. Couldn't call them reports. Mainly, just brief notes of previous jobs held."

"Where are they? Here?"

"No. Only reports on security personnel are kept here, and that's because Bronowski regards this as his base. The rest are kept in Anchorage."

"We'd like to see them. Perhaps you can arrange for them to be made available?"

"I can arrange it."

"I understand from Dr. Blake that you have a flight to Anchorage tomorrow. Is it a big plane?"

"Too big," said Black the accountant. "A 737. Only one available tomorrow. Why?"

"One or more of us might want to hitch a lift," Dermott answered. "We could, among other things, pick up those reports. Seats would be available?"

Black said, "Yes. No more questions, I trust?"

"One. You received this threatening Telex message from Edmonton today telling you to close down the line or else. What do you propose to do?"

"Carry on production, of course." Black tried to smile sardonically, but the moment was wrong. "Assuming, of course, that the criminals have been apprehended?"

"Where's the Telex?"

"Bronowski had it. It may be on his person. Or in his desk."

"I'll find it," Dermott said.

"I don't think Bronowski would like you rummaging about his desk."

"He's not here, is he? Besides, he's a security man. He would understand." Dermott shook his head. "I don't think you ever will."

"No," Black said. "Good night." He turned on his heel and left. No one said "good night" to him.

"Well, well." Brady exclaimed. "A friend for life in three minutes flat. Don't know how you do it, George. Pity he acts so suspiciously—otherwise he'd have made a splendid suspect."

"Badly ruffled feathers," Morrison said. "To put it in a restrained fashion, ruffling other people's feathers is his specialty. A martinet of the first order, they say, but an extraordinarily able man."

Dermott said, "Not, I gather, universally popular. Does he have friends?"

"Professional business contacts, that's all. Socially, nothing. If he has any friends, he hides them well." He tried to conceal a yawn. "My normal bedtime lies well behind me. In the FBI, we try to get to bed by ten P.M. Can I be of any assistance before I go?"

"Two things," Dermott said. "The maintenance crew at Pump Station Four. Fellow called Poulson in charge. Could you have their backgrounds investigated as rigorously as possible?"

"You have a reason for asking?" The FBI man sounded hopeful.

"Nothing really. Just that they happened to be there when the sabotage occurred. I'm clutching at straws. We have damn little else to clutch at." Dermott smiled wryly.

"I think we can do that," Morrison said. "And the other?"

"Dr. Blake tells me that the two dead engineers were brought back here today. Do you know where they were put?"

Morrison knew and told them, said his good nights and left.

Brady said, "I think I shall go and rest lightly in my room. Notify me if the heavens fall in. But not after the first half hour or so. I take it you two are about to indulge your morbid curiosity in viewing the departed."

Dermott and Mackenzie looked down at the two murdered engineers. They had been covered in white sheets. No attempt had been made to clean them up since they last saw them at Pump Station Four. Perhaps it had been impossible. Perhaps no one had had a strong enough stomach for the task. Mackenzie said, "I hope they're going to be sewn up in canvas or something before being taken to Anchorage tomorrow, or their relatives are going to have the screaming heebie-jeebies. Whatever you're looking for, George, look for it quick. I'm not enjoying myself."

Nor was Dermott. Not only was the sight revolting, but the smell was nauseating. He lifted the hand of the man he'd briefly examined before and said, "How would you say that forefinger got that way?"

Mackenzie bent, wrinkled his nose and said, "It sounds crazy, but it could have been broken by a pair of pliers. The trouble is that charring's obliterated any marks that might have been made on the skin."

Dermott went to a wash basin, soaked his handkerchief and cleaned up the charred area as best he could. The black carbon came off surprisingly easily. It didn't leave the skin clean—the pitting was too deep for that—but clean enough to permit a closer examination.

"No pliers," Mackenzie said. "To break the bone, pliers would have had to close right into the flesh and would have been bound to leave saw-tooth marks. No saw-tooth marks, so no pliers. But I agree with you. I'm sure that bone was deliberately broken."

Dermott rubbed some carbon off the charred clothing and smeared it on the cleaned area so that it did not look as if it had been wiped. He opened the jacket and slid his hand into the inside pocket: it came out empty. Mackenzie said, "The papers and cards have taken wing and flown. With assistance, of course."

"Indeed. Could have been Poulson or one of his pals. Could have been Bronowski when he was out there yesterday. Could have been the kindly healer himself."

"Blake? He does look like a first cousin of Dracula," Mackenzie said.

Dermott raised the damp handkerchief again and

started to clear the area around the bullet hole in the forehead. He peered closely at the wound and said to Mackenzie, "Can you see what I imagine I see?"

Mackenzie stooped low and peered closely. Still stooped, he said softly, "With the hawk eyes of my youth gone forever, I could do with a powerful magnifying glass." He straightened. "What I imagine I see is the brown scorch marks of burned powder."

As before, Dermott smeared some carbon back on the cleaned area. "Funny—my imagination runs the same way. This guy was shot at point blank range. The scenario reads that it was a very close thing indeed. The killer had a gun on this engineer and was probably searching him. What he didn't know was that the engineer not only had a gun of his own, but had it out. However it was, he must have seen it just in time and shot to kill—there could have been no time to indulge in any fancier gunwork. The engineer's gun hand must have gone into muscular spasm—irreversible contraction; not unknown at the time of violent death. To free the gun, the killer had to wrench it so violently that he snapped the trigger finger. Don't you think that fits in with the peculiar angle at which the finger was broken?"

"I think you have it. It fits, anyway." Mackenzie frowned. "There's only one thing I see wrong with your scenario. Why should the killer take the gun in the first place? He had a gun of his own."

"Sure he had, but he couldn't use it anymore," Dermott said. "More accurately, he couldn't afford to keep it anymore. Having seen no exit holes at the back of the head he knew he had left two bullets in the region of two occiputs, and that the police could match up the bullets with the gun he was carrying. Which meant he would have to get rid of it. Which meant that he would be gunless, at least temporarily. So he took the engineer's gun. My guess is that he will have got rid of both guns by this time, and he's almost certainly got another weapon by now. In these United States—and don't forget Alaska is the United States—getting hold of a hand gun is extremely simple."

Mackenzie said slowly, "It all fits. We may well be up against a professional killer."

"We may well be up against a psychopath."

Mackenzie shivered. "My Scottish Highland ancestry. Some ill-mannered lout has just walked all over my grave. Let's take counsel with the boss. Counsel and something else. If I know our worthy employer, he'll already have had half the contents of the jet's bar brought to his room."

"And you want his ideas?"

"I want some of those contents."

Mackenzie had exaggerated somewhat. Ferguson hadn't brought across more than a tenth of the plane's stock, but even that represented a goodly amount. Mackenzie had already had his first scotch and was on his second. He looked at Brady, propped up in bed in a pair of shocking heliotrope pajamas, which served only to accentuate his massive girth, and said, "Well, what do you make of George's theory?"

"I believe in the facts and I also believe in the theory, for the adequate reason that I see no alternative to it." Brady contemplated his fingernails. "I also believe we're up against a trained, ruthless and intelligent killer. I don't doubt that he might be a psychopath on the loose. In fact, there may be *two* psychopaths—an even more unpleasant prospect. The trouble is, George, I don't see how this advances us much. We don't know when this nut will hit again. What can we do to prevent it?"

"We can scare him," Dermott answered, "that's what we can do. I'll bet he's already worried by the fact that we're raking in fingerprints and records all over the shop. Let's try to worry him a little more. I'll go down to Anchorage tomorrow while you and Mackenzie stay here and do some work." Dermott sipped his scotch. "It should be a change for at least one of you."

"I could be deeply wounded," Brady said, "but slings and arrows from an ungrateful staff are nothing new to me. What, precisely, do you have in mind?"

"Drastically narrowing the range of suspects is what I have in mind. All very simple, really. This is a close-knit community here in Prudhoe Bay. They more or less live out of each other's pockets. Everyone's movements must be known to at least a handful of other people, probably a great deal more. Check on everybody and find out who has a definite alibi for being here on the morning the engi-

neers were being killed out in the mountains. If two or
more people, say, can honestly tell you that X was here at
the time of the crime, you can strike X off the suspects
list. At the end of the day we'll know how many suspects
we have. Not even a handful, I bet. I wouldn't be surprised if there were none at all. Remember that Pump Station Four is a hundred and forty miles away, and the only
feasible way of getting there is by helicopter. One would
have to have the time and opportunity and the ability to
fly a helicopter to get there, and there would be no hope
of taking a chopper without someone noticing. I think
you'll find it all very straightforward.

"Less straightforward is the next inquiry—who was in
Anchorage on the day that the original phone message was
sent from there to Sanmobil? There must have been quite
a few. Don't forget they go on holiday every three or four
weeks and, almost without exception, they go to Fairbanks
or Anchorage. It will be more difficult to establish alibis.
You won't find many people who have witnesses as to
their whereabouts at 6 A.M. of a black winter morning in
Alaska.

"In this case, though, we're more concerned about
those who are not in the clear than those who are. I'll
bring back a photostat of the prints they've taken. We
should be able to get the doubtfuls' fingerprints without
too much trouble and, with luck, match one set up with
the phone booth's set. I don't know how this sounds to
you, but it seems quite straightforward to me."

"And to me," said Brady. "I think Don and I can

manage that little chore without too much difficulty. Don't forget, though, that there's a fairly large community of people down at Valdez."

"As you're my boss," Dermott said, "I'll refrain from giving you a withering stare. Who in Valdez is going to fly a round trip of thirteen hundred miles during a winter night, stopping occasionally for fuel and so giving his identity away? And who's going to fly or helicopter the sixteen hundred miles round trip to clobber Bronowski and very possibly do away with Finlayson, especially as he would be immediately recognized as a stranger the moment he set foot in this area?"

Mackenzie said, "He has a point, you must admit. In fact, two points."

Dermott went on, "And don't tell me they could have come from one of the pumping stations. They don't have helicopters."

"I didn't say anything of the sort." Brady sounded aggrieved. "All right, we'll go along with the assumption that it's Prudhoe Bay or nothing. But what if we turn up zero?"

"Then it will be your turn to come up with the next bright idea."

"Hard day," Brady said. "You for bed?"

"Yes. I had intended to look at those records and prints tonight, but the prints aren't going to be of any use to me until I return from Anchorage. Reports can wait, too. I'll just hunt up that Edmonton Telex and take it down to the Anchorage police and see if they can help me." He stood up. "By the way, has it occurred to you that you yourself may be in danger tonight?"

"Me!" It was as if Dermott had suggested some unthinkable form of *lèse-majesté*. Then a look of vague apprehension crept into Brady's face.

"It may not be just your family who are at risk," Dermott persisted. "Why should these people bother about kidnapping when they could achieve their ends by putting a bullet in your back—which is not, if I may say so without offense, a very easy target to miss? How are you to know there isn't a homicidal maniac in the room next door to you?"

"Good God!" Brady drank deeply from his daiquiri. Then he sat back and smiled. "At last, action! Donald, get the Smith and Wesson from my case." He took the gun, thrust it deep under his pillow and said, almost hopefully, "Don't you think you two are at risk also?"

"Sure," Mackenzie said, "but not nearly as much as you. No Jim Brady, no Brady Enterprises. You're the legend. Without either of us, you could still function quite efficiently. This homicidal maniac doesn't strike me as the type who would go for a couple of lieutenants while the captain is around."

"Good night, then," Dermott said. "Don't forget to lock your door as soon as we're gone."

"Don't worry. You're armed, right?"

"Of course. But we don't think we'll be needing any weapons."

NINE

WHEN DERMOTT WOKE UP IT WAS WITH such a heavy-headed feeling of exhaustion that he could have sworn he hadn't been to sleep at all. In fact, less than an hour had elapsed since he'd switched out the light, closed his eyes and dropped off. He did not wake up of his own volition. The overhead light was on and Morrison, looking as distraught as a senior FBI agent is ever likely to look, was shaking him by the shoulder. Dermott eyed him blearily.

"Sorry about this," Morrison began, "but I thought you'd like to come along. In fact, I want you to."

Dermott peered at his watch and winced. "For God's sake, where?"

"We've found him."

Sleep, and all desire for it, dropped from Dermott like a cloak. "Finlayson?"

"Yes."

"Dead?"

"Yes."

"Murdered?"

"We don't know. You'll need warm clothing."

"Wake Mackenzie, will you?"

"Sure."

Morrison left, Dermott rose and dressed for the cruel temperatures outside. As he pulled on a quilted anorak his mind went back to his first meeting with Finlayson. He thought of the neatly parted white hair, the grizzled Yukon beard, the hobo clothes. Had he been too hard on the man? No good worrying now. He pocketed a flashlight and moved into the passageway. Tim Houston was standing there. Dermott said, "So you know too?"

"I found him."

"How come?"

"Instinct, I guess." The bitterness in Houston's voice was unmistakable. "One of those finely honed instincts that comes into operation about ten hours too late."

"Meaning that Finlayson could have been saved if this instinct of yours had been operational ten hours ago?"

"Maybe—but almost certainly not. John was murdered."

"Shot? Knifed? What?"

"Nothing like that. I didn't examine him. I knew that Mr. Morrison and you wouldn't want me to touch him. I didn't have to examine him. He's outside, it's thirty below, and all he's wearing is a linen shirt and jeans. He's not even got shoes on. That makes it murder."

Dermott said nothing, so Houston continued. "Apart from the fact that he'd never have crossed the outside doorstep voluntarily without his Arctic clothing, he'd never have been permitted to do so anyway. There are always people in the reception area, besides a person who mans the central telephone fulltime. By the same token, it would have been impossible for anyone to carry him out."

"Lugging corpses is conspicuous. So?"

"He wouldn't even have had to be a corpse. I think he was silenced in his own bedroom and bundled straight out the window. The cold would have finished him off. Here come your friends. I'll go get some more flashlights."

Outside, the cold was breathtaking. The temperature, as Houston had said, stood at thirty below. The forty-mile-per-hour gale brought the combination of temperature and chill-factor down to minus seventy. Even double-wrapped as a polar bear, without an exposed inch of flesh, the fact remains that one still has to breathe—and breathing in those conditions, until numbness intervenes, is a form of exquisite and refined agony. In the initial stages it is impossible to tell whether one is inhaling glacial air or super-heated steam: a searing sensation dominates all else. The only way to survive for any length of time is to breathe pure oxygen from a suitably insulated tank—but those are not readily available in the Arctic.

Houston led them around the right hand corner of the main building. After about ten yards he stopped, bent down and shone his flashlight between the supporting pilings. Other beams joined his.

A body lay face down, an insignificant heap already half-covered by the drifting snow. Dermott shouted, "You have sharp eyes, Houston. A lot of people would have missed this. Let's get him inside."

"Don't you want to examine him here, have a look around?"

"I do not. When this wind drops we'll come back and look for clues. In the meantime, I don't want to join Finlayson here."

"I agree," Morrison said. His teeth chattered audibly, and he was shaking with the cold.

Recovering the body from under the building provided the four men with no problem. Even if Finlayson had weighed twice as much, they would have had him out in seconds flat, such was their determination to regain shelter and warmth as soon as possible. As it was, Finlayson was slightly built, and handling him was like handling a 150-pound log, so solidly frozen had he become. When they were clear of the pilings Dermott looked up at a brightly lit window above and yelled through the wind, "Who's room is that?"

Houston shouted, "His."

"Your theory fits, doesn't it?"

"It does."

When they brought Finlayson into the reception area, there were perhaps half-a-dozen men sitting or standing around. For a moment nobody said anything. Then one man stepped forward and, with some diffidence, asked, "Shall I bring Dr. Blake?"

Mackenzie shook his head, sadly. "I'm sure he's an excellent doctor, but no medical school has yet got around to offering a course on raising a man from the dead. Thanks all the same."

Dermott said, "Have we got an empty room where we can put him?" Houston looked at him and Dermott shook his head in self-reproach. "Okay. So my mind's gummed up with cold or lack of sleep or both. His own room, of course. Where can we find a rubber sheet?"

So they took Finlayson to his room and laid him on the rubber sheet on top of his bed. Dermott said, "Is there an individual thermostat control in here?"

"Sure," said Houston. "It's set on seventy-two."

"Turn it up."

"What for?"

"Dr. Blake will want to do a postmortem. You can't examine a person who's frozen solid. We're getting experienced at this sort of thing. Too experienced." Dermott turned to Mackenzie. "Houston thinks Finlayson was silenced in this room. Killed, knocked out, we don't know. He also thinks that our friends got rid of him by the simple expedient of opening the window and dumping him onto the snow bank beneath."

Mackenzie crossed to the window, opened it, shivered at the icy blast of air that swept into the room, leaned out and peered down. Seconds later he had the window firmly closed again.

"Has to be that. We're directly above the spot where we found him. And it's in deep shadow down there." He looked at Houston. "Is there much traffic along there at night?"

"None. Nor during the day. No call for it. Track leads nowhere."

"So the killers left either by the front door or by this same window. They did the obvious thing—just stuffed him under the building, hoping the snow would have drifted over him before daylight came." Mackenzie sighed. "He couldn't by any chance have felt sick, opened the window for some fresh air, fell and crawled under the building?"

Dermott said, "You believe that's possible?"

"No. John Finlayson wouldn't get a breath of fresh air that way. He got a dearth of fresh air. Murder."

"Well, I think the boss should be told."

"He's sure going to be pleased, isn't he?"

Brady was furious. His black scowl accorded ill with his heliotrope pajamas. He said, "Progress on all fronts. What do you two intend to do?"

Mackenzie said pacifically, "That's why we're here. We thought you might be able to give us a lead."

"A lead? How the hell can I give you a lead? I've been asleep." He corrected himself. "Well, for a few minutes, anyway. Sad about Finlayson. Fine man, by all accounts. What do you reckon, George?"

"One thing's for sure. The similarities between what happened here tonight and what occurred at Pump Station Four are too great to be a coincidence. As with the two engineers, so with Finlayson. They all saw or heard too much for their own health. They recognized a person or persons whom they knew well and who knew them, and those people were engaged in something that couldn't be explained away. So they had to be silenced in the most final way."

Brady thought for a moment, and asked, "Is there a direct connection between Bronowski being clobbered and Finlayson being killed?"

"I wouldn't bet on it," Dermott said. "Tie-up looks too obvious. You could argue that Bronowski escaped because he didn't catch his assailants red-handed in whatever they were doing, and that Finlayson died because he did. But that's too easy, too glib."

"What does Houston think?"

"He doesn't appear to have any more idea about it than we do."

"'Appear?'" Brady seized on the word. "You mean he may know more than he's telling?"

"At the moment he's not saying or telling anything."

"But you don't trust him?"

"No. And while we're at it, I don't trust Bronowski."

"Hell, man, he's been savagely assaulted."

"Assaulted. Not savagely. I don't trust Dr. Blake, either."

"Because he's unhelpful and unco-operative?"

"A good enough reason."

Brady became tactful. "Well, you do tend to ride a bit roughshod over people's feelings."

"To hell with their delicate sensibilities! We're dealing here with three cases of murder. Come to that, I don't trust Black either."

"You don't trust Black? General manager, Alberta?"

"He can be the King of Siam for all I care," Dermott said forcefully. "Some of the most successful businessmen in history also number in the ranks of the biggest swindlers ever. I'm not suggesting he *is* a swindler. All I say is that he's crafty, cagey, cold and unco-operative. In short, I don't trust anyone."

"Look, friends, we're looking at this from the wrong angle," Brady suggested. "We're on the inside trying to look out. Maybe we should be on the outside trying to look in. Think of it this way. Who *wants* to hit the pipeline here and at the tar sands of Athabasca? Do you see any significance in the fact that here they receive their instructions from Edmonton while in Alberta they come from Anchorage?"

"None." Dermott was positive. "May be just coinci-

dence, at best a crude attempt to confuse us. Surely they
can't be so naïve as to try to convey the impression that
Canada is trying to interfere with America's oil supplies
and vice versa. Idea's ludicrous. In these times of an acute
oil shortage, what have two friendly neighbors to gain by
cutting each other's throats?"

"Then who *has* to gain?"

Mackenzie spoke quietly.

"OPEC," he said.

Mackenzie was just as positive as Dermott had been.
"If they could put a stranglehold on the two countries'
supplies from the north, they stand to gain immensely in
both profits and power. Both our governments have made
it clear that they're prepared to go to any lengths to shake
free once and for all from this crucifying dependence on
OPEC oil. This wouldn't suit our foreign friends at all.
They have us over a barrel—an oil barrel, if you will—and
they want to keep it that way."

"Why now," Jim Brady said, "although I know as
well as you do."

"They have tremendous leverage at the moment, and
the last thing they'd ever want to do is to abdicate this position of almost dictatorial power. Decisions are being
made now in both countries. Should North America become anywhere near self-sufficient in oil, our blackmailing
friends would lose their power base. They'd be forced to
abandon their pretensions to playing an authoritative role
in world affairs, and perhaps worst of all for them, their

profits would be reduced to such a trickle that they'd have to forgo their grandiose schemes for industrial and technological expansion, for hauling their countries into the middle of the late twentieth century, without any of the intermediate struggle or learning and developmental process. When it comes to national survival, desperate men are prepared to go to desperate lengths."

Brady paced for some time, then said, "Do you really think the OPEC countries would take concerted action against us?"

"Hell, no. Half of them are barely on speaking terms with the other half, and you can't imagine relatively moderate countries like Saudi Arabia participating in any such combined operation. But you know as well as I do that among the OPEC rulers there are some certifiable loonies who would stop at nothing to achieve their own ends. And you won't have forgotten that some of those countries play host to the most ruthless terrorist trainers in the business."

Brady said, "What would you say to that, George?"

"It's a theory, and a perfectly tenable one. On the other hand, since coming here I haven't seen a single person who looks remotely like an Arabian or Middle Eastern terrorist."

"So what would your guess be?"

"As a *wild* guess, I would suspect our troubles are caused by good old-fashioned capitalistic free enterprise. And if that's the case, the potential sources of our troubles are legion. I'm afraid we won't solve this by looking at it from the outside; we'll have to look out from the inside."

"And the motive?"

"Blackmail, obviously."

"Cash?"

"Well, the only other bargaining counter is hostages. Nobody's holding any hostages. So what's left? They're now in the process of softening us up by proving they can carry out their threats when and as they wish."

"They won't be asking for pennies."

"I shouldn't think so. To start with, the pipeline and Sanmobil have a combined investment of ten billion. For every day that delivery is held up they'll be losing millions more. Most important of all, our two countries are desperate for oil. Whoever those people are, they have us not over but in a barrel. Naked. The ransom will be high. I should imagine it would be paid."

"Who'd pay it?" Mackenzie said.

"The oil companies. The governments. They've all got a stake in this."

Brady said, "And once the blackmailers have been paid, what's to prevent them repeating the process all over again?"

"Nothing that I can see."

"God, you're a Job's comforter."

"Let me comfort you some more, shall I? There could be a lash-up between Don's theory and mine. *If* this is blackmail, and *if* the killers do collect, what's to prevent some of the OPEC countries approaching them and offering to double or triple their money if they destroy the supply lines for keeps—and get out? You've a big responsibility on your shoulders, Mr. Brady."

"You, George, are a rock of strength and compassion in times of trouble and stress." Brady sounded plaintive. "Well, if there are no constructive suggestions forthcoming, I suggest we all retire. There is thinking to be done and I must take counsel with myself. On such nights, the best company."

Dermott still felt unaccountably tired when the alarm clock dragged him up from the depths of a troubled sleep. It was just before eight in the morning. He rose reluctantly, showered, shaved, made his way to Finlayson's room, and was about to knock when the door was opened by Dr. Blake. At that time of the morning the doctor's beaked nose, hollow cheeks and sunken eyes lent him a more cadaverous look than ever—not the kind of physician's face, Dermott thought, to inspire hope and confidence.

"Ah, come in, Mr. Dermott. I've finished with Finlayson. Was just about to send for his casket. He and the two engineers from Pump Station Four are being flown out at nine-thirty. I understand you're going with them."

"Yes. You have caskets?"

"Macabre, you think? Well, we do keep a few tucked away. Apart from natural illnesses, this is an accident-prone profession, and we have to be prepared. You can't very well whistle up an undertaker from Fairbanks or Anchorage at a moment's notice."

"I suppose not." Dermott nodded at the dead man. "Any luck in establishing the cause of death?"

"Well, normally it requires a full autopsy to discover whether a victim has been suffering from cerebrovascular disease or cardiac arrest. Fortunately—or unfortunately—it wasn't necessary in this case." Blake sounded grim. "What was before only a suspicion is now a certainty. What would be natural causes elsewhere are unnatural here. John Finlayson was murdered."

"How? Beyond exposure?"

"None of your usual methods. He was rendered unconscious and left to die in the cold. Clad as he was in these abnormally low temperatures, I'd say his heart must have stopped in under a minute."

"How was he knocked out?"

"Sandbagged. In the classic spot, at the base of the neck. An expert. You can see the slight contusion and roughness there. A contusion can only be caused by blood still circulating, so he was clearly alive after the blow. The cold killed him."

"Where could the attacker have got sand in this God-forsaken frozen hole?"

Dr. Blake smiled. Dermott wished he hadn't: the long narrow teeth only accentuated the death's head effect. "If you aren't too squeamish, you can smell what they used."

Dermott bent and rose almost immediately. "Salt."

Blake nodded. "Probably slightly dampened. Makes an even more effective bludgeon than sand."

"They teach you this in medical school?"

"I was on the forensic side once. If I make out and sign the death certificate, will you be kind enough to hand it in at Anchorage?"

"Of course."

Big, burly, high-colored and irrepressibly cheerful, John Ffoulkes looked more like a prosperous farmer than a tough, competent senior police officer. He produced a bottle of whiskey and two glasses and smiled at Dermott.

"In view of those ridiculous prohibition laws they have up at Prudhoe Bay, maybe we can make up here in Anchorage . . ."

"My chief would like your style. We don't do so badly there. Mr. Brady claims to have the biggest portable bar north of the Arctic circle. He has, too."

"Well, then, to help erase the memory of your flight. I gather you didn't enjoy it much?"

"Extreme turbulence, an absence of pretty stewardesses, and the knowledge that you're carrying three murdered men in the cargo hold doesn't make for a very relaxed flight."

Ffoulkes stopped smiling. "Ah, yes, the dead men. Not only a tragic affair, but an extremely unpleasant one. I've had reports from my own State Troopers and the FBI. I wonder if you could have anything to add to what they said?"

"I doubt it. Mr. Morrison of the FBI struck me as a highly competent officer."

"He's all that, and a close friend of mine. But tell me anyway, please."

Dermott's account was as succinct as it was comprehensive. At the end Ffoulkes said, "Tallies almost exactly with the other reports. But no hard facts?"

"Suspicions, yes. Hard facts, no."

"So the only lead you really have are the prints we got from that telephone booth?" Dermott nodded, and Ffoulkes brought out a buff folder from a desk drawer. "Here they are. Some are pretty smudged but a few are not too bad. Are you an expert?"

"I can read them with a powerful glass and a lot of luck. But an expert—no."

"I've got a first-class young lad here. Like to borrow him for a day or two?"

Dermott hesitated. "That's kind. But I don't want to tread on Mr. Morrison's toes. He's got his own man up there."

"Not in the same class as our David Hendry. Mr. Morrison won't object." He pressed an intercom button and gave an order.

David Hendry was fair-haired, smiling and seemed ridiculously young to be a police officer. After introductions, Ffoulkes said, "Lucky lad. How do you fancy a vacation in a winter wonderland?"

Hendry looked cautious. "Which wonderland, sir?"

"Prudhoe Bay."

"Oh, my God!"

"Good, glad you're happy. That's settled then. Pack your equipment and, of course, your clothes. Three parkas should be enough—worn on top of each other. When's your plane leave, Mr. Dermott?"

"Two hours."

"Report back in an hour, David." Hendry opened the door to leave, then stood to one side as a lean man, white-bearded like an Old Testament prophet, bustled into the room.

"Apologies, John, apologies. Couldn't have caught me at a worse time or on a worse day. Two court cases, two suicides—people get more thoughtless every day."

"You have my sympathies, Charles—as I, one hopes, have yours. Dr. Parker—Mr. Dermott."

"Hah!" Parker looked at Dermott with an ill-concealed lack of enthusiasm. "You the fellow who's come to add to my burden of woes?"

"Through no wish of mine, Doctor. Three burdens, to be precise."

"I'm afraid I can't do anything about them today, Mr. Dermott. Snowed under, just snowed. Very likely I can't do anything about them tomorrow either. Most unprofessional."

"What is?"

"My two assistants. Coming down with the flu at the busiest time of the year. This modern generation—"

"I daresay they couldn't help it."

"Namby-pambies. What happened to those three anyway?"

"Two we know for sure. They were in the close vicinity of an explosion. After that an oil fire broke out. Savagely scarred. The fumes alone would have finished them off."

"But they were already finished off. So. Blasted to death, burned, asphyxiated. Doesn't leave very much for an old sawbones like me to do, does it?"

"Each of them has also a low-velocity bullet lodged somewhere near the back of his skull," Dermott said.

"Hah! So you want them out, is that it?"

"Not me, Dr. Parker. The State Police and the FBI. I'm no cop, just an oil-field sabotage investigator."

Parker looked sour. "I hope my efforts aren't as thoroughly wasted as usual."

Ffoulkes smiled. "What odds would you offer, Mr. Dermott?"

"About a million to one that they'll be wasted. That gun has almost certainly been tossed out of a helicopter somewhere over the Brooks Range."

"I'll still have to ask you, Charles," said Ffoulkes.

Dr. Parker was unimpressed. "What about this third man?"

"BP/Sohio's field production manager in Prudhoe Bay, John Finlayson."

"Good lord! Know the man well. Suppose I should say 'knew,' now."

"Yes." Dermott nodded to Ffoulkes' desk. "That's his death certificate."

Parker picked it up, screwed on a pince-nez and read through the report.

"Unusual," he said testily. "But it seems a straightforward medical report to me. There's no autopsy required here." He peered at Dermott. "From your expression, you appear to disagree."

"I'm neither agreeing nor disagreeing. I'm just vaguely unhappy."

"Have you ever practiced medicine, Mr. Dermott?"

"No."

"And yet you presume to take issue with a colleague of mine?"

"You know him, then?"

"Never heard of him." Parker breathed deeply. "But, damn it, he's a physician."

"So was Dr. Crippen."

"What the devil are you insinuating?"

"You read into my words what you choose," Dermott said flatly. "I'm insinuating nothing. I merely say that his examination was perfunctory and hurried, and that he may have missed something. You wouldn't claim a divine right of infallibility for doctors?"

"I would not." His voice was still testy, but only a testy mutter now. "What is it you want?"

"A second opinion."

"That's a damned unusual request."

"It's a damned unusual murder."

Ffoulkes looked quizzically at Dermott and said, "I'll look in at Prudhoe Bay tomorrow. There's nothing like adding a touch of chaos to an existing state of confusion."

TEN

DERMOTT AND DAVID HENDRY FLEW IN from Anchorage to Prudhoe Bay in the leaden twilight of late afternoon to find the weather distinctly improved, with the wind down to ten knots, the top of the drifting snow cloud not more than five feet above ground level, visibility in the plane's headlights almost back to normal, and the temperature at least twenty degrees higher than in the morning. In the administration building lounge the first recognizable face Dermott saw was that of Morrison of the FBI, who was sitting with a young, ginger-haired man incongruously dressed in gray flannels and blazer. Morrison looked up and smiled.

"Trust John Ffoulkes," he said. "No faith in the FBI." He gestured toward the ginger-haired young man. "Nick Turner. Ignore the way he dresses. He's been to Oxford. *My* fingerprint man. On your right, David Hendry, *your* fingerprint man."

Dermott said mildly, "John Ffoulkes just observed that two pairs of eyes were better than one. No developments?"

"Not one. You?"

"Largely a waste of time. Had a thought on the way up. Why don't we print John Finlayson's room?"

"No dice. We've done it."

"Clean as a whistle?"

"Close enough. Lots of unsatisfactory smudges which can only be Finlayson's, a couple belonging to a plumber who was there on his rounds, and one—would you believe it, just one—belonging to the bull cook, who must be a real whiz-kid with duster and polishing cloth."

"Bull cook?"

"Kind of housekeeper, bedmaker and cleaner."

"Could some other industrious soul have been busy in there with a duster?"

Morrison produced two keys. "His room key and the master key. Had them in my pocket since Finlayson was taken out this morning."

"Here endeth the lesson." Dermott laid the buff folder on the low table before Morrison. "Prints from the Anchorage phone booth. Now, I must go and report to the boss."

Morrison said, "It should amuse the two young gentlemen here to compare your Anchorage prints with the ones in the office safe."

"You don't sound very optimistic," Dermott said.

The FBI agent smiled. "By nature I've always been an optimist. But that was before I crossed the forty-ninth parallel."

Dermott found Brady and Mackenzie taking their ease in the only two chairs in Brady's room. He looked on them without favor.

"It's very pleasant and reassuring to see you two so comfortable and relaxed."

Brady said, "Rough afternoon, huh?" He waved a hand toward the serried row of bottles on the sideboard. "This'll restore your moral fiber."

Dermott helped himself and asked, "Any news from Athabasca? How are the family?"

"Fine, fine." Brady chuckled. "Stella passed on a lot more stuff from Norway. Apparently they've got that fire licked. No need to keep in touch any longer."

"That's good." Dermott sipped his scotch. "What are the girls doing?"

"Right now, I guess, they're touring the Sanmobil plant, courtesy of Bill Reynolds. Very hospitable lot, those Canadians."

"Who've they got to protect them?"

"Reynolds' own security men, Brinckman—the boss, you remember—and Jorgensen, his number two."

Dermott was unimpressed. "I'd rather they had those two young cops."

Brady snapped, "Your reason?"

"Three. First, they're a damned sight tougher and more competent than Brinckman's lot. Second, Brinckman, Jorgensen and Napier are prime suspects."

"Why prime?"

"For having the keys that opened the Sanmobil armor door, for having given the keys to those who did. Third, they're security men."

Brady smiled blandly. "You're bushed, George. You're becoming paranoid about the security men of the great northwest."

"I hope you don't have reason to regret that remark."

Brady scowled but said nothing, so Dermott changed the subject. "How did the day go?"

"No progress. Along with Morrison we interviewed every man on the base. Every one had a cast-iron alibi for the night of the explosion in Pump Station Four. So it's all clear there."

"Except," Dermott persisted.

"Who do you mean?"

"Bronowski and Houston."

Brady glowered at his chief operative and shook his head. "You're paranoid, George, I say it again. Shit, we *know* they were both out there. Bronowski's been hurt, and Houston didn't *have* to find Finlayson. If he *had* been crooked, it would have suited him far better to let the drifting snow obliterate every last trace of Finlayson. What do you say to that?"

"Three things. The fact that we know they were out at the pump station makes them *more* suspect, not less."

"Second guessing," growled Brady. "Hate second guessing."

"No doubt. But we've agreed that the bombers must be people working on the pipeline. We've eliminated everyone else, so it has to be them—does it not?"

Brady did not answer. Dermott went on, "The third thing is this: There must be some reason, albeit devious, why Bronowski was clobbered and Houston made the discovery. Look at it this way. What evidence do we have that Bronowski *was* assaulted? The only certain thing we know about him is that he's lying in the sick-bay with an impressive bandage around his head. I don't think there's a damn thing wrong with Bronowski. I don't think anybody hit him. I suggest that if the bandage were removed, his temple would be unblemished, except, perhaps, for an artistic touch of gentian blue."

Brady assumed the expression of a man praying for inner strength. "So, besides not trusting security men, you don't trust doctors, either?"

"Some I do. Some I don't. I've already told you that I'm leery of Blake."

"Got one single hard fact to back up your suspicions?"

"No."

"Okay, then." Brady didn't enlarge on this brief statement.

"We also rounded up the Prudhoe Bay members who were in Anchorage on the night of that telephone call," Mackenzie said. "Fourteen in all. They seemed a pretty harmless bunch to me. However, Morrison of the FBI did call up the law in Anchorage, gave names and addresses and asked them to see if they could turn up anything."

"You printed those fourteen, right?"

"Yes. One of Morrison's assistants did. Some Ivy League kid."

"No objections offered?"

"None. They seemed eager to co-operate."

"Proves nothing. Anyway, I brought along the prints found on the phone booth. They're being checked now against the prints of the fourteen."

"That won't take long," Mackenzie said. "Give them a call, shall I?" He called, listened briefly, hung up and said to Dermott, "Cassandra."

"So." Brady looked positively lugubrious, no easy feat for a man without a line in his face. "Houston's finest have run into a brick wall."

"Let's not reproach ourselves too much," Dermott said. He looked less downcast than the other two. "Our business is investigating oil sabotage, not murder, which is the province of the FBI and the Alaskan State Police. They appear to have run into the same brick wall. Besides, we may have the lead into another line of investigation— John Finlayson's autopsy."

"Huh!" Brady gave a contemptuous lift of his hands. "That's over. It turned up nothing."

"The first one didn't. But the second one might."

Mackenzie said, "What! *Another* autopsy?"

"The first one was pretty superficial and perfunctory."

"Unprecedented." Brady shook his head. "Who the hell authorized this?"

"Nobody really. I did *ask* for it, but politely."

Brady cursed, whether because of Dermott's words or because he had spilled a goodly portion of a daiquiri over his immaculately trousered knee. He refilled his glass, breathed deeply and said, "Took your own goddamned good time in getting around to telling us, didn't you?"

"Everything in its own good time, Jim. Just a matter of getting priorities right. It'll be a couple of days before we get the results of this autopsy. I really can't see why you are getting so steamed up."

"I can damn well tell you. Who the hell gave you the authorization to make such a request without first getting permission from me?"

"Nobody did."

"You had time before you left here this morning to discuss the matter with me."

"Sure I had time, but I hadn't had the idea by then. I was halfway down to Anchorage before it occurred to me that there could be something far wrong. Do you imagine I'd talk to you in Prudhoe Bay over an open line?"

"You talk as if this place is an international hotbed of espionage," Brady came back at him sarcastically.

"It only requires one disaffected ear, and we might as well pack our bags and return to Houston. We already know how good those people are at covering their tracks."

"George." It was Mackenzie. "You've made your point. What triggered your suspicions?"

"Dr. Blake. You know that as far as the murdered engineers at Pump Station Four and Bronowski's alleged accident were concerned, I already had reservations about Blake. I began to wonder if there was anything that could tie Blake in with Finlayson's death. I was the only person who saw the body between the completion of Blake's autopsy and the time the lid was screwed down on the coffin." Dermott stopped to sip.

"During that period Blake showed me marks on the back of the neck where, he said, Finlayson had been sandbagged into unconsciousness. On the plane it occurred to me that I had never seen a bruise or contusion of that nature. There was no sign of discoloration, or of swelling. It seemed to me more than likely that the skin had been roughed up after death. Blake said Finlayson had been struck by a bag of damp salt. His neck smelled of salt all right, but it could have been rubbed on during the night, after the body had been brought back up to the room. If he *had* been coshed, the vertebrae would have been depressed or broken."

Mackenzie said, "Obvious question—were they?"

"I don't know. They looked okay to me. But Dr. Parker will know."

"Dr. Parker?"

"Works along with the Anchorage police in a forensic capacity. Struck me as a very bright old boy. My request wasn't too well received at first. Like yourselves, he regarded the concept of a second autopsy as unprecedented or unconstitutional or whatever. He read Blake's death certificate and seemed to think it perfectly in order."

"But you persuaded him to the contrary?"

"Not exactly. He promised nothing. But he seemed interested enough to do something."

Brady said, "You *are* a persuasive cuss, George."

Dermott paused reflectively. "It may be nothing, or it may be another straw in the wind—but Dr. Parker has never heard of Dr. Blake."

Brady resumed his favorite steeple-fingered pontificating attitude. "You're aware that Alaska is more than half the size of Western Europe?"

"I'm also aware that in Western Europe there must be a hundred million people. In Alaska, a few hundred thousand. I'd be surprised, if, outside the few hospitals, there are more than sixty or seventy doctors, and a veteran like Parker would be bound to know or know of them all."

Brady unsteepled his fingertips and said, "There is hope for you. An immediate investigation into Doctor Blake's antecedents would appear to be in order."

"Immediate," Mackenzie agreed. "Morrison's the man

for that. Wouldn't it be interesting, too, to have a run-down on the man who appointed or recommended Blake to this post?"

"It would," Dermott said. "And it would certainly narrow the field a bit. I wonder. You remember just after we arrived here asking whether there were any ideas about the type of weapon used on Bronowski, and Morrison said —I think I quote him accurately—'Dr. Blake says he's no specialist in criminal acts of violence'?"

Brady nodded.

"So. This morning, when I was with him in Finlayson's room discussing the reasons for the man's death, he mentioned in an off-hand way that he used to be an expert in the forensic field. Obviously, he said it to lend credence to his diagnosis. But it was a slip, all the same. One time or the other, he was lying."

Dermott looked at Brady and asked, "Your agents in New York who are investigating Bronowski's security firm there—they aren't, shall we say, exactly burning up the track. Give them a nudge?"

"Negative. You said yourself that an open line . . ."

"Who's talking about an open line? We do it through Houston, in your code."

"Huh! That damn code. You encode any message you like and authorize it in my name."

Mackenzie winked unobtrusively, but Dermott ignored him and began to spell out a message to the telephone operator. It said much for his mastery of a code which its inventor found insupportably burdensome that

he encoded the words straight out of his head, without
having to make a prior transcript.

He had barely finished when a knock on the door announced the arrival of Hamish Black. The pencil moustache on the Alaskan general manager was as immaculately
trimmed as ever, the central parting of the hair still apparently drawn by ruler, the eyeglass so securely anchored
that it looked as if it could have ridden out a hurricane. He
still dressed in pure City Accountant, first class. At that
moment, however, there was a difference in his general
demeanor: he looked like a first-class accountant who had
just stumbled across proof of unmistakable and gross em-
bezzlement in the books of his favorite client. Yet he maintained his cool—or cold.

"Good evening, gentlemen." He was a specialist in
wintry smiles. "I hope I do not intrude, Mr. Brady?"

"Come in, come in." Brady was affability itself, a sure
sign that he didn't care too much for his visitor. "Make
yourself at home." He glanced around the cramped
confines of his room and at the already occupied chairs.
"Well—"

"Thank you, I'll stand. I shall not detain you for
long."

"A drink? One of my incomparable rum drinks?
How about a cigar?"

"Thank you. I neither smoke nor drink." The minus-
cule twitch of the left-hand corner of his upper lip clearly
indicated his opinion of those who did. "I have come here
because in my capacity of general manager of Sohio/BP I

felt it my duty to ask how much progress you have made in your investigations to date."

Dermott said, "What have we found out so far? Well—"

"Will you please be quiet, sir. I was addressing—"

"George!" Brady made a downward placatory movement of the hand toward a Dermott who was already halfway out of his seat. He looked coldly at Black. "We are not employees of yours, Mr. Black. We are not even retained by you, but directly by your head office in London. I suggest that if you want to leave this room the way you entered it, you watch your language."

Black's lips had disappeared somewhere. "Sir! I am not accustomed—"

"Okay, okay. We all know that. You're obviously in a hostile mood. Our progress so far? Not much. Would there be anything else?"

Black was clearly taken aback. It is difficult for an old-time man-of-war to attack when the wind has been taken out of its sails.

"So you admit—"

"No admission. We're just making a statement. Can we be of further help?"

"Indeed you can. You can explain to me the justification for your staying on here. The firm can scarcely afford the fees you seem likely to charge, if it gets no advantage. You have achieved nothing, and seem unlikely to achieve anything. You investigate industrial sabotage, specifically oil-flow interruption. There is, I suggest, a considerable difference between the spilling of oil and the spilling of blood. One cannot but suspect but that you are out of your depth and that events are beyond your control. One further suspects that the investigation should be left to those qualified to investigate criminal matters—the FBI and the Alaskan State Police."

"We'd be interested to know what they've found out. Or don't you feel free to tell us?"

Black compressed his lips still tighter. Mackenzie said, "May I have a word, Mr. Brady?"

"Certainly, Donald."

"Mr. Black. Your attitude here is singularly reminiscent of the one you adopted when first we met you. Have you the power to make us leave?"

"Yes."

"Permanently?"

"No."

"Why not?"

"You know very well why not. London head office would reinstate you."

"Possibly with the qualification that if any such situation arose again it would be the general manager, Alaska, who would be required to leave."

"I couldn't really say."

"I can. Or didn't you know that Mr. Brady is a close personal friend of the chairman of your company?"

From the way that Black touched his collar, it was clear that this was news to him. From the way Jim Brady experienced a sudden, suppressed difficulty in swallowing a mouthful of daiquiri, it was clear that it was news to him also.

"To return to your earlier attitude, Mr. Black," Mackenzie persisted, "on that occasion Mr. Dermott said he thought you might have something to hide. Mr. Brady suggested you were being unduly secretive and had—what was it again?—some undisclosed and possibly discreditable reason for choosing to obstruct the best interests of your company. Reasonable requests you regarded as being preposterous. Finally, as I recall, Mr. Dermott said that you were either standing on your high horse as general manager, Alaska, and were above such petty annoyances, or that you were concealing something you didn't want us to know about."

Black was possibly a shade or two paler, but his pallor could well have been caused by anger. He reached for the door handle.

"This is intolerable! I refuse to be the subject of character assassination."

As he pulled open the door, Mackenzie said, reproachfully, "I think it's impolite to interrupt a man's speech."

Black's eyes matched well the icy conditions outside. "What does that mean?"

"Just that I would like to finish what I've been saying."

Black looked at his watch. "Make it short."

"I know you have a great deal to do, Mr. Black"—two tiny spots of pink appeared on the pale cheekbones, for

Mackenzie's tone had made it abundantly clear he didn't believe Black had anything to do—"so I'll keep it short. Your intransigence interests us. You have made it abundantly clear that you would be happy to be rid of us. By your own admission you've acknowledged that we would be back very soon afterward, perhaps even in a matter of days. The conclusion is that you want us out of the way even if for only a brief period. One wonders what you intend to do or have done during that short time?"

"I see. You leave me with no alternative other than to report your gross incompetence and insolence to my board of directors in London."

When the door had closed Dermott said, "Not a bad exit line. He'll do nothing of the kind, of course—not when he's had time to reflect on Mr. Brady's close personal relationship with his board chairman." Dermott looked at Brady. "I didn't know—"

"Neither did I." Brady was positively jovial. He smacked one fat fist into the other pudgy palm. "Tell me, Donald, how much of what you said did you mean?"

"Who's to know? Not me. I just don't like the bastard."

"Hardly the basis for a dispassionate judgment," Dermott said. "But a splendid demolition job, Donald. There are times when a man rises above himself." He paused for a moment, then looked at Brady. "Remember the last time we had a run-in with our friend, you said that it was a pity that he acted so suspiciously, otherwise he would have made a splendid suspect? Maybe we're outsmarting our-

selves. It's barely possible that he should be a suspect.
Maybe, in addition, he's outsmarting us. This won't have
escaped you?"

Brady stopped being jovial. "Double-guessing again.
How often do I have to tell you, George, I hate this goddamn double-guessing. General manager, Alaska. Jesus,
George, *somebody*, by definition, has to be beyond suspicion."

In Dermott's cabin Mackenzie said, "Took you a long
time to transmit that coded message to Houston. Your
brief was merely to ask them to expedite the boss's earlier
instructions. What the hell else did you say?"

"I asked them to find out if anybody had left Bronowski's security firm within six months before or after
Bronowski's leaving."

"Maybe Brady's right. Maybe this security bit is getting to you. And even if Bronowski has hauled some of his
old associates along with him, they may have changed
their names."

"Hardly matters. Descriptions will be enough. And as
for my being bitten by the bug, it's high time you and Jim
were too. How would you try to account for the fact that
the bastards in Alberta know the Alaskan company's code,
while the villains in Alaska know the Albertan code, the
private Sanmobil code?"

"Ever since the first identical messages were received at Prudhoe Bay and Sanmobil, we've known our Alaskan and Athabascan friends were in cahoots, nicely co-ordinating their efforts to keep us wrong-footed and ensuring that we were in A while we should have been in B, and vice versa. There's no doubt in my mind that both security corps have been infiltrated. Our only suspects on both sides are security people."

"So you think the overall co-ordinator must be a security man?"

"Not necessarily. But what I'm sure of is that pretty soon we're going to hear of some fresh calamity that has struck in Athabasca. The master puppeteer must be thinking it's time the puppets were dancing again."

"Co-ordination," Mackenzie said darkly.

"In this instance?"

"You heard what I said to Black. That he wants us out for a few days for some purpose. If he can't get rid of us in one way—by asking us to leave—then he'll do it in another by arranging a fresh Athabascan calamity."

Dermott sighed, drew a line under a list of names he had printed, and handed it over. "Names for investigation —let's hope—by our friend Morrison of the FBI. What d'you think of it?"

Mackenzie took the list and studied it. His eyebrows went up. "Make Morrison jump, for sure," he said.

"I don't care if he jumps over the moon, as long as he gets on with it when he comes down," said Dermott heavily. "We've got to get action somewhere." He was about

to say something else when the telephone rang. He picked
up the receiver to listen, and gradually his face went chalk
white. He seemed not to notice when the glass in his left
hand shattered, crushed by the pressure he had put on it,
and a little rivulet of blood ran down his palm.

ELEVEN

"WHAT A *PLACE!*" EXCLAIMED STELLA AS she came back into Corinne's office. "Heavens—I had no idea it was so big. We seem to have driven about fifty miles."

"Well, it's quite a size, that's for sure." Corinne grinned, pleased that her guests had enjoyed themselves. "I hope *you* found it interesting too, Mrs. Brady?"

"Incredible!" Jean eased off the hood of her parka and shook her hair loose. "Those draglines—I've never seen anything like them. They're—they're sort of prehistoric monsters, burrowing into the bowels of the earth."

"That's right!" Stella's imagination had been fired no less. "Brontosauruses. Absolutely. Sure was kind of Mr. Reynolds to fix our tour. *And* to ask us to supper."

"Don't mention it." Corinne tried out the deprecating smile she had been cultivating. "We all like having visitors —makes a change. You'll enjoy meeting Mary Reynolds, too. Now, let's see if the boss is ready to leave."

She buzzed the intercom and announced that the ladies were back. Over the loudspeaker they heard him say, "Fine—I'll be through in a minute."

"Be right with you," she said. "All set?" She tidied her desk, locked the drawers, put the keys in her handbag and pulled on a fetching, roly-poly combination suit of powder-blue quilted nylon, as well as a pair of blue fur-topped boots. A moment later Reynolds himself came through the connecting door, similarly muffled in navy blue and white.

"Evening, ladies," he said pleasantly. "Had a good tour, I hope. Not too dull?"

"Not at all!" Jean had no trouble sounding enthusiastic. "It was wonderful. Fascinating."

"Good." He turned to Corinne. "Where are our strong-arm boys, then?"

"Waiting for us in the lobby."

"Great. We'd better not leave them behind, or your father'll give us hell." He winked at Stella and ushered her through the door.

Terry Brinckman, Sanmobil's security chief, and his deputy Jorgensen were hovering in the entrance hall. As the party approached the two men opened the outside door and let in a blast of the Arctic evening. Out on the tarmac one of the firm's yellow-and-black-checkered mini-buses stood ready, with its engine running. Reynolds opened the passenger door, helped Jean and Stella into the front seat, nipped around to the driver's side and slammed the door, cursing the knifelike wind. Corinne hopped into the back seat between the two security men.

As they cruised down toward the main gates Reynolds called up the guard on his two-way radio and identified the vehicle, to save the man coming out into the cold. At the bus's approach the high weldmesh gates began to roll open, driven by electric motors. A few snowflakes drifted fast through the blaze of the arc lamps that illuminated the perimeter fence. Reynolds gave a couple of toots on the horn to signal his thanks, and a moment later they were out in the open, with the headlight beams boring into the frozen darkness ahead.

The bus was warm and comfortable. The journey would take only twenty minutes. Yet Corinne somehow felt uneasy. Her boss had been on edge all day, and although she had maintained a sunny enough exterior, she wasn't looking forward to the evening. It could be sticky. Maybe they could get a bit of a concert or singsong going —that would help. She leaned forward and asked Stella if she could play guitar.

"Why, sure—if no one else is listening."

"Ah, come on! I thought we could maybe have a singsong."

"Course she can play," Jean said firmly. "Pick up any tune you care to sing."

"That's great." Corinne settled back between her two solid escorts. The bus had left the inhabited outskirts of the site and was winding through the low hills that separated the tar sands from Fort McMurray. Reynolds drove smoothly, without violent acceleration or braking, for the surface of the road was dusted with the ever-traveling snow, which flashed and glittered in the headlight beams.

They had just passed a sharp corner which Brinckman said was known as Hangman's Turn when Reynolds *did* jam on his brakes. He cursed as the bus slewed to the left, then corrected the skid. Ahead, the road was blocked by a black truck which had also skidded sideways-on.

"Look out!" Corinne shouted. "There's someone on the road!"

The bus shuddered to a halt a few yards short of the huddled figure lying face down. The flying snow cleared for a few seconds to reveal another body, also on its belly, but moving.

"Oh, my God!" Jean cried from up front. "There's been an accident!"

"You ladies sit tight," Reynolds ordered sharply. "Terry, go see what's happened."

Brinckman opened his door and got out. Corinne felt the blast of air hit her from the right. Then she saw another figure running, or rather staggering, toward them from the stranded vehicle. The man had his hands up, as if to shield his eyes from the minibus's lights. He was limping and lurching; she thought: he's been badly hurt.

Corinne felt Brinckman yank the first-aid box out from under the back seat. Next thing she knew, he was flat on his side, his feet having gone from under him on the ice. He got up at once and advanced more cautiously, with his feet apart, apparently to the aid of the injured man.

What happened next was so fast that Corinne afterward wondered a hundred times whether or not she had remembered it right. Everything seemed to go into a blur. One moment Brinckman was advancing to meet the crippled figure. Next second the cripple seemed suddenly to shake off his injuries: he stood upright and let fly an expertly timed blow that felled Brinckman like a tree. The instant the man lowered his shielding hand, Corinne saw he was wearing a stocking mask.

Stella screamed, "Back up—quick!" Corinne also shouted something. But before any of them could move the attacker was at Reynolds' door. In a second he had wrenched it open and thrown in something that hissed.

Instinctively Corinne threw herself down flat on the floor in the back. From the front she heard stifled screams and ghastly tearing noises as people struggled for breath. Then the gas got her too, and she found herself fighting and choking as if for her life.

In spite of her distress she became aware that the people in front were being dragged out into the snow. She crouched flat on the floor, struggling to control her stinging throat and eyes. Then she heard a man shout, "Where's the other chick? We've only got two." In the next second she felt someone seize the hood of her combination suit and drag her bodily out onto the road.

Without knowing why, she pretended to be unconscious. Somehow it seemed safer. She felt herself sliding
easily along the icy surface, being dragged like a sack of
potatoes. Her backside skidded smoothly over the snow.
As she was pulled around the front of the minibus, into the
headlights, she noticed that the supposedly injured men
had vanished. The bus's engine was still running, but the
vehicle blocking the road had started up as well. Suddenly
she was hoisted and dumped in the open back of the truck.

For the first time she felt afraid—not of being kidnapped, but of freezing to death. In spite of her thick suit
she was shivering already, and if they were going to be
driven miles in an open truck, the cold would soon kill
them all . . .

Her fears on that score proved groundless. After a
rough, bumpy drive of only a few seconds the truck
crunched to a halt. The noise of its motor was suddenly
swamped by a far louder, heavier roar that burst out all
around and over them. Corrine opened her eyes in terror
and saw that they had pulled up beside a gray-white helicopter. Even as she looked up one of the rotor blades
moved past her line of sight.

She felt she should scream or run—but would it do
any good? Even a second's hesitation was too long. She
felt herself grabbed by shoulders and ankles and swung
aboard, again like an inert sack.

The noise was terrific. The engine-roar increased to a
furious pitch, but through it she could hear a woman
screaming and men yelling. She saw a bundle she recog-

nized as Stella struggling frantically with one of the men in stocking masks, rolling across the bare steel. Another of the men slid the door in the side of the fuselage nearly shut, but he kept his head stuck out through the gap, bellowing at someone still on the ground.

The engine-note rose and fell, rose and fell, as though the pilot was having mechanical difficulty. Then it went up and stayed up—but only for a few seconds. Again it dropped. Corinne had never been in a helicopter before and did not know what to expect. She didn't know whether the pilot was going through his normal take-off routine, or whether he had some problem. What she did notice, however, was that the man who'd been shouting to his colleague on the ground had failed to close the door properly: It still stood a few inches ajar. A desperate idea flashed into her head: At the moment of take-off, whenever it came, she would dart to the door, drag it open, and fling herself out.

Before she'd had time to evaluate the risks, she felt the floor tilt—they were off already. Then came a heavy bump. Down again, she thought. Next time they did lift. It was then or never.

She rolled over, flung herself at the door and hauled it back. She was hit by a stunningly cold wash of wind. Too late she realized that they were already off the ground. She was caught by the slipstream, whirled around and sucked out. She clutched wildly at the door frame but her gloves slipped uselessly over the bare metal. At the edge of her consciousness she heard a man screaming, "You're crazy!

You'll be killed!" Then she was falling through the snow-laden wind. She tumbled over in mid air and glimpsed a pair of headlights snaking through the night way below. That was the last thing she saw. The next couple of seconds would bring her nightmares for the rest of her life. Time stopped. She fell endlessly through the freezing sky, convinced that her body would be smashed to pieces any instant. She tried to scream, but could not. She tried to breathe, but could not. She tried to turn over, but could not alter her attitude in the slightest. She dropped helplessly, rigid with terror. Then she screamed.

The impact was unbelievably gentle. Instead of smashing into iron-hard tundra, she landed in something soft and yielding. She hit it back-first, and went right on down through several feet of blessed cushioning. She was winded by the impact, but that was all. She lay on her back gasping and groaning for breath, but once she had got it back, she began to shake with relief. To her own amazement, she found she was laughing as well as crying. She had landed on her backside in a great big drift of snow.

Jay Shore was just about to leave his office at the Sanmobil plant when the telephone rang. He picked up the receiver and said, "Yes?"

"Switchboard operator here," said a voice high with

stress. "Got an emergency. Driver Pete Johnson is on the radio. Wants to talk to you immediately."

"I'll take it. Patch him through." Shore waited.

"Hullo? Hullo?" Johnson's voice crackled through, even more excited than the operator's. "Mr. Shore, sir?"

"Speaking. Take it easy. What's the problem?"

"I'm on my way down to Fort McMurray, sir. Driving bus MB Three. Just come around a corner and found Bus MB Five abandoned in the middle of the road."

"*Abandoned?*"

"That's right. Doors open, motor running, lights on. Point is, it's the bus Mr. Reynolds took to go home in."

"Jesus! Where are you?"

"About a mile past Hangman's Turn. Mile toward Fort McMurray."

"Okay. I'll get someone right out there."

"Mr. Shore?"

"What is it?"

"I just saw a chopper take off from near the road, and *somebody fell out of it*. And two of our security guys— Mr. Brinckman and Mr. Jorgensen—are lying in the road, like they've been hurt real bad."

"Damn!"

"Yeah, and there's a truck stuck in the snow by where the plane took off. It's trying to get back on the road, facing toward Fort McMurray."

"Keep away from it," Shore ordered. "Stay in your own vehicle. Back off a bit. But don't go near the truck. I'll get someone right down."

"Okay Mr. Shore, sir."

Shore banged down the receiver and snatched up another, an outside line. He dialed and waited. He knew that Carmody and Jones, the two RCMP men assigned to protect the Brady family, were also due at the Reynoldses' for supper, so he called directly there. Someone answered— Mrs. Reynolds.

"Mary? Jay Shore speaking. Look—I'm afraid there's been some sort of a . . . mix-up. George and the ladies have got delayed. What's that? No—I hope not. Nothing to worry about. Have you the two constables there already? Great. Yes please. Either will do."

John Carmody came on the line.

"Emergency," said Shore quietly. "I think your party's been hijacked. Yes—I do." He explained all he knew in a couple of sentences. "What I want *you* to do is come right up the road to Hangman's Turn. You see anybody coming to meet you, stop him. It could be the gray truck we're after. Okay?"

"Okay. We're on our way."

"That's fine. Get moving."

Carmody drove. Jones rode shotgun, his .38 revolver ready in his hand. The Cherokee Jeep station wagon, in four-wheel drive, held the road better than a regular sedan, but even so they had to go carefully.

Carmody swore steadily as he nursed the wheel. "Goddamn it to hell!" he kept muttering. "The first time we leave them, *this* happens. What in hell were the Sanmobil security guys doing, for Christ's sake?"

They drove on, snow whirling through the headlight beams. Suddenly they saw lights coming the other way.

"Block the road!" Jones ordered. "Get sideways."

"Better to keep head on—dazzle him. He can't get past, anyway."

Carmody stopped in the middle of the road and switched on the station wagon's flashers. The oncoming driver rounded a bend, saw them, braked and slewed violently from side to side before sliding to a halt.

Jones got out and moved toward the vehicle. He'd only gone three or four yards when a spurt of fire flashed from the driver's window, followed instantly by the crack of a gun. Jones spun sideways, clutching his left shoulder. The other driver slammed into gear and let out the clutch. For a second his tires raced griplessly on the snow. Then he shot forward, cannoned into the Jeep, shunted it sideways enough for him to scrape past, and accelerated away in the direction of Fort McMurray.

Carmody tried to open his door but found it jammed: the bodywork was buckled all down that side. He hunked across to the other side and ran to the aid of his wounded colleague. Jones was conscious but bleeding badly from a wound in the top corner of his chest—a large, dark stain had spread out across the snow beneath his body.

Carmody thought fast. It was too cold to administer

first aid to the wound. If he took off any of Jones's clothes, the man would die of exposure and shock. First priority was to get him somewhere warm, then to hospital. He ought to call up an ambulance.

"Come on, Bill," he said gently. "You gotta get up."

"Okay," Jones muttered. "I'm okay."

"On your feet, then." Carmody got him around the waist, avoiding his chest and shoulders, in case he made anything worse there, and hoisted him upright. Then he propelled him gently toward the Jeep and opened one of the back doors.

"In there," he said. "Front door's jammed."

He got the wounded man safely in, closed the door, climbed aboard himself and turned up the heater to maximum. Then he addressed himself to the radio. To his chagrin, he could get nothing out of it. The set was live, but no signal came through. Something had been broken by the impact of the truck.

For a moment Carmody considered turning and giving chase. Then he realized the other driver had too much start on him. Even with his four-wheel drive, he would never overtake him in the short distance between there and Fort McMurray. He was closer to the Sanmobil plant, in any case. Better get on and make contact with the bus driver who had first raised the alarm.

He set off as fast as he dared. Jones was ominously silent, not answering questions about how he felt. Carmody set his jaw and drove through the snow.

Five minutes later he came on the stranded minibus.

Immediately he recognized the black-and-yellow check-ered MB Five, which he had seen and ridden in many times before. Beyond it a line of vehicles had piled up, the drivers being kept at bay by Johnson, who had told them that the police were about to arrive, and that no one must touch the bus until the cops had checked it out. The beaten-up security men were hunched in the seats of John-son's bus, apparently comatose.

Carmody sized up the position in a moment. "Get it out of the way," he ordered. "Let everybody else through."

They pushed the Reynolds' bus to one side and waved the other vehicles past. Three back in the line was a Sanmobil truck with two crewmen aboard—the only men Shore had been able to conscript immediately at that late hour. Over Johnson's bus radio Carmody called for police reinforcements and alerted the Sanmobil sick-bay, warning them that three injured men were being brought in. Then he detailed one of the Sanmobil men to drive his own Jeep right onto the plant, with Jones still in it. Brinckman and Jorgensen, unsteady on their feet, also climbed aboard.

"Get back in the warm," Carmody told them. "I'll talk to you guys later." As they drove off he turned to Johnson: "Okay, so what happened?"

"I just came on the bus in the middle of the road, like you saw it. The two security guys were lying in front of it, trying to get up. I got out to see what the matter was, and heard the racket of a helicopter engine, right close."

"Where was it?"

"Just over there. I'll show you."

He switched on a big flashlight and led the way over the frozen tundra. "Sounded like he had a problem with the motor—kept running it up and letting it die again. Then he *did* go. Lifted off and headed thataway—north. Here—you can see the ski marks."

In the flashlight beam the imprint of long, heavy skis was still visible, though dusted over with the snow blown about by the rotor's down-draft.

"Any markings on the chopper, identification?" Carmody asked.

"Nothing—it was just like a big black shadow against the sky. Couldn't even tell the color exactly, but it looked off-white. Pair of small fins near the tail too."

"And then what happened? Where did the person fall?"

"A woman, it was. She screamed. Someplace over there." Johnson pointed. "Not too far."

"How high did she fall from?"

"Maybe a hundred feet. Maybe more."

"Must be dead. We'd better look, all the same. Oh, my God! One of the Bradys killed."

They went up an incline into the teeth of the wind. On top of the slope the ground was rounded into smooth, gentle humps. The flashlight beam, sweeping the snow, revealed nothing.

"Must have been around here," said Johnson doubtfully. "Can't have been much farther, or I'd never have seen the body at all. Try over there a bit."

They cast a little to their left. Suddenly Carmody, who had been walking on hard-frozen tundra, sank to his waist in snow. As he exclaimed and struggled to extricate himself from the drift, Johnson called, "Listen, I thought I heard something."

They waited, catching only the whine of the wind. Then Johnson heard the sound again—a cry that sounded faint yet close at hand.

"There it is!" he shouted. "Sure as hell, someone calling. This way!"

They tried to move eastward, but both lunged into the deep snow again and realized that a rift in the ground ran in that direction.

"She's in the snow," cried Carmody. "Must be. Only way she could have survived the fall."

They regained the hard edge of the invisible miniature valley and followed it another twenty steps. Then they heard the cry again, almost beneath them. This time they shouted back and got an answer. A few more steps brought them to the lip of a hole about a yard across that had been punched vertically downward into the drift. Shining the light down it, they saw a bundle of powder-blue snowsuit.

"Hey! You! Mrs. Brady? Stella?" Carmody called. "Are you hurt?"

"No," came the muffled answer. "I'm not Mrs. Brady or Stella, and I'm not hurt. Just stuck."

"Who are you, then?"

"Corinne Delorme."

"Corinne! Heaven's sakes! John Carmody here. Hold on, and we'll get you right out of there." He sent Johnson running to the truck for a shovel and a rope, and in five minutes they had dug and hoisted the girl out. Considering she had been outdoors for more than half an hour, she was in remarkably good shape, mainly because the snow had insulated her and given her complete protection from the wind. But as soon as they got her into the warmth of the truck cab, reaction set in and she began to shudder uncontrollably.

Carmody's first impulse was to drive her to hospital, but then he changed his mind. Something—he could not quite tell what—made him favor a more devious approach. The guys in the helicopter must reckon she was dead. They must think they had another murder on their hands. It was a million-to-one that she had fallen into the drifted-up ravine rather than onto the ground: five yards to either side, and every bone in her body would have been broken. Something might be gained, Carmody thought, if the kidnappers did not realize anyone had survived. Therefore he decided to move her away into safekeeping, at any rate until Brady and his team returned.

"Know what I want you to do?" Carmody said to Johnson. "Drive Miss Delorme to the isolation unit on the plant. The *isolation* unit. When you reach the main gates, have her keep down out of sight, on the floor. I don't want anyone to know where she is. Any bother, say you're on a special run for Mr. Shore. Okay?"

Johnson nodded.

"You hear that, Corinne?" Carmody lifted up her chin. "He'll take you to a good place at Athabasca. Nice and warm and comfortable. Out of the way, too. I'll see you back there as soon as I can make it."

Shock and reaction had knocked the girl to pieces for the moment, and she could not answer.

"Go on, then," Carmody told Johnson. "Drive."

TWELVE

IT WAS PAST MIDNIGHT AND STILL SNOW-
ing heavily when Jim Brady arrived back in Fort McMurray, but the lobby of the Peter Pond Hotel was as crowded
and bustling with activity as if it had been just after noon.
Brady sank wearily into a chair and for the first time
waved off a drink. The flight from Prudhoe Bay had been
a grim one: between them, Brady, Dermott and Mackenzie had uttered hardly a word.

A tall, lean man, dark-moustached and heavily tanned,
approached. "Mr. Brady? My name's Willoughby. Glad to
make your acquaintance, sir, though not in these damnable
circumstances."

"Ah—the police chief." Brady smiled without humor. "And rough for you, Mr. Willoughby, to have this happen in your territory. I was sorry to hear that one of your men had been killed."

"I'm glad to say that report was premature. There was a great deal of confusion around here when we made that phone call to you. The man was shot through the left lung and certainly looked bad, but now the doctor says he has a more than even chance."

"That's something." Brady smiled wanly again.

Willoughby turned to two other men. "D'you know . . . ?"

"Those two gentlemen I've met," said Brady. "Mr. Brinckman, Sanmobil security chief, and his deputy, Mr. Jorgensen. Odd—for a couple of reportedly injured men, you look remarkably fit to me."

Brinckman said, "We don't exactly feel it. Like Mr. Willoughby said, things got exaggerated in the heat of the moment. No broken bones, no knife or gun injuries, but they did knock us about a bit."

"Pete Johnson—the guy who raised the alarm—will vouch for that," said Willoughby. "When he got there, Jorgensen was lying on the road, out cold, and Brinckman was wandering around in a daze. He didn't know if it was last night or last month."

Brady turned to another man who had appeared at his side. "Evening, Mr. Shore. Morning, rather. The Brady family seem to have disturbed a lot of people's sleep, I'm afraid."

"To hell with that." Shore was visibly upset. "I helped show Mrs. Brady and your daughter around the plant yesterday. That this should happen to her. Just as bad, that this should happen to you when you and your family were virtually our guests and you were trying to help us. A black day and a black eye for Sanmobil."

"Maybe not all that black," said Dermott. "God knows, it must be a traumatic experience to be kidnapped, but I don't believe any of the four is in immediate danger. We're not dealing with political fanatics such as you get in Europe or the Mideast. We're up against hard-headed business men with no personal animosity against their victims. They almost certainly regard them as bargaining counters." He clasped and unclasped his big hands. "They're going to make demands, probably outrageous, for the return of the captives, and if those demands are met, they'll honor the bargain. Professional kidnappers usually do. In their own twisted terms, it's sound business practice and plain common sense."

Brady turned to Willoughby. "We haven't really heard what happened. I assume you haven't had time to make wide-ranging inquiries?"

"Afraid not."

"They've just vanished into thin air?"

"Thin air is right. Helicopter, as you heard. They could be a few hundred miles away in any direction by this time."

"Any chance of airfield radars having picked up their flight path?"

"No, sir. It's a million to one that they were flying below radar level. Besides, there are more palm trees in northern Alberta than there are radar stations. Down south, it's different. We've alerted the stations there to keep a watch, but nothing's been reported so far."

"Well"—Brady steepled his fingers, sinking back in his chair—"it might help if we could have a brief chronological account of what happened."

"That won't take long. Jay?"

Shore said, "Yes. I was the last person to see them, apart from these two"—he pointed at Brinckman and Jorgensen. "They left in one of Sanmobil's minibuses, with Bill Reynolds driving."

Mackenzie cut in, "Were there any phone calls before they left?"

"I wouldn't know. Why?"

"Let me ask another question." Mackenzie looked at Brinckman. "How did the kidnappers stop your bus?"

"They had a truck slewed across the road. Blocked it completely."

"It couldn't have been there long. There's a fair bit of traffic on that road, and drivers wouldn't take kindly to being held up. Was there, in fact, any other traffic at the time?"

"I don't think so. No."

Willoughby said, "Your point, Mr. Mackenzie?"

"Plain as a pikestaff. The kidnappers were tipped off. They knew the precise time when Reynolds' bus left and when it could be expected at the interception point. Phone or short-wave radio—even a CB would have been enough. Two things are for sure—there was an informer, and he came from Sanmobil."

"Impossible!" Shore sounded shocked.

"Nothing else makes sense," said Brady. "Mackenzie's right."

"Good God!" Shore sounded outraged. "You make Sanmobil sound like a criminals' den."

"It's not a Sunday school," said Brady heavily.

Dermott turned back to Brinckman. "So Reynolds pulled up when he saw this truck across the road? Then?"

"It was all so quick. There were two men lying in the road. One was face-down and very still, as if he were hurt real bad. The other was moving—he'd both hands clutching at the small of his back and was rolling from side to side. He seemed to be in agony. Two other men came running toward us—well, hardly running, more staggering. One was limping badly, and he had an arm stuck inside his mackinaw jacket as if he was trying to support it. Both of them had a hand up in front of their faces, covering their eyes."

Dermott said, "Didn't that strike you as odd?"

"Not at all. It was dark, and we had our headlights on. It seemed natural they should shield their eyes from the glare."

There was a pause. Then Brinckman went on, "Well —this guy with the damaged arm—as I thought—came weaving up to my side of the bus. I grabbed the first-aid box and jumped out. I slipped on the ice, and by the time I had my balance I saw the man had dropped his hand and was wearing a stocking mask. Then I saw his left arm coming up. It was almost a blur, but I could see he had some kind of a sap in his hand. I had no time to react." He fingered his forehead gingerly. "That's all, I guess."

Dermott crossed to him and examined the contusion on the side of his forehead. "Nasty. Could have been worse, though. An inch or so further back and you'd likely have had a fractured temple. Looks as if your friend was using lead shot. A leather bludgeon wouldn't have done that."

Brinckman stared at him in an odd fashion. "Lead, you reckon?"

"I should think so." Dermott turned to Jorgensen. "I take it you hadn't much better luck?"

"At least I wasn't blackjacked. I just thought my jaw had been broken. The other guy was either a heavyweight champion, or he was clutching something heavy in his fist. I couldn't see. He jerked open Mr. Reynolds' door, flung in some kind of smoke bomb, then banged the door shut again."

"Tear gas," said Willoughby. "You can see his eyes are still inflamed."

"I got out," Jorgensen went on. "I waved my gun around, but it might have been a water pistol, the use it was. I was blind. Next thing I remember, Pete Johnson was trying to shake some sense into us."

"So, of course, you don't know how Reynolds and his

passengers made out." Jim Brady looked around. He was taking over. "Where's Carmody?"

"Down at the station," said Shore. "Still making his report. Pete Johnson's with him. They'll be here presently."

"Good." Brady turned back to Brinckman. "The man who attacked you—was he wearing gloves?"

"I'm not sure." Brinckman thought and then said, "Once he'd passed out of the beam of the headlights, he was in pretty deep shadow, and, as I said, it all happened so damn quickly. But I don't think so."

"Your man, Mr. Jorgensen?"

"I could see his hand pretty clearly as he threw the tear-gas canister. No—no glove."

"Thank you, gentlemen. Mr. Willoughby, a few questions if I may."

"Go ahead." Willoughby cleared his throat.

"This truck the kidnappers used—you say it was stolen?"

"That's right."

"It's been identified?"

"Belongs to a local garage proprietor. It was known he was off on a couple of days' hunting trip."

"At this time of year?"

"Your true enthusiast goes hunting any time. At all events, it was seen passing through the streets yesterday afternoon, and we assumed the owner was taking it along for his trip."

"Which argues a fairly intimate local knowledge?"

"Sure, but no help to us." Willoughby smoothed his dark moustache. "Fort McMurray's no longer a village."

"Have you fingerprinted the truck, inside and out?"

"Being done now. It's a long job—there are hundreds of prints."

"May we see them?"

"Of course. I'll have them photostated. But, with respect, Mr. Brady, what do you hope to achieve that we, the police, can't?"

"You never know." Brady smiled enigmatically. "Mr. Dermott here is an international expert in fingerprinting."

"I didn't know!" Willoughby smiled at Dermott, who smiled back. He hadn't known either.

Brady changed his tack. "Any chance of identifying the helicopter from the measurements of the ski marks that Carmody took?"

Willoughby shook his head. "It was a good idea to record them, but no—the chances of identifying any one machine from its skiprints are extremely remote, because there will almost certainly be dozens of its particular type around. This is helicopter country, Mr. Brady, like Alaska. Here in northern Alberta our communications are still very primitive. We have no divided highways—freeways— in this part of the world. In fact, north of Edmonton there are only two paved roads that reach up north. Between them—nothing. Apart from ourselves, and Peace River and Fort Chipewyan, there are no commercial airports in an area of two hundred thousand square miles."

"So," Brady nodded. "You use choppers."

"The preferred form of transport at all times. In winter, the only form."

"It's a good bet that an intensive air search wouldn't have a hope in hell of locating the getaway machine?"

"None. I've made a bit of a study of kidnapping, and I can answer you best by a comparison. The world's most kidnap-happy place is Sardinia. It's a kind of national pastime there. Whenever a millionaire is snatched, all the resources of the law and the Italian armed forces are brought into play. The Navy blockades harbors and virtually every fishing village on the coast. The Army sets up roadblocks, and specially trained troops sweep the hills. The Air Force carries out exhaustive reconnaissance by plane and helicopter. In all the years these searches have been carried out, they've never yet located a single kidnapper's hideout. Alberta is twenty-seven times larger than Sardinia. Our resources are a fraction of theirs. Answer your question?"

"One begins to feel the first faint twinges of despair. But tell me, Mr. Willoughby, if you had four kidnapped people on your hands, where would you hide them?"

"Edmonton or Calgary."

"But those are towns. Surely . . ."

"Cities, yes—and the population of each must be crowding half a million. The captives wouldn't be hidden —they'd be lost."

"Well." Brady pulled himself up in his chair. He looked weary. "Okay. I suppose we have to wait word from the kidnappers before we make a move. You two gentlemen"—he turned to Brinckman and Jorgensen—"I don't think we need keep you any longer. Thank you for your co-operation."

The two security men said their good nights and left. Brady hoisted himself to his feet. "No sign of Carmody yet? Let's go and make ourselves more comfortable while we wait for him. The desk will no doubt inform us when he arrives. This way, gentlemen."

Once in the privacy of his own room, armed now with a fresh drink, Brady seemed suddenly to shake off his exhaustion.

"Okay, George," he said briskly. "You've been holding out on us. Why?"

"In what way?"

"Don't pussyfoot. You said you were more concerned about the demands the crooks are going to make than about my family. You love my family. Now what did you mean?"

"The first demand will be that you, Don and I take off for Houston. They must be convinced we're on the verge of a breakthrough.

"The second demand will be a ransom message. To keep things within reasonable bounds they can hardly ask for more than a couple of million dollars. But that would

be peanuts compared with the stakes our friends are playing for.

"Third, the greater stakes. Obviously, they'll demand
a fortune to cease their harassment of both Prudhoe Bay's
and Sanmobil's oil supplies, and the increasing destruction
of their equipment. That's where they hold all the aces. As
we've seen, both systems are embarrassingly vulnerable to
attack. For as long as the criminals' identity remains undis-
covered, they can keep on destroying both systems piece-
meal.

"Their price will be high. I imagine they'll base it on
the development cost of the two systems—that's ten billion
for starters—plus the daily revenue, which is the cost of
over two million barrels a day. Five per cent of the total?
Ten? Depends what the market will bear. One thing's for
sure—if they demand too much and price themselves out of
the market, the oil companies are going to cut their losses
and run, leaving the insurance companies to hold the baby
—and it will surely be the most expensive baby in insurance history."

Brady said querulously, "Why didn't you bring this
up downstairs?"

"I have an aversion to talking too much in crowded
hotel foyers." Dermott leaned toward Jay Shore. "Did
your Edmonton office send the fingerprints we asked for?"

"I have them in the safe at home."

"Good." Dermott nodded approval, but Willoughby
was curious, "What prints?"

Shore hesitated until he received an all-but-impercep-
tible nod from Dermott, and said, "Mr. Brady and his men
seem pretty well convinced that we have at Sanmobil one
or more subversives actively aiding and abetting the men
trying to destroy us. Mr. Dermott particularly suspects
our security staff and all those who have access to our
safe."

Willoughby shot Dermott a cool, quizzical look. It
was clear that he considered the matter one for the Canadian police and not for foreign amateurs. "Would you
mind explaining why?" he asked coldly.

"They're the only suspects we have—especially the
men in charge of the security shifts. Not only do they
have access to the key of the armory from which the
explosives were stolen, they actually carry the damn thing
around with them on duty. More, I have good reason to
suspect the security staff on the Alaskan pipeline. Further,
it appears more than likely that both security staffs are
working hand-in-glove under the same boss or bosses.
How else can you explain how the terrorists here know
the Sohio/BP code, while the criminals there know Sanmobil's?"

Willoughby said, "This is just conjecture . . ."

"Sure. But it's conjecture shading into probability.
Isn't it a basic police philosophy to set up a theory and examine it from all sides before discarding it? Well, we've set
up our theory, examined it from all sides, and don't feel
like discarding it."

Willoughby frowned, then said, "You don't trust the
security men?"

"Let me amplify that. The majority are straight, no doubt; but until I know for sure, they're all under suspicion."

"Including Brinckman and Jorgensen?"

" 'Including' is not the word. 'Especially'."

"Jesus! You're talking crazy, Dermott. After what they went through?"

"Tell me what they went through."

"They told you already." Willoughby had become incredulous.

Dermott was unmoved. "I've only got their word for that—and I'm pretty sure in both cases that word's worthless."

"Carmody corroborated their story—or rather, Johnson did. Maybe you don't trust him either?"

"I'll decide that when I meet him. But the point is, Johnson *didn't* corroborate the story. All he said—correct me if I'm wrong—was that when he arrived on the scene he found Brinckman unconscious and Jorgensen staggering around. That's all he said. He had no more idea what went on before that than you or I do."

"Then how d'you account for their injuries?"

"Injuries?" Dermott smiled sarcastically. "Jorgensen didn't have a mark on him. Brinckman did, but if you'd been watching him, you'd have seen him jump when I told him he'd been struck by a lead-filled club. That didn't fit. There was something wrong with the scenario.

"I suggest both men were in perfectly good health until they saw the lights of Johnson's minibus approaching, whereupon Jorgensen, acting on instructions, tapped

Brinckman on the head just hard enough to lay him out briefly."

"What do you mean, 'on instructions'?" Willoughby demanded doggedly. "Whose?"

"That remains to be discovered. But you might like to know that these aren't the first peculiar injuries we've come across. A doctor in Prudhoe Bay, for one, has discovered that we have highly suspicious minds on this subject. Donald and I had to examine a murdered engineer whose finger had sustained a curious fracture. The good doctor explained it away to his own apparent satisfaction, but not to ours. He probably gave orders that if any other such—ah—marginal incidents happened, any security agents in the vicinity were to display proof of injuries sustained in the loyal execution of their duties—such as, in this case, their attempts to protect those whom they were supposed to be protecting."

Willoughby stared at him and muttered, "You have to be fantacizing."

Dermott answered, "We'll see." But his reply was cut short by the sudden arrival of Carmody and Johnson. Both men looked pale and exhausted—a condition Brady sought to remedy by providing them with very large scotches.

After a suitable pause for congratulation on his night's work, Carmody was taken through his account, step by step. The exercise proved disappointing until, when he came to describe the scene of the helicopter ski marks, he suddenly became tongue-tied. He broke off in mid-sentence and stammered, "Say, Mr. Brady, could I—er—could I talk with you *privately?*"

"Well!" Brady was somewhat taken aback. "By all means—but what purpose would it serve? These gentlemen enjoy my fullest confidence. Say what you want in their hearing."

"Okay, then. It's about the girl—Corinne . . ." Whereupon he told them the story of the rescue. Amazement swiftly and thoroughly woke up his audience. They crowded forward, listening intently.

"Maybe I was wrong," Carmody ended up, "but I just figured that if news of her survival didn't get out, it might be a card up our sleeve."

"You figured correctly," Jim Brady said.

"Where is she, then?" asked Dermott sharply.

"Right now she's in the isolation unit at the plant. She went a bit hysterical, with the reaction, but she's all right."

Dermott let out a whoosh of air and said, "My, oh my!"

"A very original observation, George," Brady remarked wryly. "Do I detect a certain . . . pleasure on your part that the young lady is alive and well and in safe hands?"

"You do," said Dermott. Then he added quickly, as if feeling he had been overenthusiastic, "And why not?"

"Point is, I took a statement from her," Carmody went on. "Want to hear it?"

"Certainly," Brady said. "Fire away."

The statement still existed only in Carmody's note-book, and so took some time to read. The beginning of it merely confirmed what had been established already—but then came a revelation. After the hold-up, the girl re-ported, "One man came staggering toward us along the road."

"*One* man?" snapped Dermott, half-rising out of his chair. "Did she say *one* man?"

"That's what she said." Carmody resumed his recita-tion, backtracking a sentence to emphasize her account. " 'I saw two men lying in the road, like they were hurt. One was dead still. The other could move a bit. Then one other man came limping back toward us. He had a hand up in front of his eyes. Mr. Brinckman was sitting on my right. He jumped out and grabbed the first-aid box from under the seat. I think he slipped and fell over. Then he got up again. Then I saw the other man straighten up and hit him. He went down—Mr. Brinckman, that is. The other man had a stocking mask on—I could see that by now. He opened the door where Mr. Reynolds was sitting and threw something into the bus . . .' "

"That's it!" cried Dermott, smiting his fist on the coffee table. "We got them!"

Brady glowered at him. "Would you favor us slower brethren with an explanation?"

"The whole thing was a frame-up. They told us a load of garbage. They said *two* men came at them, to make it seem more realistic that they hadn't put up any re-sistance. Now it's obvious they didn't *try* to resist. They were part of the act. Jorgensen just sat there watching his partner get slugged."

"How come he wasn't much affected by the tear gas?" Brady asked.

"He was prepared for it, of course," Dermott replied instantly. "If you screw your eyes shut and hold your breath, tear gas has very little effect on you. Jorgensen only had to hold out for a couple of seconds before opening his own door and getting into the fresh air. Listen to what the girl said. There were no bodies left on the road when she was dragged away. Every damn one of them had got up, right as rain, to help get the captives aboard the chopper. It was only when they saw Johnson's headlights coming that Brinckman and Jorgensen resumed their artistic poses on the road."

Willoughby muttered a curse. "I believe you're right," he said slowly. "I really do. And we haven't a shred of hard evidence against them."

"No way you could dream up a charge and haul them in for preventive detention?" asked Dermott hopefully.

"None."

"I wish you could," said Dermott. "I'd sleep happier for the rest of the night. As it is, I don't intend to sleep at all. I've got a slight aversion to being murdered in bed."

Brady nearly choked on his drink. "And what the hell does that mean?"

"Just that I think an attempt will soon be made to murder me. And Donald. And you."

Brady looked as though he might explode, but remained speechless. Dermott addressed him with some acerbity.

"Whenever you spoke down there in the foyer just now, you were tightening another screw in your own coffin lid." He turned to Willoughby. "Could you spare a guard for Mr. Shore's house tonight?"

"Of course, but why?"

"Simple. Mr. Brady unfortunately made it clear that he wanted copies of fingerprints found on the stolen truck. Brinckman and Jorgensen know that we've asked your people for what could be damning prints from your Edmonton H.Q. They'll discover, if they haven't already, that the copies of their own prints which we took earlier are in the safe in Mr. Shore's house."

"What good would it do them to get the copies?" Brady asked edgily. "The originals are at police H.Q. in Edmonton."

"How far d'you think this rot has spread?" said Dermott. "The originals may still be there, but they won't be much help once they've been through a shredding machine."

"Where's the problem?" asked Willoughby. "We just print 'em out again."

"On what grounds? Suspicion? Just one moderately competent lawyer, and the town would be looking for a new police chief. They'd refuse point-blank. What could you do then?"

"Point out to them—which is the case—that it's a condition of employment at Sanmobil."

"So you'd have mass resignations on your hands. Then what?"

Willoughby didn't answer. Mackenzie broke in, "You said I was the other grave digger?"

"Yes. You said the kidnappers must have been tipped off from Sanmobil as to when to expect Reynolds' bus. You were right, of course. But Brinckman and Jorgensen must have thought you meant it was they who gave the tip. They may even think we can trace the call to them, even though outgoing calls from the plant aren't normally tapped."

"Well, I'm sorry." Mackenzie shifted uneasily.

"Too bad. The damage has been done. And it wouldn't have helped to reproach you and Mr. Brady in public."

The phone rang. Dermott, the nearest, picked it up, listened briefly and said: "One moment. I think the person you should talk to is Mr. Shore. He's right here with us."

He handed the phone over and listened impassively to Shore's half of the conversation, which consisted almost entirely of muttered expletives. The phone rest settled as he replaced the receiver, so badly was his hand shaking. His face had gone white.

"They've shot Grigson," he gasped.

"Who's Grigson?" snapped Brady.

"Sanmobil's president. That's all."

THIRTEEN

THE POLICE DOCTOR, A YOUNG MAN named Saunders, straightened and looked down at the unconscious man on the pile of blankets. "He'll be all right, eventually, but that's all I can do for him now. He needs the services of an orthopedic surgeon."

"How long will it be before I can question him?" Brady asked.

"With the sedative I've given him, it'll be several hours before he comes around."

"Couldn't that damned sedative have waited a little?"

Dr. Saunders looked at Brady with a marked lack of enthusiasm. "I hope, for your sake, you never have your shoulder and upper arm shattered, the bone structure completely fragmented. Mr. Grigson was in agony. And even had he been conscious, I wouldn't have let you question him."

Brady muttered something about medical dictators, then looked at Shore and said testily, "What the hell was Grigson doing here anyway?"

"Dammit, Brady, he's more right to be here than you and I and the rest of us put together." Shore sounded shocked and angry. "Sanmobil is the dream-come-true of one man and one only, and he's lying there before you. Took him nine years to turn his dream into reality, and he had to fight all the way. He's the president. Do you understand that—the president?"

Mackenzie said pacifically, "When did he arrive?"

"Yesterday afternoon. Flew in from Europe."

Mackenzie nodded and looked around Reynolds' office. It wasn't a small room, but it was fairly crowded. Apart from himself, Brady, Shore, Dr. Saunders and the unconscious Grigson, there were Willoughby and two young men who had clearly been in the wars during the recent past. One had a bandaged forehead, the other an arm strapped from wrist to elbow. It was to this last person, Steve Dawson, that Mackenzie addressed himself.

"You were in charge of the night shift?"

"Nominally. Tonight there *was* no night shift. The plant's closed down."

"I know. So how many of you were here tonight—yourself apart?"

"Just six people." He glanced down at the wounded

man. "Mr. Grigson was asleep in his private room along the corridor there. Then there was Hazlitt—supervisor of the night security shift—and four security guards deployed around the plant."

"Tell us what happened."

"Well—I was patrolling, reinforcing the security team, as I had nothing else to do. I saw a light come on here in Mr. Reynolds' room. First I thought it must be Mr. Grigson—he's a very active, restless person, and an erratic sleeper. Then I got to wondering what he could be doing, because he'd already spent a couple of hours with Mr. Reynolds yesterday. So, quiet as I could, I came along the passage to Grigson's room.

"The door was closed, but not locked. I went in, and there he was asleep. I woke him, told him there were intruders in the plant, and asked to borrow a gun. I knew he had one, because he used to practice on a little private target range he'd set up here.

"He'd have none of it. He produced his automatic, but kept it himself. He said he'd had it for years and knew how to use it. I couldn't argue with him—after all, I'm only twenty-eight, and he's crowding seventy.

"Anyway, in here we found a man with the door of that safe open. He'd smashed Corinne's desk open with a fire ax to get at the keys. He was wearing a stocking mask and examining a bunch of keys he had in his hand.

"Mr. Grigson told him to turn around, real slow, and not to try anything, or he'd kill him. Then suddenly came two pistol shots, right close together, from behind, and

Mr. Grigson pitched headlong to the floor. He was wearing a white shirt, and blood from his right shoulder and arm was pumping through it. I could see he was hurt real bad.

"I dropped to my knees to help him. The man who'd fired the shots probably figured I was going for Mr. Grigson's gun. Anyway, he fired at me too."

Dawson was breathing quickly, his distress evident. Brady poured him a scotch and handed the glass over. "Take this."

Dawson's smile was wan. "I've never had a drink in my life, sir."

"Maybe you'll never have another," said Brady agreeably. "But you need this one, and we need your story."

Dawson drank, spluttered and coughed. He screwed up his eyes and drank some more. He clearly detested the stuff, but his system didn't, for almost immediately some color began to return to his cheeks. He touched his bandaged forearm.

"Looks worse than it is. The bullet just grazed me, wrist all the way to elbow, but very superficial. Stung, more than anything. One of the masked men forced me to help lug Mr. Grigson to the armory. On the way out I picked up two first-aid kits—they didn't object. They pushed us into the armory, locked the door and left.

"Then I took off Mr. Grigson's shirt and stanched the wound as best I could. It took a lot of bandages—there was so much blood coming. I thought he was going to bleed to death."

"He could have," Saunders said with certainty. "No question, your quick action saved his life."

"Glad I was of some use." Dawson shuddered, looked at the doctor and went on, "Then I bandaged my own arm and had a go at the door, but there was no way I could get it open. I looked around and found a box full of detonators, each with a fuse attached. I struck one and dropped it out through one of the ventilation grilles. It went off with quite a bang. I must have let seven or eight of them off before Hazlitt came hammering on the door and asked what the hell was going on. I told him, and he ran off to fetch a duplicate key."

Dawson drank some more, spluttered, but less than before, and put his glass down. "I guess that's about all."

"And more than enough," said Brady with unaccustomed warmth. "A splendid job, son." He looked around the assembled group, then asked sharply, "Where's George?"

Until then no one had noticed that Dermott was missing. Then Mackenzie said, "He slipped out with Carmody some time back. You want me to go find him?"

"Leave him be," said Brady loftily. "I have little doubt our faithful bloodhound is pursuing some spoor of his own."

In fact the bloodhound was pursuing a fancy, not a line. He had taken Carmody aside and whispered in his ear that he urgently wanted to question the girl, Corinne. Where was she?

"In the isolation ward, like I said," Carmody replied. "But I doubt you'll find it on your own. It's way out by itself, near Dragline One. Want me to come with you?"

"Sure. That'd be real kind." Dermott swallowed his disappointment. He wanted to go alone. The instincts at work inside him made him feel uncomfortable. Nothing like this had happened to him in years. But he had better be realistic and accept the offer of guidance.

By then the wind had increased, as it often did late in the night, and was whistling across the flat, open site with a deadly chill. The noise made it almost impossible to talk in the open—not that anyone in his senses would remain in the open for more than the minimum time.

Carmody had been reunited with his damaged Cherokee. Shouting an excuse into the wind, he got in first at the passenger door and slid across behind the wheel. Dermott heaved his massive frame in close behind him and slammed the door.

Carmody drove steadily across an apparently unmarked plain. The film of drifting snow had obscured the road, and the flat ground all looked the same.

"How the hell do you know which way to go?" Dermott asked.

"Markers—there." Carmody pointed as a small stumpy, black-and-white post went past, with the number 323 stenciled on it in bold figures. "We're on Highway Three. In a minute we'll turn onto Highway Nine."

Altogether they drove for nearly ten minutes before lights showed up out of the darkness ahead. Dermott was amazed once again at the sheer size of the site: by then they were four or five miles from the administration buildings.

The lights grew to a blaze of several windows, and they pulled up outside a single long hut. As they went through the door the heat hit them like a hammer, as did a smell of disinfectant. Dermott at once began to wrestle his way out of his outdoor clothes. He felt he would stifle if he kept them on for one more second.

They found Corinne propped up on a pile of pillows, looking white but (to Dermott's eye) very sweet in a pair of pea-green pajamas. Contrary to Carmody's predictions, she was wide awake. She'd been asleep, she said, and had woken up thinking it was already morning.

"What time is it, anyway?" she asked.

"Four o'clock, near enough," Dermott answered. "How d'you feel?"

"Fantastic. Not even a bruise, as far as I can tell."

"That's wonderful. But my, were you lucky!" Dermott began asking routine questions, to which he didn't really want the answers. He wished to hell Carmody would go away someplace and leave him alone with the girl. What he would say to her if that happened, he didn't quite know. All the same it was what he wanted.

"You've given us a real good lead, you know," he said enthusiastically. "Can't say just what it was, but it may be the breakthrough we needed. Mr. Brady's delighted . . ."

His voice tailed off as a heavy rumble suddenly shook the building. "Jesus!" He looked up sharply. "What was that?"

Carmody was gone already, out of the room and down the short passage. Dermott caught up with him at the outside door.

"Helicopter!" Carmody snapped. "Made a low pass right over the building. There he is, burning now." Way out in the blackness a red and a green light converged and then separated again as the aircraft swung around. As the two men stood watching, a pair of car headlamps snapped on from a point about a hundred yards in front of them. The vehicle moved forward, turned and stopped, with its headlights steady on a patch of snow.

"It's a marker!" Carmody cried. "He's gonna land. Quick, get the girl out of here. They must have come for her."

"How in hell do they know she's here?" said Dermott.

"Don't worry about that. Let's get her away." Moving like a sprinter, Carmody slipped back into the building, bundled Corinne up in a cocoon of blankets and carried her out to the jeep, where he dumped her in the back seat. Dermott lumbered behind him, envying his speed, and hauled himself into the front.

Without putting on any lights Carmody started the engine and moved off into the inky night, heading out into the open behind the parked marker vehicle. A couple of hundred yards beyond it he swung around and faced in the same direction as the lights, so that he and Dermott could watch what happened through the windshield.

They sat there with the heater going full blast.

"Warm enough?" asked Carmody over his shoulder.

"Plenty, thanks." Corinne sounded as though she was enjoying herself. "I've got enough blankets to keep an elephant warm."

Dermott wondered uneasily whether that was any sort of a joke at his expense, but his speculation was cut short by the arrival of the helicopter. Suddenly it was there, large and gray-white, riding down on a storm of snow into the headlight pool. The rotor flashed brilliantly in the silvery beams, and the snow flew outward from the downdraft.

"That's the one!" said Carmody in a voice charged with excitement. "The getaway chopper. Description tallies perfectly with Johnson's: gray-white, no markings, small fins by the tail. That's our baby. Damn!"

As soon as the machine had landed, the car's headlights cut. The watchers sat blinded by the sudden darkness. They saw a flashlight bobbing about in the blackness, but nothing else.

"Boy, will they be mad when they find you've gone!" Carmody said happily.

"D'you think they're still in it?" Corinne asked. "The others, I mean?"

"Could be—easily. Depends where the chopper's been these past few hours. Must have been waiting on the ground someplace."

"Come on!" snapped Dermott. "Let's get out of here."

"Wait a minute," Carmody said easily. "I wanna see what they do. Any moment now they'll be at the building. There—I can see them now."

Two figures moved swiftly past the lighted windows. More light showed as the door opened and shut."

"Can't we ram the helicopter or something?" Corinne suggested. "Stop it taking off?"

"Too big," said Carmody immediately. "You notice the legs and skis? Higher than our roof. All we'd do would be to damage the landing gear, which wouldn't stop them getting off. Besides, if I know them, there's a couple of guys with guns guarding the thing, at least. Hey—what was that?"

"What?" Dermott looked at him.

"I heard something. Machinery. Sure I did." Carmody looked out past Dermott into the darkness. "Open your window a minute."

Dermott obeyed, and instantly the noise was far louder: a huge squealing and clanking, as of some giant engine.

"Jesus Christ!" Carmody shouted. "The dragline. It's right here beside us."

Dermott opened his door and got out. His eyes, accustomed to the dark, could just make out the gigantic outline towering above them. Suddenly the noise seemed terrific. "Good God!" Dermott yelled into the wind. "It's alive. It's *moving!*"

Instinctively he began to run toward the machine, or rather, around it, for already he was alongside. Beside him he could hear the whine of electric motors, the squeal of metal and the crunch of frosted dirt as the mighty shoe ground forward. The coldness of the wind seared his lungs and made his eyes stream briefly before they froze. In spite of the discomfort, he felt fired by excitement and by rage, for here was a final and outrageous act of sabotage taking place right on top of him. In a flash of intuition he saw what they intended: to drive the monster machine over the edge of the pit which it had been excavating.

The facts and figures that had been flung at him came crowding into his head. Six and a half thousand tons. It could move at some 250 yards an hour. The pit was 150 feet deep. Although he was no engineer, he knew instinctively that if the monster went over the edge, it would never come out again.

He came around the front of it and got another shock. The edge of the pit, showing as a limitless black hole, was less than thirty yards away. Perhaps only twenty-five. That meant he had a tenth of an hour—six minutes—to get the damn thing stopped. He looked up desperately. The boom disappeared into the night, like an Eiffel Tower tilted over. Somehow he had to get into the cab and throw the right switches.

He ran back right under the thing, between the shoes. Somewhere there must be a ladder. At last he found it. But as he looked up toward the cab, far above him, he saw someone moving there in a faint glow of light. He hesitated, one foot on the steel ladder, wishing he had a gun and wondering whether he should go back for Carmody. That was the last thought that entered his head for a couple of minutes, for the blow caught him squarely on the back of the neck, and brilliant points of light seemed to shoot outward through his head as he slumped to the ground.

He came around shaking from the cold and stuck in an awkward position. His hands were jammed, somehow—jammed behind him. He needed to straighten his arms and get them back into action. He strained to sort himself out and realized with a shock that his wrists were manacled together, *and manacled to something.*

He gave a grunt and heaved, whereupon a man spoke out of the dark behind him.

"Ah, Mr. Dermott," said a voice he half-recognized but could not place. "Struggling will not help. You are anchored to a steel ring let into concrete. The ring is directly in the patch of Dragline One, which, as you can see and hear, is now only a few feet from you. The controls have been preset and locked in position so that the middle of the right shoe will pass over you. Good-bye, Mr. Dermott. You have less than two minutes to live."

Fear cleared Dermott's head. "Bastards!" he roared. "Sadistic bastards! Come back!" But even as he shouted, he knew it was useless. In the whistle of the wind and the monstrous grinding of the dragline, his voice was nothing and carried nowhere. He twisted around and discovered that he was tethered almost on the lip of the pit: the edge of the black abyss was no more than a yard away. In the opposite direction, the front of the dragline's shoe had ground remorselessly to within fifteen feet of him. The front of it was coming on like a tank. Above him, the steel tracery of the boom seemed to fill the sky with an angry black pattern.

Dermott stopped shouting and began to fight the manacles. At least there was some movement. He could feel that a length of chain had been passed through the shackle on the ground. He jerked it furiously back and forth in the faint hope that the chain would break, but all he achieved was to chafe his wrists viciously and expose them to the cold. He could feel the icy steel biting into his bare skin. Frostbite, he thought dully. But what did frostbite matter if he was going to be crushed like a beetle?

"Carmody!" he yelled desperately. "Help!" Where the hell had Carmody gone? Why didn't he come looking?

Dermott fought the chain again and flopped flat, gasping. The shoe was only twelve feet off, scrunching on inch by inch. The whine of the electric motors seemed to fill the night, as if hell had claimed him.

He threw his body feverishly to left and right, experimenting to see if he could get clear of the shoe's line of advance. Nothing he tried was the slightest good. The shoe was ten feet wide, and he was tethered right in the middle of its track. The monster had been set marching with hideous precision.

He lay still again, panting, beaten. Suddenly images began flashing through his mind, conjured up uninvoked by the extremity of his desperation. Once again he witnessed the final terrifying seconds of the car crash that had killed his wife, the time when an explosion had blown him clean off a rig in the Gulf of Mexico, into the shark-owned sea . . .

All at once he became aware of a light flashing over him. Then someone was crouching, pulling at his arms. Then he heard a high, feminine cry.

"Corinne!"

"My God!" she cried. "What's happened? Oh, Jesus!" She leaped to her feet and began to run. "*Wait!*" she screamed over her shoulder.

Dermott saw her fall, get up again, and go like a greyhound, around the corner of the shoe, the flashlight swinging wildly in the blackness. He shouted something after her, but she was gone. *Wait*, she'd said. Wait! What a hell of a thing to say! How could he wait? The shoe was scarcely ten feet from him: one minute, give or take a few seconds.

He found his eyes were full of tears, though whether they were of fear or relief or gratitude or what, he couldn't tell. He was crying like a baby.

Seconds were passing. He began to count. He got to ten and couldn't go on. He had been overtaken by a horrific vision of the exact physical process of destruction that was about to annihilate him. He would feed his feet and legs to the monster first. Or could he? Could he listen and watch while his ankles, shins and knees were crunched and flattened on the tundra? No—he would have to get the end over quickly and give it his head. But what would *that* be like, for God's sake? To hear his skull crack and feel that unthinkable weight! Impossible! Never!

He roared again, "CARMODY!" As if by a miracle, his shout was answered. Headlights come boring up out of the night and swept across him as the vehicle turned. Dermott stared incredulously as the lights came on at speed, heading right for him and the front of the shoe. At the last moment the vehicle slowed, but not enough to stop. The driver deliberately slid it into the front of the shoe, using it as a last-ditch barrier to stop the monster's progress. There was a sharp crash and the tinkle of falling glass. Then the door of the Jeep opened and Corinne leaped out.

There was so little space left that Dermott had all but been run over. The Jeep's left-hand wheels were almost on him. The next thing he saw was the tires being forced bodily sideways toward him by the irresistible pressure of the dragline's advance.

Corinne had the tail gate of the Jeep open. She dragged out a steel box—the emergency equipment—and dumped it behind Dermott with a crash.

"Keep still!" she shouted above the noise. "No—come back a bit. There. Keep there!"

Dermott leaned backward in the attitude she ordered, speechless with tension. He saw the wheels of the Jeep come sideways at him again. The back wheel was touching his feet already. The Jeep was being pushed like a toy. At that rate it was going to do more harm than good. It was merely acting as an extension of the shoe, and would crush him before the dragline itself reached him.

He felt Corinne struggling behind him. Suddenly she gave a desperate cry. "Oh my God! I can't do it. I'm not strong enough."

Dermott's voice returned. "What's happening?" he shouted.

"The cutters!" she sobbed. "The bolt shears are biting into the chain, but I can't get enough pressure on them. It's too bloody hard!"

"Put one end on the ground," he ordered calmly. "One handle on the ground. Then get your weight on the other."

He felt her try, but she slipped and went down with a crash. "Try again!" he yelled.

By then the noise of the dragline was overwhelming: its roaring and grinding filled the night. But suddenly a new sound: a sharp crack told him that the great steel treads of the shoe had hooked into some part of the Jeep's bodywork. Instead of being pushed back, the vehicle had been gripped and held down. Dermott stared incredulously as the Cherokee began collapsing like an eggshell. The remaining headlight was snuffed out. Cracking, snapping noises accompanied the collapse of the hood and front wheels.

Behind him Corinne gave a despairing scream. "I just can't do it. I've got halfway through, but that's all."

"Look for a hacksaw!" Dermott shouted. "In the emergency pack."

"Got one!" She began working again frantically.

For Dermott time seemed to have stopped. He saw that the Cherokee's engine block had at last offered the dragline a spot of serious resistance: only a spot, it was true, but a definite token. Ponderous as a dinosaur, the machine lifted one foot slowly into the air as it ground the little vehicle beneath its steel sole. As if in a trance, Dermott saw the windshield shatter, the front of the roof crumple down, the passenger compartment flatten. Right in front of him a back wheel snapped off and was squashed flat onto the ground. If his arms had been free, he could have reached out and touched the front of the shoe—it was that close.

But his arms were *not* free.

"I can't!" Corinne screamed in desperation.

Dermott's head cleared, and he shouted, "Is there an ax?"

"A what?"

"An ax."

"Yes—here."

"Smash the chain with that. Aim for the link you've been working on."

"I might hit you."

"To hell with that. Belt it."

He felt the thump as she let drive. The chain snatched sharply at his wrists and nearly jerked his arms from their sockets. Suddenly he smelled the stink of gasoline: the tank had been crushed.

Clank! She brought the ax down, then again. When Dermott twisted to see how she was doing, the clawing thread of the shoe scraped down past his shoulder. The thing was touching him. He shrank away from the monstrous beast, and brought out his last, terrible idea.

"Chop my hands off!" he ordered, quite calmly.

"I can't!"

"Go on. It's them or me."

"*NO!*" She gave a piercing shriek and swung the ax down with every ounce of her behind it. Next second she was on her knees sobbing, "Oh my God, it's gone! It's gone!"

Dermott fought his instinct to leap up. He held himself down as she struggled with the severed link. The tread was bumping and bruising him now. In another few moments it would hook him under, as it had the car.

"For Christ's sake!" he shouted. "Quick!"

Miraculously, his hands came free. He got his arms back to their normal position and twisted sideways. "Look out for the pit!" he yelled. He himself was on the very lip. Hardly had he rolled clear of the dragline when there was a huge *whumph* and a roar of dark-red flame shot sideways at ground level. A chance spark had ignited the car's gasoline. By a fluke he had rolled into the wind, so that the

fiery blast went the other way and left him unscathed.
Corinne was there behind him, also intact.

The blaze made no difference to the monster's advance. The flames roared for a few seconds, then went out,
and the dragline continued without faltering toward the
brink.

Dermott felt weak with reaction—but not as weak as
the girl. One moment she was standing behind him; the
next, as Dermott struggled to find the words to express his
gratitude to her, she had collapsed in a heap on the ground.
He picked her up as tenderly as he knew how, laid her
gingerly over his shoulder in a fireman's lift, and began
carrying her toward the still-lighted windows of the isolation quarters. His eyes seemed to have gone blurred with
the strain. Or was it just ice? He scrubbed them with his
free hand and saw better. Out in the patch of white light
ahead of him, the helicopter was preparing to take off,
lights flashing, rotor spinning. Even as he watched, it lifted
off and slanted away into the sky.

At once the car whose lights had provided the marker
moved off and accelerated. Once again, Dermott realized,
the unspeakable murderers had melted into the night. He
knew he ought to feel disappointed. As it was, he could
concentrate on nothing except getting back into the
warmth of the hut and lying down.

He was very close to the building, going slow, when
he saw someone pass across the lighted windows in front
of him. Fear seized him. Maybe it was one of them. Was

he going to be shot after making such an effort? Before he had time to put down his burden or alter course, a flash-light came on, searched briefly and found his face.

"Good God! Dermott!"

"Carmody! Where in hell have you been?"

"Trying to ditch the chopper. What about you?"

"Had a . . . had a bit of bother." Suddenly Dermott found he could hardly talk. He was about to break down. "Take her, will you?" he croaked. "I've had it."

With an exclamation Carmody relieved him of his inert burden. "Quick," said the policeman. "Inside."

They laid Corinne on one bed and Dermott collapsed onto another with the manacles still dangling from his wrists. "Ring Shore!" he gasped. "Tell him for Christ's sake to switch off the power to Dragline One. Tell him and Brady to get up here like they never drove before."

They had turned on the floodlights to illuminate the 150-foot depths of the pit below. They had also hammered in spikes ten yards back from the lip, and to these they had attached ropes so that the vertiginously inclined or the less-than-sure-footed could cling to them as they peered over the edge.

Dragline One had ended up on its nose, tilted back-ward toward the near-vertical face at an angle of thirty degrees. The massive casing appeared undamaged, as did the triangular arm over which the control cables passed. Even the boom, its enormous length stretched out horizontally across the uneven valley floor, seemed undamaged, at least from above.

Brady had prudently wrapped his belaying rope three times around his mighty girth. "Surprisingly little damage," he said. "Or so it looks. I suppose some of the electric motors were wrenched free from their beds."

"That'll be the least of our troubles." Jay Shore looked stricken, ashen-faced in the floodlights. The sight of the crippled monster had far more effect on him than on any of the others. "It's getting the damn thing out of there."

"Wouldn't it be easier to get a replacement?" asked Brady.

"Jesus! Do you know what a replacement would cost at today's prices? Forty million dollars. Probably more. And you don't order one up, just like that. If we could have one on our doorstep tomorrow, I'm sure Sanmobil would order it. But it can't be done that way. You can't transport a thing that size overland. Electric motors apart, the whole caboodle comes crated in tens of thousands of pieces, and it takes a team of skilled engineers months to assemble it."

"Cranes?" Brady suggested. He seemed fascinated by the sheer size of the problem. Or he was trying to be diverted; trying not to think of his missing wife and daughter.

Shore made a dismissive gesture with his gloved

hands. "The biggest cranes in the world—a whole battery of them—couldn't lift the dragline an inch off the floor. We'll either have to dismantle it piece by piece and raise the bits up here for reassembly, or build a road from down there back up to surface level and have it towed up on bogies—or, perhaps, under its own steam. The road would have to be a very gentle gradient, which would mean a length of over a mile, heavily metalled on massive foundations. Whatever we do, it'll cost millions." He swore at some considerable length. "And all this in just seven minutes' work!"

"Why in hell couldn't you *stop* it, when we phoned you?" asked Carmody.

"The bastards knew what they were doing," said Shore savagely. "They'd gone into the generator room, thrown the breaker that fed power to Dragline One, locked the door from the outside, left the key in the lock and smashed it so thoroughly that it'll need an oxy-acetylene torch to open it again. We just couldn't get in to shut down the power."

"They sure knew how to cause the maximum damage and disruption with the minimum of effort," said Brady. "I suggest, Mr. Shore, there's no point in our remaining here a moment longer. All you're doing is twisting the knife deeper into your wound. Let's all get back inside and ask George what happened."

"Okay. Let's go." Shore, who had supervised the construction of the dragline, working along with the contractors, Bucyrus-Erie, seemed strangely reluctant to leave the fallen giant. It was as if he were abandoning an old friend. Brady could appreciate how he felt. But he could also appreciate how he felt himself—he had become acutely conscious of the cold.

Shore took one last look at the dragline and turned back toward the heated haven of the minibus. "Okay," he repeated automatically. "Let's go hear Dermott's story."

They drove the short distance back to the isolation block, where they found Dermott lying on a bed, already being questioned by Willoughby. Corinne was sitting on a chair in the corner of the small room, looking in better shape than the man she'd rescued.

"How is he?" Brady whispered to the nurse out in the corridor.

"His wrists look pretty bad—they got chewed up by the manacles, and frostbitten as well. They're going to be real painful for the next few days. They'll mend, though."

"What about his general condition—exposure?"

"What are you *talking* about? He's got the constitution of an ox."

By the time Brady, Mackenzie and Carmody had filed into the room, the place was crammed full. Brady seemed much moved by the sight of his senior operative brought low, with hands and forearms heavily bandaged.

"Well, George," he began, clearing his throat heavily, "I am informed that you plan to survive."

"Sure do." Dermott grinned up at them. "But boy—I wouldn't want to go through *that* again."

"I got the story," Willoughby cut in, brisk and businesslike. He gave a quick precis of what had happened, including the arrival and departure of the helicopter. "I'm sorry to say it, Mr. Shore, but it seems the plant is riddled with corruption. Number one, somebody sabotaged the generator room, so that you couldn't turn the power off. Number two, somebody else set the controls of the dragline to take it over the edge. Number three, somebody else hit Dermott and manacled him to the steel ring. Number four, somebody else again informed the kidnappers that the girl had survived her fall out of the helicopter and was back here in the isolation unit. That makes quite a lot of saboteurs for one plant."

"Too right, it does," Shore said bitterly. "You don't think the chopper came back to do the dragline job—that somebody on board got out and set the controls?"

"Impossible. The dragline was moving before the chopper landed. Isn't that right, Mr. Dermott?"

"Right. At least—no—not quite. But we saw men from the chopper go straight to the building here—and then we heard the dragline moving, right near us. The guys from the helicopter didn't have time to reach the dragline and set up the controls."

"What I'd like to know is whether your family, Mr. Brady, were still on board the helicopter," Willoughby said.

"Yes, they were." Carmody startled them all with his sudden pronouncement. "And Mr. Reynolds. He was with them."

"How d'you know?" Jim Brady asked. Dermott sat up abruptly.

"I *saw* them. That's what I was doing all the time you were involved with the dragline. I made a wide circle on foot and approached the helicopter from the back. There was a man armed with a machine gun guarding the ladder, but I climbed up onto the skid-struts from the opposite side and got a look in through the cabin windows. They were all there—Mrs. Brady, Stella, Mr. Reynolds."

"How . . ." Brady faltered. "How did they look?"

"Fine—just fine. Quite calm, all of them. But they weren't quite as passive as they looked."

"What d'you mean?" Dermott asked quickly.

"One of them managed to drop this out of the door, or out of a window." From his breast pocket Carmody drew a brown leather billfold, which he handed to Brady. "Looks like one of yours—J.A.B., nicely embossed in gold."

"My God!" Brady took it. "That's Jean's. Her middle name's Anneliese. This was a birthday present. Anything in it?"

"Sure is. Take a look."

With his fingers trembling a little, Brady opened the billfold, unbuttoned a flap and drew out a small scrap of paper. "*Crowfoot Lake Met. Station*," he read out loud. "Well I'm damned."

Dermott was elated. "I knew it! I knew it!" he kept saying. "I knew the bastards would overreach themselves.

Didn't I say they'd make a major mistake through over-confidence or desperation? Well, they've made it. Some-body couldn't resist the temptation to talk. Jean heard the name and wrote it down. Great, Jean!"

"Sheer luck I found it," said Carmody. "When the chopper took off it blew hell out of the snow and all but buried the billfold. I was just having a quick look around when I saw the corner sticking up out of a drift."

"We got it, anyway," said Dermott. "What are we waiting for?"

"Not so fast," Brady countered. "For one thing we don't know where Crowfoot Lake is."

"Oh yes we do," said Willoughby. "It's up beyond the Birch Mountains, seventy, eighty miles north. I know it well."

"How do we get there?" Dermott asked.

Willoughby looked at him reproachfully. "Helicop-ter. No other way."

"It's four o'clock in the morning, gentlemen," Brady said heavily. "An error to pursue further tonight. For one thing, we are all exhausted."

"And for another we don't have a helicopter," said Dermott.

"Precisely, George. I must say, your ordeal doesn't seem to have blunted your wits any."

"Thank you." Dermott lay back happily. "Maybe Mr. Willoughby can help us in the morning—I mean, later this morning."

"Sure, sure." Willoughby stood up. "But everyone please be careful. We're up against professionals. Their performance has been pretty impressive to date. Nothing would please them better than to catch one of your gentlemen, Mr. Brady. Or you, for that matter." He turned to Corinne, only to find she had fallen asleep, sitting upright, in the corner. "Okay," he said gently to Mackenzie. "Look after her. But whatever you do, all keep together."

"Like now," said Brady. "We'll all get in that bus together and drive back to town. Mr. Carmody—it doesn't sound as though your vehicle's too serviceable. May I offer you a ride?"

"Flat as a pancake," said Carmody wryly. "Never saw anything to match it. Thank you."

They all piled in, with Shore driving. But before they even reached the administration block a radio message caught them.

"Mr. Shore—urgent." It was Steve Dawson, of the night shift. "We got another emergency."

"Oh *no!*" Shore groaned. "I'm coming. Be right there."

Dawson met them and led them straight into a room off the main corridor which held six beds and was obviously a dormitory. On one of the beds lay the body of a fair-haired young man whose sightless eyes gazed at the ceiling.

"Oh my God!" said Shore.

"Who is it?" Dermott snapped.

"David Crawford. The security man we were talking about."

"The one we suspected?"

"That's him. What happened?"

"Stabbed through the heart, from behind," said Dr. Saunders, who was standing by the bed. "He's been dead some hours. We only just found him."

"How come?" Dermott demanded. "Isn't this the security men's dormitory?"

"One of two," said Saunders. "The other's larger. Normally both are occupied by off-duty shifts. But since the shutdown, the men have been living at home. Nobody had any cause to come in here tonight."

"Ruthless bastards," said Brady, very low. "Four dead and two critically injured so far. Well, Mr. Willoughby. You've got a murder investigation on your hands."

FOURTEEN

A T 11:30 THAT SAME MORNING BRADY and his team were the sole occupants of the hotel's dining room. Outside, the wind had gone, the snow had been reduced to the occasional flurry, and the sun was making a valiant effort to shine through the drifting gray cloud. Inside, the mood was one of expectancy and suppressed excitement.

"One thing's for sure," said Brady firmly. "*You*'re not coming on this little jaunt."

"Oh yes I am," Dermott countered. "I most certainly am. You try leaving me behind."

"What can you *do?*" Brady was half-scornful, half-sympathetic. "You can't use a gun, knock anybody down, tie anybody up."

"All the same, I've got to be there." Dermott was gray from lack of sleep and the pain in his savaged wrists. He could use his hands for gentle tasks, but his fingers were stiff, and to ease the discomfort he kept both elbows propped on the table with his forearms sticking straight up. "I really need two slings," he muttered. "One for each arm."

"Why not stay here and look after your gallant savior?" Mackenzie suggested slyly.

Dermott colored perceptibly and grunted: "She's okay, I guess."

"She's being guarded, sure," Mackenzie agreed. "But she might be even safer if she came with us. With the rot spreading as far as it has . . ." He broke off and went back to eating as he saw Willoughby, the police chief, approaching across the room.

"Good morning, chief." Brady beamed at him. "Get any sleep?"

"One hour." Willoughby tried to smile, but his heart wasn't in it. "Call of duty. Can't complain."

"News," Brady announced abruptly. "Take a seat." He handed a letter across the table. "Communication from our friends. Mailed yesterday in the local post office."

Willoughby read the first paragraph without alteration of expression. Then he looked slowly around the watching faces and said matter-of-factly, "One billion dollars." Suddenly his calm gave way. "One billion dollars!"

he cried. "Jesus!" He qualified the word "dollars" several times. "The sonsabitches are crazy. Who's going to pay attention to this kind of drivel?"

"You think it's drivel?" Dermott asked. "I don't. Probably a rather optimistic estimate of what the market will stand, but not very, I would think."

"I can't believe it." Willoughby threw the letter down on the table. "A billion dollars! Even if they mean it, how could the money be transferred without being traced to the recipient?"

"Nothing simpler," said Mackenzie, forking a pancake. "You could lose Fort Knox in the labyrinth of Eurodollars and offshore funds."

Willoughby glared at him over the breakfast cups. "You'd actually pay this blackmailing monster?"

"Not me," Mackenzie answered. "I couldn't. But somebody sure enough will."

"Who'd be so crazy?"

"There's no craziness involved," said Dermott patiently. "Just calculating, common business sense. The people who stand to lose most—our two governments, and the major oil companies who've invested in Alaska and Alberta. I don't know what the position is in Canada, but this is going to pose an intriguing problem in the States, because any governmental operation in tandem with the oil companies requires Congressional approval—and as every schoolkid knows, Congress would cheerfully immolate the oil companies. Looks like it'll make a highly diverting spectacle."

Willoughby looked baffled.

"Read some more," Brady prompted. "The next paragraph is only a minor shock to the nervous system."

The policeman picked up the letter and started again. "So they want you out of Alaska and Alberta—specifically, south of the forty-ninth parallel."

"As predicted," said Brady.

"But no mention of any ransom?"

"Again, as we predicted." Brady sounded smug.

"You're not getting out, I take it."

"Oh no? I'm going to contact my pilot in a moment and have him file a flight plan for Los Angeles."

Willoughby stared at him. "I thought you wanted to go to Crowfoot Lake?"

"We do. But we don't want to advertise our destination to any ill-natured persons who may be listening in. Therefore, we file a flight plan for L.A."

"Okay, I get it." Willoughby grinned. "What do you want *me* to do?"

"Well . . ." Brady became evasive. "First, we need a guarantee from you."

"You can't make deals with the police." Willoughby's tone suddenly hardened.

"Rubbish!" said Brady comfortably. "It's done all the time. Felons even make deals with judges in court."

"Okay. So what do you want?"

"What we *don't* want is a company of paratroopers. Sure, they could mop this lot up with their hands tied behind their backs, but they might mop up a few wrong people too. Softly, softly on this one. Finesse. Stealth. Secrecy. Our way or not at all."

"You making a point or something?"

"Tell me about Crowfoot Lake," said Brady.

"It's an ideal place for this sort of thing. Tucked right away in the hills. Big, covered helicopter shelter right by the station. A chopper would never be spotted from the air. I was up there a year back, investigating a reported murder which turned out to be death by misadventure. Couple of young city boys newly arrived at the weather station. Happens at the beginning of the hunting season every year, without fail—all the Dan'l Boones and Buffalo Bills dropping like flies all over the place."

"How big's the lake?" Dermott asked. "Can a plane land on it?"

"Well, you *can* land on it." Willoughby paused. "But I don't think it would do you much good. See here, the lake's only two miles long, so wherever you came down on it, the people in the Met. Station would be bound to hear you. I've got a better idea."

"We need one."

"Now, Mr. Brady. I've got a request. I'm in a delicate position. I am the law around these parts, and I'm supposed to know what's going on. I'm also a blackmailer. In return for guaranteeing that I can get you to the Met. Station undetected, I'd like some degree of participation in your expedition. You can't operate without police authority, and

I'm the authority. All cards very close to the chest, okay. But I'd like an official watching brief—a presence."

"I know whose presence I'd like," Mackenzie said. Up till then he had been chewing steadily throughout the conversation, but a delicate patting of his big face with the napkin indicated that his meal was over. "I'd like Carmody."

Willoughby said, "That's not a bad idea. I'll get him right away."

He went off to telephone, came back and said, "A couple of minutes."

"Fine." Brady turned to Mackenzie. "Don, tell Ferguson to go out to the airport and file a flight plan for Los Angeles. Tell him to expect people with provisions out there in just over an hour. Ask the kitchen to give us provisions for two or three days."

"Just food, Mr. Brady?"

Brady loftily ignored the insinuation. "Ferguson is in charge of the commissariat. He'll know of any shortfalls. George, we'll need some hand compasses and, I guess, ammunition. Be generous with the ammunition."

Willoughby said, "Hand compasses we have in abundance. What guns?"

"Colt .38's."

"No problem."

Dermott said, "Well, thank you. Tell me, Mr. Willoughby, you have a deputy chief?"

"Indeed. And a good one."

"Good enough to be left in sole charge here?"

"Sure. Why?"

"Why don't you come with us? Giving us the directions is all very well, but it's not the same as having you on the spot."

"Don't, Mr. Dermott. You tempt me. You tempt me sorely." From the momentary gleam of anticipation in his eyes, it was clear that he spoke the truth. "Duty, alas, before pleasure. I have a murder investigation on my hands."

"You've just reported zero progress. There are shortcuts, Mr. Willoughby. You wouldn't want us foreign amateurs to do the job for you, would you now?"

"I'm afraid I'm not quite at my best."

"You would be when we introduced you to Crawford's murderer. Where else would he be but at Crowfoot Lake?"

"Mr. Dermott, forget my last remark. I'm back at my very best. Ah, here he is."

Carmody looked as large and formidable as ever.

Dermott said, "With Mr. Willoughby's consent, a request to make on behalf of Mr. Brady, Mr. Mackenzie and myself. As alien civilians we can only request. Those kidnappers—you're aware they are multiple killers, desperate men. They'll shoot on sight and shoot to kill."

Carmody looked around in slight puzzlement but politely said nothing.

Dermott went on, "Mrs. Brady, her daughter and Mr. Reynolds—we know where they're being held."

Carmody, almost like a man in prayer, clasped his two hands lightly together and said, in a suitably churchlike whisper, "Boy, oh boy. Let's go get them."

Brady said, "Thank you. We appreciate it. One hour from now, okay?"

Willoughby said, "I'll just nip back to the office and put in a call to Edmonton."

"Aha! I thought secrecy was the watchword?"

"It still is."

"Then may I ask?"

"You may not. A surprise. To be revealed at Crowfoot Lake. Or in the very close vicinity. You wouldn't rob me of my surprises?"

As the jet lifted off, Brady looked across the aisle to where Carmody had just withdrawn a peculiar metallic device from its chamois-lined leather casing. It appeared to consist of a small telescope attached to a curving, semicircular arm which in turn was bolted to a rectangular metal box. Brady said, "What do you have there, Mr. Carmody?"

"John, please Mr. Brady. Makes me feel less self-conscious. We cops are used to being called many things, but not 'Mister': This? This is an infrared telescopic night sight. These are the securing clamps. Fits on a rifle."

"You can see in the dark with that?"

"A little light helps. But total darkness is rare."

"You can see the enemy, but he can't see you?"

"That's the idea behind it. Unsporting and unfair. Never give the bastards a break—especially, Mr. Brady, if they're pointing guns at wives and daughters."

Brady turned to Willoughby who was in the window seat. "And what lethal armaments are *you* carrying?"

"Apart from the regulation revolver? Just this little number here." He reached down and picked up a zipped leather bag some eighteen inches by ten.

"Funny shape for a gun," Brady said, intrigued.

"Two pieces that screw together."

"It wouldn't be a submachine gun?"

"It would."

There was a short silence and then Brady said, "No chance you'd be carrying a few hand grenades on you?"

Carmody gave a deprecating shrug. "Only a few."

"Infrared sights, submachine guns, grenades—aren't those illegal?"

"Could be." Carmody sounded vague. "I'm not sure they are at Crowfoot Lake. You'd have to ask Mr. Willoughby about that."

The angle of climb had leveled off, and Brady nodded his thanks as Mackenzie brought a daiquiri to him.

"Cruising altitude, Donald? No way could we possibly have reached that yet."

"Maybe this is high enough. You'd have to ask our

police chief there." He nodded forward. Willoughby had gone up to the co-pilot's seat and was bent over a map with Ferguson. "Doing his navigator's bit, I see."

Some five minutes more passed before Willoughby rose and headed back to sit by Brady.

"How long, Mr. Willoughby?"

"Seventy minutes."

"Seventy minutes! But I thought Crowfoot was only seventy miles away?"

"We filed a flight plan for Los Angeles, remember. Our first leg takes us through the radar control at Calgary. So, we're flying south. We're also flying low to lose the radar control at Fort McMurray. When we do, we'll circle to the west and then north. After ten minutes, northeast. We'll keep low. No danger of bumping into anything; it's pretty flat all the way." He spread out a chart. "Even the Birch Mountains here are really nothing of the sort. The highest peak is less than twenty-seven hundred feet. Really, it's just a low divide, a watershed. The streams on the west side flow west and northwest into the Peace and Birch rivers. The streams to the east flow east and southeast into the Athabasca River."

"Where's Crowfoot Lake?"

"Here, just on the west side of the divide."

"It doesn't have a name printed."

"Too small. Neither does Deerhorn—here—on the east side of the divide. That's where we're going. It's a lake, too, but it's always called just Deerhorn."

"How far from Deerhorn to Crowfoot?"

"Six miles. Maybe seven. Far enough, I hope. We go into Deerhorn low and we go into Deerhorn slow—as near stalling speed as possible. The chances of our being heard at that distance are remote. The only time we'll make any real noise is when we land. The only way a fast-landing jet like this can stop on a relatively short stretch of ice is to use reverse thrust on the engine. That makes quite a racket. But I'm pretty sure that the divide between the two lakes will act as a suitable baffle. I'm a little more concerned about the helicopter."

"Helicopter?" Brady said carefully.

"Yes. Left Edmonton about half an hour ago. Due in about an hour after us."

"You promised me—"

"And I keep my promise. No troops, no police, not even a peashooter. Just some Arctic gear I want. It's due to arrive just after dark."

"And without radar transmission or airfield landing lights, how's he going to find his way here?"

"A signal from us by radio beacon. He's only to follow his nose. What worries me slightly is the noise the helicopter will make in landing. It's the biggest you've ever seen, and the racket is corresponding."

"Of course." Brady showed his disquiet. "Our friends at Crowfoot Lake have their own helicopter. Won't they hop in and come over to investigate?"

"I hope not. I want them," Willoughby said grimly,

"to stand trial, and they won't be able to if they're dead. If they come across, I'll have no option but to shoot them down."

"Fair enough." Brady seemed unperturbed at the thought. Then he added, "You can do that?"

"We came here equipped with weapons for the express purpose of doing just that."

"Ah! I was asking Carmody about some of his equipment and he mentioned this infrared night sight. But I thought that was for shooting people."

"It can do that, too. Did he mention the fact that he's also got a rifle that can switch from single-shot to automatic at the touch of a switch? The combination of that, the night-spot and a squirrel-hunter's eye, makes for a fairly lethal outcome. You know I have a submachine gun? Did I also mention that it has a special large capacity magazine—the old circular-drum type—and that every sixth shell is a tracer so that I can see how I'm doing?"

"No."

Willoughby smiled. "And of course we didn't mention my own modest contribution—the jumping jacks. For use when we're not seeing too well what's going on up above. Just like fireworks, really—except that you get no fancy explosion of color, just a blinding magnesium flare that drifts down slowly on a parachute. Lasts only ninety seconds, but if you can't accomplish what you want to in ninety seconds, you should have stayed at home in the first place."

"If I were a devout Christian, I could almost weep for my adversaries."

"Don't."

"Who said I was a devout Christian?" Jim nodded to Carmody. "He really goes about killing people?"

"He *leans* on people."

"What, with submachine guns and high-powered rifles?"

"We'll use them if we have to."

Brady said dryly, "You surprise me. Those weapons are illegal, of course—for police use. Right?"

"That's the trouble with being in a remote northern town—you don't keep up as much as you might with all the notes, minutes and regulations that Edmonton issues every other day."

"Of course not."

Sometime later, Brady winced as the jet engines went into reverse thrust. Even though reason told him that the decibel level was no higher than normal, his apprehensive frame of mind made him feel he was listening to a continuous thunderclap of sound. When they had landed, he said to Willoughby, "You could have heard that racket clear back in Fort McMurray."

"Wasn't all that bad." Willoughby seemed unconcerned. "Well, stretch the legs, a little fresh air. Coming?"

"What? Out in that mess?"

"What mess? It's not even snowing. And it's seven miles to Crowfoot Lake. A little exercise, a little acclimatization. Remember what you told me back in Sanmobil? Inside the human frame there's no room for both cold and daiquiris. Let's put it to the test, shall we?"

"Hoisted on your own petard," Dermott said behind him. Brady scowled, hauled himself upright and followed Willoughby to the fore end of the cabin. He looked at Ferguson and stopped.

"You look worried, boy. That was a perfect touchdown."

"Thank you. But I am, as you say, a little concerned. Aileron controls got a bit stiff as I came in to land. Nothing much, I daresay. Soon locate the trouble. First landing on ice, and maybe I was being a little oversensitive."

Brady followed Willoughby out and looked around. Deerhorn was a singularly bleak and unprepossessing place. Snow-dusted ice beneath their feet, flat, barren land, devoid of any form of vegetation, stretching away in featureless anonymity on three sides. To the northeast lay a range of low hills, sparsely covered with a scattering of stunted, snow-laden trees.

"Those are the Birch Mountains?"

"I told you. I don't think the person who named them knew much about mountains."

"And those are *birch* trees?"

Willoughby said, "He wasn't much of a botanist either. These are alders."

"And seven miles beyond—"

"Look out! Stand back!" Both men whirled around to see Ferguson racing down the boarding steps clutching in one hand a cylindrically-shaped object about ten inches long and three in diameter.

"Keep clear, keep clear!" He sprinted by them, covered another fifteen yards, arched his back while still running and, like a cricket bowler, overarmed the cylinder with a convulsive jerk of his body. The cylinder had traveled not more than three yards when it exploded.

The blast was powerful enough to knock both Brady and Willoughby, even at a distance of almost twenty yards, off their feet. For several seconds they lay where they had fallen, then made their way unsteadily toward the prone figure of Ferguson. Even as they reached him they were joined by Dermott, Mackenzie and Carmody, who had been inside the plane.

Ferguson had fallen face down on the ice. Gently, they turned him over. His face and body appeared unmarked. It was difficult to tell whether or not he was breathing.

"Into the plane with him," Brady said. "Warm blankets and heating pads from the Red Cross chest. His heart may have stopped. Anyone here know anything about heart massage?"

"We do," Carmody said. He picked up Ferguson and headed for the plane. "First aid certificates."

Three minutes later, Carmody, still kneeling in the aisle, sank back on his heels and smiled.

"Ticker's going like a watch," he said. "Bloody fast watch, mind you, but it's going."

"Good work," Brady said. "We leave him there?"

"Yes," Dermott said. "Even when he regains consciousness—no reason why he shouldn't, there's no sign of any head injury—he's still going to be in shock. Heat pads we have in plenty. That's all we can give him, and probably all he requires. Can someone tell us what the hell happened? He came running up the aisle shouting, 'Stay where you are!' and clutching this damned thing in his hand. He was out through the door like a greyhound clearing his trap."

"I know what happened," Brady said. "He complained that the controls were a bit stiff when he came in to land. That was because whoever placed this charge did a sloppy job. The thing stayed in place while we were climbing or cruising at a steady altitude but slid forward and wedged itself against the ailerons when we started to descend. As we left the plane he told me he was going to look for the cause of the stiffness." Brady pursed his lips. "He found it all right."

"He was lucky," said Dermott. "Had it been a metal-cased bomb, the casing would have turned into shrapnel when it exploded and the backlash would have caught him. Not a mark on him. So, a plastic bomb. For plastic bombs, plastic fuses—chemicals, really. You have two acids separated by some synthetic plastic barrier. One of them eats through the barrier, and when the two different acids meet they detonate. When an acid eats its way through the plastic barrier it generates considerable heat. I'm sure Ferguson not only felt this heat but knew right away what it meant."

Brady looked somber. "If we weren't such a devious bunch, we'd have been flying at thirty-thousand feet on the way up. Our last trip, gentlemen."

"Right," said Dermott. "Even flying low, like we did, we had the luck of the devil. The drawback of a chemical detonator is that it's almost impossible to get timing accuracy within ten or fifteen per cent. The timing could have gone off ten minutes earlier—and that would have been curtains for us. Our friends didn't want us out of this country—they wanted us out of this world. What better way to do it, neatly, cleanly and efficiently than have your plane's tail fall off six miles up?"

The Sikorsky Sky-Crane landed in darkness just after three-thirty in the afternoon. It was, as Willoughby had promised, the biggest helicopter they had ever seen. The engines cut, the huge rotors idled to a standstill, and there was left only the sound of a generator whining somewhere inside the massive hull. Telescopic steps snaked down from an opened door and two men climbed nimbly down to the ice and approached the waiting group.

"Brown," the leading figure said. "Lieutenant Brown, Air Force, alleged skipper of this craft. This is Lieutenant Vos, co-pilot, also alleged. Which of you gentlemen are Mr. Willoughby and Mr. Brady?"

They shook hands and Brown turned to introduce a third person who had joined them. "Doctor Kenmore."

"How long can you stay?" Willoughby asked.

"As long as you wish."

"Very kind. You have some cargo for me?"

"We have. Okay to unload now?"

"Please."

Brown shouted instructions. Brady said: "Two requests, Lieutenant?"

"You have but to ask."

"I wish we had some more of this civility in the United States Air Force," Brady said. He addressed Dr. Kenmore. "My pilot's been hurt. Would you look at him?"

"Of course."

"Donald?" The two men left for the aircraft. "George? Lieutenant, this is Mr. Dermott. Second request. We have an excellent transmitter on our plane, Lieutenant, but unfortunately the pilot who operates it, is out of action . . ."

"We've got an excellent transmitter and a first-class radio operator who's ready for action. James!"

A young man appeared at the head of the steps. "Take Mr. Dermott to Bernie, will you?"

Bernie was a bespectacled fellow seated by a huge RCA transceiver. Dermott introduced himself and said, "Could you get me some numbers do you think?"

"Local, sir? Albertan, I mean."

"Afraid not, Anchorage and New York."

"No problem. We can patch in through a radio link via our Edmonton H.Q." Bernie's professional confidence was reassuring in the extreme. "Numbers and names, sir?"

"I have them here." Dermott handed over a notebook. "I can actually speak to those people?"

"If they're home, sure."

"I may be gone for a few hours. If I am, and you get through, will you ask them to hold themselves available or let me know where I can reach them?"

"Of course."

Dermott rejoined the group outside. Two low-profiled vehicles were already on the ice. A third was being lowered. "What are those?" Dermott asked.

Willoughby said, "My surprise for Mr. Brady. Snowmobiles."

"They're not snowmobiles," a black-haired slender youth said.

"Sorry." Willoughby turned to Dermott. "John Lowry, an expert on those machines. The Edmonton people sent him up to show us how to operate them."

"They're everything-mobiles," Lowry said. "Snow, roads, rough terrain, marshes, sand—you name it. Comparatively, the American and Canadian snowmobiles belong to the age of steam radio. Made by the firm of VPLO—initials only, the full name is unpronounceable—in Oulu, Finland. Called, naturally, the Finncat. Made of fiber glass. Unlike the ordinary snowmobile, it has no skis up front. That motor-driven traction belt you see extends under the full length of the body."

"Where did they come from?"

"We got three to put through extended tests—you know, the old test-to-destruction bit. Those are the three."

Dermott said to Willoughby, "Nice to have friends."

"Not quite standard models," Lowry went on. "The front compartments are usually for stowage of gear. We've converted them into jump seats."

Brady said, "You mean I can ride in one of those right now?"

Dermott said, *sotto voce* to Willoughby, "Test to destruction is right."

Lowry said, "I should think so, sir."

"That's great, just great." Brady's tone was hushed and reverent. The prospect of trudging a fourteen-mile return journey through Albertan snows had held singularly little appeal to him.

"Driving is simple," Lowry said. "Changing the inclination of the traction belt changes the direction of travel. Done by the handlebars. You have forward and reverse gears and—a very sophisticated touch—hydraulic disc brakes. It can also do forty miles an hour."

"Forty?" Dermott said. "It looks as if it would be hard pushed to touch five."

Lowry smiled. "Forty. Not on rough terrain, of course. Incidentally, these don't come cheap—four thousand dollars—but then the unique never does. I understand that you gentlemen are in a hurry. First three drivers up, please."

Dr. Kenmore returned from the plane with Mackenzie while Willoughby and his two men were learning the controls of the Finncats. Kenmore said, "Concussion. Nothing very serious, not the blast, he must have hit his head on the ice—there's a beauty of a bruise just above his right ear. I'll have him brought across here—we have a heating and lighting generator running all the time when the motors are switched off."

Brady said, "Thank you, doctor. We appreciate it."

"Nothing. May one ask where you're off to in those toys?"

"Don't let young Lowry hear you. He'd have a fit," Dermott said.

Brady said, "Please understand we don't mean to be churlish. We'll tell you when we come back. How's your expertise on shotgun wounds and bones shattered by high-velocity bullets?"

"Not very extensive, I'm afraid." Kenmore's expression hadn't altered. "You plan to remedy that before the night is out?"

"I hope not." Brady's face was suddenly serious. "But it may come to that."

The six men left at four-thirty, exactly one hour after the Sikorsky had touched down. The helicopter's crew were there to see them go. Lieutenant Brown said, "Air Force personnel are not as stupid as they look. We know where you're going, naturally. Good fortune." He looked at the arsenal of weapons they carried, ready for action, shoulder-slung or in holsters. "Dr. Kenmore may be in for a sleepless night."

The Finncats were everything that Lowry had promised, nimble, maneuverable and possessed of remarkable
traction. Two carried small but efficient headlamps which
picked out a path through the straggling alders. It said
much for the dogged willingness of the little two-cylinder
engines that a heroically suffering Brady had to get out
only twice—the Finncat on those occasions had refused to
budge another inch—and walk a total of two hundred
yards on the way to the gently rounded convexity which
marked the watershed of the Birch Mountains. Shortly before the little army reached this point, they had switched
off their headlights.

The descent was simple but just as slow as the ascent
because, in the absence of lights, the half-seen alders had to
be negotiated with care. The engines, no more than idling,
were gratifyingly quiet. Willoughby called softly and the
three Finncats came to a halt.

"Far enough," he said. "We can't be more than three
hundred yards from the shore."

"Okay." Dermott agreed. "How many crew at the
Met. Station, Willoughby?"

"Just two. I shouldn't imagine that any harm has
come to them. They have to keep sending their regular
radio reports. Any breakdown in those would have
brought an official helicopter out here very quickly. So the
reports must have continued to go out—under duress."

They made their way down to the lake's edge, keeping their voices low—sound travels as well over ice as it
does over water. Tall reeds grew by the frozen shore. Carmody parted these, unpacked his infrared night sight,

pressed his face against the rubber eye piece and switched on.

The Crowfoot Lake meteorological station consisted of only two huts, one about three times the size of the other. The smaller one had a variety of poles, boxes and what appeared from that distance to be uncovered recording instruments on its roof. This smaller hut was dark: the larger, presumably the living quarters, showed two brightly lit windows. Beyond this hut was parked a large, white-painted helicopter.

Jones passed the night sight to Brady, who studied the station briefly, then handed the instrument on. The last man to use it, Dermott, took the sight from his eye and said, "As a target for tonight, I've seen worse. We go now?"

"We go now," Brady said. "And we don't treat them like human beings. No warnings. No fair play. No sportsmanship. Shoot first, questions afterward. People who plant time bombs in aircraft—or steal my Jean and Stella—aren't full of finer feelings or the rules of civilized warfare."

Willoughby said, "Fair enough. But shoot to cripple, not to kill. I want those men to stand trial."

Brady said, "Of course, the conduct and termination of the trial would be greatly speeded if we had their confessions in advance."

"And how do you figure on getting those?" Dermott asked.

"Simple, George. It all depends upon how intrepid you're feeling this afternoon."

FIFTEEN

THE WICKED WIND HISSED THROUGH THE clump of alders some twenty yards behind the meteorological station. The trees offered little in the way of cover, but it was the best and closest that the men could find. Luckily, the night was moonless: the buildings showed as black lumps in the snowy landscape.

Bulky as bears in their Arctic gear, the raiders silently watched another figure, flattened to the snow, inch his way up toward them, propelled only by elbows and toes. Arrived in the shelter of the trees, John Carmody rose to a kneeling position.

"They're there," he whispered. "Reynolds and the ladies. The ladies are handcuffed together, but they seem all right. Don't look as though they've been maltreated. There are five other men in there, smoking and drinking, but not drinking too much. A little room leads off the big one. Could be there's someone asleep in there, but I don't think so. The door's ajar and the light's on. Any person who wanted to sleep would have switched the light off."

"Well done, boy," said Brady.

"Three other things, sir. At least three of the men are armed, although none actually had a gun in his hand. The whole group is sitting around the table listening to a radio. They're listening pretty hard, too—trying to catch something. That made me think there wouldn't be another of them in the small room—he'd have been out there listening too."

"Could be the two station operators are in there," said Dermott. "Tied up, I mean."

"I thought that too," said Carmody.

"I know what they're listening for," Brady whispered. "News of a certain jet having crashed in Alberta this afternoon. What was the third thing you saw?"

"All five men are wearing stocking masks."

Dermott said, "Which they wouldn't bother with if they intended to dispose of the hostages." His husky murmur dropped to a whisper. "Keep low. Keep quiet."

A rectangle of light had appeared at the side of the cabin. A figure walked through the opened doorway and headed toward the smaller building. Moments later lights came on there.

"One of them," Brady said. "Hardly likely to let one

of the operators stroll across there and send off an S.O.S.
Perfect. Come, George, this is where you earn your congressional medal of honor or whatever."

Brady moved out, traveling quickly and silently, no
trace of the comfort-loving fat man left. Arriving at the
main cabin door, Brady looked over his shoulder to check
the smaller cabin. The light was still on, the door still
closed. Brady turned back to the cabin door, gripped the
handle, opened the door and walked inside, .38 in hand,
closely followed by Dermott and Mackenzie, with their
guns leveled. Brady advanced on the four stocking-masked
men sitting around the table. Several started up.

"Keep your hands on that table," he said, "if you're
not entirely mad. We're just looking for an excuse to
shoot you through the head. One of you turn that radio
off—the good news you're waiting for has just arrived."

"Jim! Jim!" Jean Brady was on her feet. "You've
come!"

"Of course." Brady's voice held a curious mixture of
irritation and smug self-satisfaction. "You thought I
wouldn't? Brady Enterprises always delivers." As his wife
made to approach him, he raised his left hand. "Just a minute. Don't come too close. These are desperate men. Mr.
Reynolds, Stella. Sorry we took so long about this but—"

"Dad!" Stella was on her feet, a desperate urgency in
her voice. "Dad, a man—"

"Drop your guns." The deep voice came from the
doorway. "Don't turn around or you're dead."

"Do what the man says." Brady set the example.

Within a second the other two guns had clattered to the floor.

"Stay where you are," the same voice ordered. "Billy."

Billy didn't have to be told what to do. His search was quick but thorough. He stepped back and said, "Clean, boss."

"So." The door closed and a burly man appeared before them. Like the others, he was masked. "Sit on that bench there." He waited until they had done so, seated himself by the table and said, "Watch them." Three of his men produced pistols and covered the three seated men. He put away his gun.

"The ladies, I must say, seem very disappointed. They shouldn't, really."

Brady looked at them. "What he means is that things could be worse. If his plan had worked, we three would be dead. As it is, Ferguson is critically ill and two others seriously injured." He looked at the leader. "You placed that bomb in the plane?"

"I can't take all the credit. One of my men did." He lit a cigarette and stuck it through a hole in the stocking mask which had been cut out for that purpose. "So now I have Mr. Jim Brady and his two invaluable associates. A full hand, one might say."

Brady said, "Designed to blow our tail off at thirty thousand feet?"

"What else? It would be interesting to know how you're alive."

"*We're* alive. But one man's probably dying, and two are seriously injured. God, man, what are you—a psychopathic killer?"

"Not psychopathic. Just a businessman. How come *you* didn't die?"

"Because we landed before the bomb went off." Brady sounded very tired. "We got a report from a forest ranger saying that an off-white helicopter had been seen in these parts. Nobody paid attention except us—we knew you had a white helicopter."

"How did you know that?"

"A lot of people saw it around the plant at Athabasca."

"No harm done." He waved a hand. "All the aces in the pack."

"Whoever placed that explosive charge in my plane made a lousy job of securing it," said Brady sarcastically.

"I can vouch for that. He was interrupted."

"The package moved forward and jammed the controls—the tail ailerons. The pilot had to land—it was on the way down that we caught a glimpse of your helicopter. We crash-landed on another lake. Pilot told us to get out. He tried to remove the charge, and the two others stayed with him. I guess they felt they had to—they were cops."

"We know that, too."

"So they were expendable. You had no compunction about murdering them, too?"

"Compunction is not a word in my vocabulary. Why did you come here?"

"For your helicopter, of course. We have to get those injured men to hospital."

"Why hold us up?"

"Don't be so stupid. We can't fly the damn thing."

The leader shrugged. "Sorry about that."

"And of course, you people killed Crawford."

"Crawford?" He turned to another of his men. "Fred, that lad you attended to—"

"Yeah. That was him."

"And you critically wounded Grigson, Sanmobil's president, and a policeman?"

"Seems to have been an awful lot you didn't prevent."

"And, of course, it was you who blew up the plant and destroyed the dragline. A pity you had to kill and wound so many in the process."

"Look friend, we don't play kiddies' games. Too bad if someone gets in our way. This is a man's world, and we play for keeps."

Brady bowed his head in apparent acceptance, raised his hands to cross them behind his neck. His fingers touched.

What should have been the tinkling of shattered glass was lost in the crash of three shots that sounded almost as one. The masked men with the guns yelled out in agony and stared in shocked disbelief at their shattered shoulders. The door was kicked violently open and Carmody jumped in, machine gun steady in his big hands. He moved a couple of steps forward. Willoughby ran into the cabin carrying a revolver.

Dermott said, "Your words. This is a man's world, and we play for keeps."

Carmody advanced on the masked leader and thrust the barrel of his machine gun hard against the man's teeth. "Your gun. By the barrel. Do you know what is my one ambition in life right now?" The man, apparently, did. Carmody pocketed the gun and turned to the remaining and unwounded member of the quintet, who had his gun on the table before Carmody could even speak to him.

Brady said, "Satisfactory, Mr. Willoughby? The floor is yours."

"An Oscar, Mr. Brady. They sang beautifully." He advanced to the table. "I think you all know who I am?"

Nobody spoke.

"You." He indicated the person who had so hastily placed his gun on the table. "Towels, cotton wool, bandages. Nobody's going to mind very much if your three friends bleed to death, but personally I would sooner see them die legally. After they've been tried, of course. Let's see your faces." He walked around ripping off masks. The first three faces apparently meant nothing to him. The fourth, belonging to the man he'd just appointed to first aid duty, clearly did.

"Lucky Lorrigan," Willoughby said. "Erstwhile helicopter pilot, more recently a murderer on the run from Calgary. Severely wounded a couple of officers in your breakout, Lucky, didn't you? My, aren't they going to be pleased to see you again!"

He tore the mask from the leader's face. "Well, well, would you believe it? No less than Frederick Napier himself, second senior supervisor in Sanmobil security. You've strayed a bit from home, haven't you, Freddie?"

"All five of you are hereby taken into arrest and charged with murder, attempted murder, kidnapping and industrial sabotage. I don't have to remind you about your legal rights, silence, access to lawyers. You've heard it all before. Not that it will do any of you the slightest good. Not after the beautiful way Napier sang."

Brady said, "Would you say he was the best singer of the lot, Mr. Willoughby?"

Willoughby stroked his chin. "A moot point, Mr. Brady." He had no idea what Brady was talking about, but had learned to listen when he suggested something.

Brady said, "You really are extraordinarily naïve, Napier. I told you that Mr. Willoughby and his officer were severely injured when our plane crash-landed, yet you seemed hardly surprised to see them here. Perhaps you're just stupid. Perhaps events have moved too fast for your limited intellect. Our plane, of course, did not crash-land. No forest ranger pilot spotted you. We never saw your helicopter on the way to our alleged crash-landing.

"Deerhorn, the lake just over the hill there, was our destination from the time we left Fort McMurray, because we knew exactly where you were. You sing like a lark,

Napier. But Brinckman and Jorgensen sing like angels. They're going to turn State's evidence. Should get off with five years."

"Brinckman and Jorgensen!" Napier jumped to his feet then collapsed back in his chair with a whoosh of expelled air as the barrel of Carmody's machine gun caught him in the solar plexus. He sat there gasping for breath. "Brinckman and Jorgensen," he wheezed, and had just started in on a résumé of their antecedents when Carmody's gun caught him lightly on the side of the head.

"Ladies present," Carmody said pleasantly.

"State's evidence!" Napier said huskily. "Five years! Good God, man, Brinckman's my boss. Jorgensen's his lieutenant. I'm only number three on the totem pole. Brinckman is the one who fixes everything, arranges everything, gives all the orders. I just do what I'm told. State's evidence! Five years! Brinckman!"

Willoughby said, "Would you swear to that in court?"

"Too damn right, I would! Treacherous bastard!" Napier stared into space, his mouth no more than a compressed white line.

Willoughby said, "And before all those witnesses, too."

Napier shifted his gaze from faraway places to Willoughby. His expression was one of total incomprehension.

"Mr. Brady was quite right, Napier. You really are a

rather simple person, but as a singer you just got raised to the rank of angel. Until this moment we didn't have a single solitary thing we could pin on either of them. Thanks to you, they'll join you behind bars tonight. It should be a fascinating get-together."

The big white helicopter touched down on Deerhorn at five forty-five in the afternoon. Lucky Lorrigan with a muzzle of Carmody's gun screwing into his ear, had flown the seven-minute hop in impeccable style. The two meteorological station operators had been freed and, when told why, had willingly sworn themselves to secrecy for the next twenty-four hours.

Brady was first off the plane, followed by Dermott and the wounded men. A curious reception committee from the Sikorsky, headed by Lieutenant Fraser, was there to greet them.

Fraser said, "That was fast work. Congratulations! No problems?"

"Routine exercise." Brady was a master of the throwaway phrase. "Some for Dr. Kenmore, though. Three silly people got in the way of flying bullets."

Kenmore said, "I'll fix them up, Mr. Brady."

"Thanks. But you look mighty young to me to be an orthopedic surgeon."

"So it's like that?"

"Patch them up as best you can. Nobody's going to take your license away from you if they peg out during the night."

"I understand." The young doctor's eyes widened as the women descended the steps. "Well, well."

"Brady Enterprises," Brady said with a smirk in his voice, "associates only with the best and the most beautiful. Well, Mr. Lowry, we'll have to see about getting back those splendid machines of yours. And now, Lieutenant, if you will excuse me—a matter of some urgency."

He had taken some few steps toward his aircraft, when the lieutenant overtook him. "It got pretty cold in your plane, Mr. Brady, so I took the liberty of transferring some essential supplies to our nice warm Sikorsky."

Brady turned ninety degrees without breaking stride and headed purposefully toward the Sky-crane. He patted Lieutenant Fraser on the arm. "Lieutenant, a very promising future lies ahead of you."

Dermott said to Bernie, the Sikorsky radio operator, "Any luck?"

"Got through to all three, sir. Your New York number and one of your Anchorage numbers—a Mr. Morrison —said they had no information for you yet and probably wouldn't have for the next twenty-four hours. Your other Anchorage number—a Dr. Parker—asked if you would be kind enough to call him back now."

"Would you get him please?"

"No bother." Bernie smiled. "And then you'd like some privacy?"

Brady had been reduced to the discomfort of sitting on a packing box—admittedly a large one—in the fore part of the Sikorsky's cavernous hold. He appeared not to be suffering too much. He was speaking to a fully conscious Ferguson.

"You've made it, son. You're damned lucky, but not nearly as lucky as we are, thanks entirely to you. We'll discuss this—ah—later, in private. Sorry your eyes are still troubling you."

"Just a damned nuisance, Mr. Brady. Otherwise, I could fly the plane with no trouble."

"You're not flying anything, anywhere," Kenmore said. "It may be two or three days before we can be sure that your eyesight is stabilized. I know a specialist in Edmonton."

"Thank you. How are our wounded heroes, by the way?"

"They'll live."

"Ah, well. We can't have everything."

Two and a half hours later Brady was again presiding over a cheerful company, but this time rather more comfortably ensconced in the best armchair in the Peter Pond Hotel. Doubtless inspired by the thought of the enormous fees he would extort, he was positively Maecenas-like in his hospitality. Reynolds had been joined by his wife. The atmosphere was festive, but Dermott and Mackenzie didn't seem very jovial. Dermott approached the beaming Brady —he wasn't beaming at anything in particular but was just sitting there, wife's hand in his left, daiquiri in his right— and said, "Donald and I would like to slip away for a bit, sir. Do you mind?"

"Of course not. Do you need me?"

"Minor matters, only."

"Go right ahead, George." The beam, which had faded slightly, lit up again. Brady would now have the field to himself, and it was possible that his retailing of recent events might vary slightly from the one he would have given if his two lieutenants had been present. He glanced at his watch. "Eight-thirty. Half an hour or so?"

"About that."

On their way out they stopped by Willoughby's chair. Dermott smiled at a rather misty-eyed Mrs. Reynolds, then said to Willoughby, "Brinckman and Jorgensen?"

Willoughby smiled happily. "Are guests of the Canadian Government. Heard fifteen minutes ago. Look, gentlemen, I don't know how to—"

"Wait." Mackenzie smiled. "We aren't through with you yet."

"Some more matters to be attended to?"

"Not in Alberta. But we have to cast a net again. Can we see you in the morning?"

"When?"

"Late. May we call you?"

Dermott and Mackenzie spent not half an hour but an hour and a half in Dermott's room, talking, planning, and mostly, telephoning. When they returned to the lounge Brady greeted them effusively. He was totally unaware of how much time had elapsed. The number of the company had increased. Dermott and Mackenzie were introduced to a couple who turned out to be the mayor and his wife. Jay Shore had returned from the plant and they were introduced to *his* wife, too. They were introduced to a charming lady who turned out to be Mrs. Willoughby. After that they were introduced to two other couples whose names they failed to catch. Jim Brady was spreading his wings that night.

Willoughby came up and spoke to them quietly. "Another item, although it's just another unnecessary nail in the coffin. We retrieved the prints from Shore's house and compared them to the ones in the kidnap truck. Two matching sets were found—Napier and Lucky Lorrigan's."

At eleven o'clock, Dermott and Mackenzie approached Brady again. He was still in sparkling form: his tolerance for rum passed mortal understanding. Dermott said, "Mr. Brady. We're bushed. We're off."

"Off? Bed? I'll be damned." He glanced at his watch. "The night's young." He made a grandiloquent gesture with his arm. "Look at *them*. Are *they* thinking of bed?" Jean gave Dermott a rueful smile which indicated that she was thinking of just that herself. "They're happy. They're enjoying themselves. Just look!"

Wearily they looked. No question, Brady had the right of it. They were enjoying themselves, not least young Carmody, who had discreetly withdrawn from the main body of the group to sit in a corner with Stella.

"We wish you luck. You want us to collapse dramatically in front of all your guests?"

"That's the trouble with you young people of today. No get-up-and-go." When the occasion arose Brady could conveniently forget that his associates and himself were of the same generation. "No stamina. Not fit." He seemed totally unaware of how preposterous he sounded, but they knew he wasn't.

"We'd like to talk to you in the morning."

"You would?" He eyed them both suspiciously. "When?"

"When you're fit, unlimited stamina, the lark singing."

"Damn it all, *when?*"

"Noon."

Brady relaxed. "In that case, why don't you stay?"

Dermott went and kissed Jean good night, Mackenzie did the same. They made the rounds with punctilious good nights and left.

They got to bed just after one in the morning. The previous two hours had been spent on the telephone.

Dermott awoke at seven-thirty. By eight, he was showered, shaved, eating off his breakfast tray and busy on the telephone. At nine he was joined by Mackenzie. At ten they were both closeted with Willoughby. At noon, they joined Brady at his breakfast table and explained what they had in mind. Brady chewed through the last of his ham omelette, which had originally been the size of a soup plate, then shook his head in a decisive fashion.

"It's out of the question. It's all over. Okay, there are a few stray threads in Alaska, but who am I to devote my time to that sort of small potatoes?"

"So it is in order if Donald and I resign?"

Fortunately for Brady he was neither eating nor drinking at the moment, so he had nothing to choke over. "Resign? What the hell do you mean?"

"It's Donald's fault, really. Half Scots, you know. He hates to see good money being thrown away."

"Money being thrown away?" Momentarily, Brady looked almost appalled, but his recovery was swift. "What's this nonsense?"

"How much are you charging Sanmobil for our services?"

"Well, I'm not one to prey on the misfortunes of others. A half million I guess. Plus expenses, of course."

"In that case, I reckon Donald and I would rate a quarter of a million for picking up stray threads and small potatoes." Brady was silent, his eyes fixed on something beyond infinity. "With your name," Dermott persisted, "one can see no reason why the Prudhoe Bay oil companies shouldn't also come up with a half million. Plus, of course, expenses."

Brady brought his gaze back from outer space to the dining-room table. "It's not, as you may think, that I'm not at my best in the morning. It's just that I have so much on my mind. What time is this meeting tonight?"

SIXTEEN

THE MEETING WAS HELD THAT EVENING in the Sanmobil canteen, which was drably lit and decorated in dingy cream and pea-green. Nevertheless, the room had much to recommend it for such a gathering, not least the fact that it was large and warm and a place from which the public could easily be excluded.

The tables and chairs had been rearranged so that the men conducting the proceedings sat in a line—on stage, as it were—facing down the long room. The rest of the seats had been set out in two blocks, divided by a gangway.

In the middle of the top table sat Willoughby, acting as host in his own parish. On his right was Hamish Black, general manager of BP/Sohio, Alaska, who had flown down from Prudhoe Bay to be present. On Willoughby's left sat Brady, overflowing a rickety wooden chair, and beside him were his two trusty henchmen.

Down on the floor, the home team was represented by Bill Reynolds, Jay Shore and a handful of others. On the Alaskan side there were eight men, among them Dr. Blake, gaunt and cadaverous as ever; Ffoulkes, the Anchorage police chief; and Parker, the police forensic surgeon. Morrison of the FBI had come on the same plane, and behind him sat four of his agents. At the back of the room were nearly thirty other men from Sanmobil brought in so that they could hear the full report of what had been happening. Finally, in an unobtrusive position at one side, John Carmody and a couple of fellow policemen occupied a flat bench, with their backs against the wall; and sandwiched between them was Corinne Delorme, looking small and wan and rather scared.

Willoughby stood up to open the proceedings.

"Good evening, ladies and gentlemen. As the senior representative of the law here in Alberta, and as your nominal host, I would like to thank all you people who've been good enough to come from places as far afield as Prudhoe Bay, Anchorage and even New York."

A murmur went around the room.

"That's right," Willoughby confirmed. "Two gentlemen at least have come all the way from New York. Now, the purpose of this meeting is to explain to the senior employees of Sanmobil and BP/Sohio just what's been going on these past few days, and, if possible, to clear up the few final questions to which we don't yet have the answers. I call on Mr. Hamish Black, general manager of BP/Sohio, Alaska, to put you in the picture."

Black rose to his feet, all disapproval and severity. Yet when he began to speak, he seemed to acquire a stature and authority that thoroughly surprised Brady and his associates.

"I hardly need tell you," he began, "that both the Alaskan pipeline and the Sanmobil tar-sands complex here at Athabasca have recently been subjected to deadly and intensive industrial sabotage. The action effectively closed down the flow of oil from both centers, and in the process of the sabotage at least four innocent people have been murdered, while several others have been gravely injured.

"We devoutly hope that the savage and brutal attacks are at an end. They certainly seem to be so in Alberta—and for this the sole credit goes to the investigation team of Brady Enterprises, headed by Mr. Jim Brady himself and his two senior assistants, Mr. Dermott and Mr. Mackenzie."

With the ghost of a smile softening the line of his pencil moustache, Black indicated the Brady team. To his dismay, Brady found himself blushing for the first time in years. He ground his teeth and contrived to look sideways at Dermott without moving his head. The guy they'd treated like dirt was praising them!

"Unfortunately," Black went on, "no such happy conclusion has been reached in Alaska. Up there, we have no positive guarantee that the sabotage is at an end, for the simple reason that the individuals responsible for the criminal activity have not yet been brought to justice.

"Brady Enterprises have been as deeply involved in making inquiries in Alaska as they have here, and since they are the only people with an overall view of the present position, I should like to call upon Mr. Brady himself to give us a report."

Brady heaved himself upright and cleared his throat.

"Thank you, Mr. Black. Ladies and gentlemen, I promise to be as brief as possible, and to waste none of your time. First I will ask for a word from Mr. John Young, who is director of City Services, a Federally backed investigative agency in New York. One of its functions is to oversee and regulate the conduct of private detective and investigative agencies in the state of New York. Mr. Young?"

In the front row of the Sanmobil team seats, a lean, bald-headed man with thick-rimmed glasses rose to his feet. He looked at the papers in his hand, smiled at Brady, and turning to face the body of the hall, he began.

"City Services was asked by Brady Enterprises—this was with governmental consent—to investigate the background of a private security agency owned and run by one Samuel Bronowski, who later became head of security on the Alaskan pipeline.

"Apart from the fact that an unusually large percentage of valuables entrusted to the firm's safekeeping had been missing—for readily explainable reasons—we found no evidence of any outright misconduct. But I was further asked to find out the names and identities of any of Bronowski's associates who left the firm at about the same time as he did—that is to say, within six months either side of his departure date. We came up with ten names—not a particularly high wastage rate in such an agency—but Brady Enterprises were particularly interested in four of them." Here Young consulted the notes in his right hand. "Their names are Houston, Brinckman, Jorgensen and Napier."

Young sat down and Brady rose again to thank him. "Well," he continued, "for those of you who do not already know, three of the four just mentioned are already in jail, charged with various crimes from murder downward. The other man, and Bronowski, you can now see for yourselves."

He made a small sign to Willoughby, who nodded to one of his uniformed men at the door. Next moment the door opened, to admit Bronowski and Houston, manacled together. They were hustled to seats in the front row of the Alaska-side stalls. Bronowski still sported his impressive head bandage, and beneath it, his broad, strong face was sullen.

"So." Brady purred. "I promised we would not waste time. We have established that at least two security agents from the pipeline and three from Sanmobil were old acquaintances, that they were acting in concert, organized widespread sabotage, exchanged codes and were responsible for murder. We have also established that Bronowski was the undisputed leader. These facts have been put on record by many witnesses, who will testify in court. But let us move on, I would like to call on Dr. Parker."

"Yes, well." Parker paused reflectively. "I act in a forensic capacity for the police at Anchorage. Mr. Dermott brought down three corpses from Prudhoe Bay. I examined one of them—an engineer who had been murdered in Pump Station Number Four. He had sustained a most unusual injury to his right index finger. I understand that Dr. Blake here attributed this to the force of the explosion which destroyed the pump station. I have to disagree. The finger was deliberately broken—there is no other way it could have happened. Mr. Dermott?"

Dermott stood up. "Mr. Mackenzie and I have a theory. It's our belief that this dead engineer was carrying a pistol when he was held up by the people who had planted the explosives. We further believe that he recognized his assailants, and they, knowing this, killed him before he could use his gun in self-defense. We also believe that his dead finger locked over the trigger grip. That would be possible, doctor?"

"Indeed—quite possible."

"We surmise the criminals had to break the man's forefinger to get the gun away. A dead man found with a gun in his hand would have raised serious doubts as to whether the explosion had been a genuine accident.

"Further, papers seen in his coat pocket were later missing. Neither my colleagues nor I know what those papers were. We can only assume that he had accumulated incriminating evidence against someone—which would account for the fact that he was carrying a gun."

Dermott paused. Then he said, "I would like to ask Mr. Brady to discuss the vital question of who is ultimately responsible for this spate of crime."

Brady hoisted himself upright again. "Mr. Carmody— would you be so kind as to stand by Bronowski? I am aware that he is handcuffed, but I'm also convinced he's a man of violence. Dr. Parker?"

Dr. Parker rose leisurely and walked across to Bronowski. Carmody was already there. The doctor said to him, "Get behind him and hold his arms."

Carmody did so. Bronowski yelped with pain as Parker reached forward and ripped away the bandage that covered his forehead and temple. The doctor peered closely at the temple, touched it, then straightened.

"This is a delicate area of the head," he said. "A blow such as he is alleged to have received would have left a bruise for at least a fortnight. Probably longer. As you can see, there is no such bruise, no sign of any contusion. In other words," he said, pausing for effect, "he was never struck."

Brady said, "Things look rather black for you, Dr. Blake."

"They're going to look a damn sight blacker," Parker said. He had resumed his place. "Mr. Dermott, in Anchorage, made what I then regarded as an extremely strange request. I no longer regard it as such. Despite the fact that you, Dr. Blake, had carried out an autopsy on John

Finlayson, Mr. Dermott asked me to carry out another. Unheard of, but, as it turns out, justified."

"Your certificate said that Finlayson had been struck on the occiput with some form of loaded salt bag. As in the case of Bronowski, there was no sign of any contusion. The skin had been somewhat abraded, which could have occurred before or after death. What is important is that one of my younger associates discovered traces of ethyl oxide in the blood. It is difficult to conceal such trace elements. On closer examination, we discovered a tiny blue puncture just under the rib cage. Further investigation proved beyond any doubt that a needle or probe had been inserted through this puncture and pierced the heart. Death would have been pretty well instantaneous. In other words, Finlayson had been anesthetized, then murdered. I do not think there is one medical authority in either of our countries who would dispute my findings."

Brady said, "Comment, Dr. Blake?"

He appeared to have none.

The FBI's Morrison said, "I have. He's not a doctor. He was trained in an English university and flung out in his fourth year for reasons as yet undisclosed but which I'm sure we can readily ascertain. No doubt he learned enough in that time to use a needle or probe."

Brady said, "Comment, Blake?"

Again he had none.

"I do not know, but I'm pretty sure that this is what happened," Dermott said. "Finlayson came across Bronowski and Houston tampering with the fingerprint card index. I suggest that Bronowski was removing his own prints from the file. I suggest he was substituting some other prints for his own. Whose, I do not know, but that again we can ascertain. The next suggestion is straightforward and obvious. The prints on an Anchorage telephone booth were Bronowski's. We have only to take his prints to confirm."

Brady said, "Comment, Bronowski?"

Silence.

"Well." Brady looked around the room. "Guilty as hell. That almost wraps it up." He stood up, as if to end the meeting. "But not quite. None of the accused has the intelligence or knowledge to mastermind an operation of this nature. This required a highly specialized degree of knowledge. Someone who had the inside track."

Willoughby asked, "We have an idea of this person's identity?"

"I know who he is. But I think I'll let Mr. Morrison and the FBI take over here. My colleagues and I had our suspicions as to the identity of the mastermind behind the killings and sabotage both here and in Alaska, but it was Mr. Morrison who got the proof."

"I got the proof," Morrison said, "but that was only because my nose was pointed in the right direction. Bronowski claimed to have owned—and maintains he still owns—an investigative agency in New York. This is untrue. As Mr. Young discovered in the course of his investigations, Bronowski only acted in the capacity of a front man, a figurehead. The real source of power, the owner, was someone else. Right, Bronowski?"

Bronowski scowled, clamped his lips and kept his counsel.

"No matter. At least you don't deny it. Mr. Young, accompanied by New York detectives and armed with a search warrant, examined the firm's private correspondence. The firm had been so naïve as to file away, instead of destroying, fatally damaging and incriminating evidence. This evidence not only revealed the identity of the true owner, it also revealed the astonishing fact that this same individual owned no fewer than four other protection or investigative agencies in the city of New York." Morrison glanced to one side. "Mr. Willoughby?"

Willoughby nodded and looked aside. Carmody nodded, rose and walked leisurely to the back of the room.

"This owner," Morrison went on, "was an absentee landlord, but only during the past couple of years. Before that he was on the New York stock exchange and an investment counselor on Wall Street. He wasn't too successful. Not really a financial man at all, though he liked money. More like a bull in a china shop. Too extroverted.

"The landlord's most recent absence was caused by the fact that he had become busy elsewhere. He was busy in Athabasca, at an inconvenient distance from Wall Street. He was, in fact, working for Sanmobil. He was busy being Sanmobil's operations manager."

"Don't move. Keep quite still." Carmody leaned over

Reynolds' shoulder and relieved him of a silenced automatic which he had begun to slide out of a shoulder holster. "You could cause yourself an injury. What's a law-abiding citizen like you doing carrying a gun?"

Gasps of surprise broke out all around the room. Almost everybody stood up to get a better view. Reynolds' face, normally so rubicund, had gone gray, making an unpleasant clash with his corn-colored hair. He sat as if paralyzed while Carmody slipped manacles on him.

"This is in no way a trial," Brady announced. "So I do not propose to question him. Nor will I adumbrate the factors that made him turn the way he did—save to say that his main grievance appears to have been that he had been passed over for promotion. He found his way ahead blocked. He conceived the idea that outsiders were always brought into the firm to occupy senior positions. You may think his reaction a little excessive."

Brady stopped. He had, at this point, intended to have a dig at Black, by mentioning the oil companies' practice of installing accountants in senior management positions. As things had turned out, however, he decided against it, and merely asked Black to sum up.

This Black did, in a surprisingly warm and human manner. Again he praised Brady Enterprises effusively, and he ended by reassuring everyone present that the campaign of terror and destruction was over. The meeting was closed. Police officers escorted Reynolds, Blake, Bronowski and Houston away to the cells, and everyone else began to disperse.

Brady, feeling unwontedly nervous, sidled up to Black.

"My apologies," he muttered. "Must offer you my sincere apologies. My associates were infernally rude to you that time . . . no cause for it."

"My dear fellow—not at all," said Black magnanimously. "I daresay it was my fault anyway. I hardly realized what deep trouble we were in. I thought your investigations were superfluous. Now I know different."

"I'd like to apologize, too," muttered Dermott, stiff with embarrassment. "Trouble was—if I may say so—you seemed so unco-operative."

"It was the *cost* that frightened me. Don't forget, I'm an accountant by training." To the amazement of the Brady team, Black actually laughed. They laughed too, from sheer release of tension—and the next second, Black caught them neatly on the rebound.

"Well now, Mr. Brady," he said briskly, "as to the question of your fee . . ."

"Oh . . . now!" Brady spluttered, caught right off-balance. "I assumed all along I would negotiate that with your London office."

"No need, I'm glad to say." Black was all breezy sunshine. "London has empowered me to deal directly with you. Our chairman felt that despite your close friendship, or perhaps because of it—I should settle this."

"That's . . . well . . . NO! I mean, I . . . I never discuss fees myself." Brady sounded lame, and knew it. But he pulled himself together fast. "I have to consult *my* accountant, even if you don't."

"Forty love, and Black to serve," muttered Dermott as they moved away. He was about to go for his coat when, down one side of the room, he spotted Corinne Delorme still sitting on a bench, as if in a trance. He went along to her.

"Come on, honey," he said gently. "Time to go."

"I just can't believe it," she said. "It's not possible."

"Well—it happened. Are you upset?"

"Not really—no. I didn't care that much about him. It's just that I kind of got used to believing what he said."

"I know, one does. But you saw how devious he was. Anyone who had himself kidnapped to add verisimilitude to the proceedings—anyone who does that is hardly straightforward."

"I guess that's right. All those murders, too. Oh God, it's awful."

"It *was* awful. But it's over. Coming?"

"I suppose so." She stood up, and Dermott helped her into her coat.

"You and I were the two luckiest people in the whole damn business," he said. "We both ought to be dead. Without you I would be."

Suddenly her blank eyes lit up and she smiled.

Dermott smiled back. "What are you going to do now you've got no boss to work for?"

"I don't know. Find another job, I suppose."

"Not many good jobs in Fort McMurray. Why not come south and work for me?"

"For *you?*" Her eyes widened. "I haven't thought of that."

"Think of it now. Shall we go?"

"Okay."

"I'd offer you my arm, if it wasn't still so damned sore."

"And I might even take it." She looked upward and snuggled close against him as they went out through the door.

The sight seemed to occasion the most immense merriment in Brady and his one remaining associate. They both rolled in their seats like clowns, giving vent to noisy explosions.

"Stay me with flagons, Donald," cried Brady, as he recovered. "I am seriously in need of liquids. I was beginning to think we had a romance on our hands."

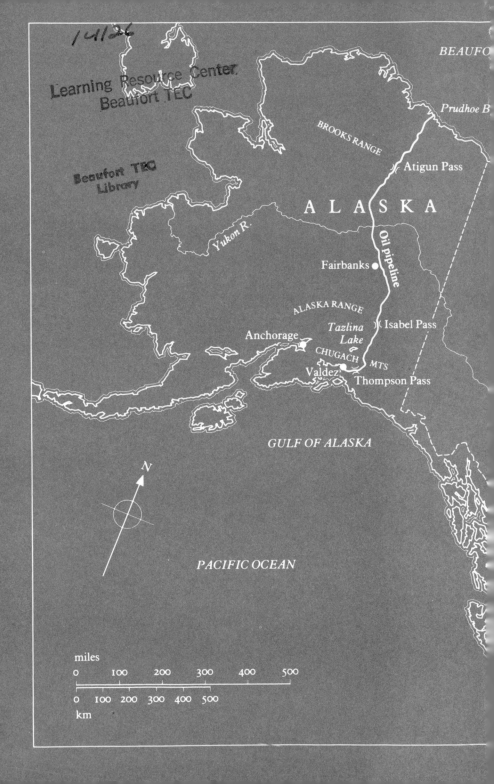

BEAUFO

Prudhoe B

BROOKS RANGE

Atigun Pass

A L A S K A

Yukon R.

Oil pipeline

Fairbanks ●

ALASKA RANGE

Tazlina Lake

Isabel Pass

Anchorage ●

CHUGACH MTS

Valdez ● Thompson Pass

GULF OF ALASKA

N

PACIFIC OCEAN

miles

0   100   200   300   400   500

0   100   200   300   400   500
km